THE WATCH

KAREN WOODS

Harper
North

HarperNorth
Windmill Green,
Mount Street,
Manchester, M2 3NX

A division of
HarperCollins*Publishers*
1 London Bridge Street
London SE1 9GF

www.harpercollins.co.uk

HarperCollins*Publishers*
Macken House,
39/40 Mayor Street Upper,
Dublin 1
D01 C9W8

First published by HarperNorth in 2024

1 3 5 7 9 10 8 6 4 2

A catalogue record for this book
is available from the British Library

ISBN: 978-0-00-865686-7

Printed and bound in Great Britain by
CPI Group (UK) Ltd, Croydon

MIX
Paper | Supporting
responsible forestry
FSC™ C007454

This book contains FSC™ certified paper and other controlled
sources to ensure responsible forest management.

For more information visit: www.harpercollins.co.uk/green

To my mother, Margaret.
I miss you every day and I know you're still proud of me.

To our kid, Daz. Hope you're looking down on me and
smiling at all my stories.

To my son, Dale, rest in peace. Goodnight, God Bless xxx

The Manor estate in North Manchester was the kind of place where people would sell a kidney for the chance to live there. Each garden was nicely kept, with flowers and hanging baskets fronting the smart semi-detached houses set back from the roadside. The people who walked by assumed you had to have a few quid to live there and maybe they were right; compared to most places nearby, these houses cost dough. The gleaming front doors and litter-free streets were a world away from the gloomy avenues and run-down estates only a little way across town. Those neglected estates, riddled with rubbish, where residents didn't care about the place they lived attracted trouble. But the Manor was well kept, and had the kind of community that ensured it stayed that way: older residents always out on the street cleaning up any litter, keeping an eye out for anyone loitering without good reason, and they always had a keen eye for any dog fouling the pavements too. God help anyone who broke the rules on this street; they would take photographs of you, follow you, name and shame you and make you clean the mess up. No, the Manor was peaceful and if some of the residents looked out of their upstairs windows they could see greenery, trees, fields in the distance. No one would have thought this was the same Manchester you saw on the news. But that's the thing about peace – it shatters easily.

So perhaps it was no surprise that locals were wary of newcomers. At 4 Manor Road, right at the entrance to the estate, Brooke and Vincent McQueen were exactly that. When they moved in, the woman in the shop at the end of road had joked that there wasn't enough room for another Queen Bee on this street and Brooke had looked puzzled.

'Just wait til you meet Bronwen or Bridie. Each of them think they're Queen Bee already. They won't know what to make of you moving in.'

'Well a bee can only sting you once before they die, that's all I know,' Brooke had said. But she wasn't after any bother with her new neighbours. She had enough of that closer to home.

Brooke and Vince had been together for years but only married recently, and only now had saved the kind of money it took to buy a place. Vincent was out at work from six o'clock each morning, you could set your alarm clock by him. And Brooke often worked long hours at the salon, grafting to make ends meet and make sure they could afford the nice things they wanted for their new home. From the outside, they seemed like just the type who'd fit into Manor Road – hard-working, respectable people. But before long, the whispering going on behind their backs grew. In a quiet place like the Manor, noise travelled and soon the neighbours were sure theirs was the house the shouting and screaming was coming from in the small hours.

It was a mild autumn night when Vincent McQueen staggered up the road, stumbling against the neatly trimmed bushes, mumbling to himself, wobbling from side to side. Manor Road was not the kind of street where it would pass unnoticed. Bridie and Bert Hammond from number 8 were at their front bedroom window, like a couple of plant pots. They would tell anyone they met the next morning about seeing Vincent steaming drunk walking past their house. Bridie had a sour look on her face as she stood back from the window, desperate to see what the man was up to but scared of being spotted. 'How on earth does he get that drunk, he can't even stand up? I don't know what's going on in that house but something strange is happening. If you came home drunk like that, Bert, I'd hit you over the bleeding head with the frying pan. Shameful it is, especially on a weeknight.'

Bert let out a laboured breath and went back to his bed. 'He's probably had a hard day's work, needed to unwind. Give the man a break, will you? Get away from that window and back to bed, it's well past midnight and you've got a busy day tomorrow, haven't you?'

Bridie stood looking at Vincent through the window and shook her head. 'I'll call and see Brooke after work, just to see if she needs someone to talk to. You never know what goes on behind closed doors, do you?'

'You bloody do, Bridie, because you're never away from that window. I'm sure if anything is going on at that house, you'll be the first to know.'

Bridie climbed back into bed and lay staring at the ceiling. She had a bad feeling about their new neighbours.

Chapter One

Joanne and Frank Drury had lived at number 6 for over fifteen years, along with their daughters, Emma and Susan, now almost grown. Emma was eighteen and Susan sixteen – nearly seventeen, as she always told everyone. A neat family of four, good parents, both working hard, with a lovely house that they were proud of. Exactly the kind of people you'd expect on a street like Manor Road.

But the smiles in the perfectly posed family photo that hung on the living room wall were rarely seen these days. People had warned Joanne about what it would be like to have two teenage girls on her hands, but to say they were a handful was an understatement. Susan had been expelled from school and Joanne was at her wits' end. Where had it all gone wrong? She'd asked herself this time and time again and she could never figure out why her youngest daughter had turned out the way she had. Joanne always seemed to be at the high school for meetings regarding

Susan and her behaviour. Susan had never liked school but until now, all the times she'd been sent home had been for minor slips – not having the correct uniform or giving backchat to a teacher. Privately, Joanne had thought they were a bit over the top, but rules were rules. And now she'd been caught vaping in class one too many times, and then they'd found laughing gas canisters in her bag, there was no getting out of this one. Not that her daughter cared. Deep down inside, Joanne had known this day would come when her daughter would no longer be welcome in school, but she supposed she should be relieved she had lasted this long – she only had a few weeks left anyway. Susan had no respect for anybody, and thought she knew as a mother she shouldn't admit it, her daughter had turned into a proper gobby cow.

Joanne sat down at the kitchen table and looked into her coffee cup. Ten times she'd shouted her daughter to get up out of bed and up to now she was still lying in her pit. Every morning it was the same old story. Joanne bolted from her seat and ran up the stairs like a woman on a mission. She ran into her daughter's bedroom and straight over to the bed. 'Get out of that bed! How many times do I have to tell you you're not lying in bed all bleeding day while we're out at work. You can do some cleaning, tidy your room, anything but lie in your bed all day dossing.' Joanne yanked at the duvet and dragged it from the bed. She flung it to the side of her and stood looking at her daughter with her hands firmly placed on her hips. Susan was bright orange, tan-stains all over the white bedding. 'Up,' she growled.

Susan opened her eyes slowly and folded her pillow under her head as she stretched her arms above her head. Cocky as ever. 'Chill, Mum. I'll do the cleaning when I wake up. Just go to work, woman, and leave me alone. I told you it wasn't my fault I got expelled, so stop taking it out on me. The teachers hated me at that school. I was set up. I told you time and time again and you never listened. Anyway, you set me up for shit at school giving me some 1950s name – I've had to give as good as I got from day one. What did you expect?'

'I expect my daughter to go to school and get a bloody education, that's what. I'll tell you something for nothing too, don't think you're going out tonight either. No school, no going out.'

Susan sprung up from her bed and grabbed her blue dressing gown. 'You can't keep me in, I'm sixteen.'

Joanne started to pick up dirty washing from the floor and walked around the bedroom as she replied, 'Don't think I've not heard the rumours about you on the estate. Everyone's talking about you, drinking, smoking weed, and God knows what else you've been up to. Have some bleeding respect for this family and stop showing us up. We work hard to give you and Emma a good home and you just don't care. Go on, tell me what's next for you with no GCSEs.'

'You're so old fashioned. I don't need qualifications, Mother. I'll earn money my way. Just get off my case, or, if you're that arsed about me, get back onto the school and tell them it wasn't my fault.'

Joanne stood at the bedroom door and let out a laboured breath. 'Don't be smart with that mouth, Susan, because I'm on a short fuse with you and, trust me, I'll knock your bleeding block off. Your dad's the same. Sort your shit out and give us all a break, will you?'

'I will. I'll get a job and show you all. You all think Emma is the bees' knees and she's worse than me.'

'She's got a job, paying her way, and she left school with good grades – unlike you will at this rate.'

'Yeah, whatever, Mam. Go on, I'm up now, no need to stand there gawping, is there?' Joanne was beetroot, her hands squeezing at the clothes in her hand. 'Just get up and do what I've asked you.'

Joanne walked out of the room and she could hear Susan shouting after her. 'I'm still going out tonight, you won't stop me.'

Joanne headed into the kitchen and threw the dirty clothes next to the washer in a huff, then turned to her husband, shaking her head. 'Frank, you better have a word with that mouthy cow up there, before I say something I can't take back. On my life, she has no respect for nobody, did you hear her shouting she's still going out tonight when I've told her she's grounded.'

Frank was reading the morning paper, plainly sick to death of the drama each morning. 'She's not stepping foot out of this house. I'll tell her that too. You know, since she's been hanging about with that Sabrina Clarke from the Two Hundred estate, she's got so bleeding cheeky. She's lucky we didn't throw her out when she got expelled. Old Bert asked me the other day why she wasn't in school, and I said she had time off to study for her exams. I mean, why am I lying to everyone about her?'

Joanne agreed and stood looking at her husband. 'It's embarrassing, Frank. I'm at the end of my tether. If we had family in another country, I would ship her out, believe me. Yep, pack her stuff and have done with her. She doesn't realise how good she's got things here.'

'Well, we don't have anywhere we can send her, so we just have to deal with her.' Frank looked at the white clock on the wall and stood up, folding his newspaper under his arm. 'We need to curb the spending some more, too. The leccy and gas have gone up a hundred pound each. I rang the suppliers and tried to get it lowered, but they weren't having any of it.'

'I'll try and get an extra shift at work. That's the last thing we need, getting into more debt.' There was a nervous look in her eye as she spoke to her husband again. 'You're not gambling again, are you?'

Frank started to put his coat on and walked towards the door. 'Am I bleeding hell, I've been down that road before and messed up. I won't make that mistake again. It's a fool's game.'

Joanne let out a long breath. 'Sorry for asking, love, but I needed to make sure. It's a disease it is, and a wicked one.'

But Frank was gone.

Susan lay on her bed, scrolling through her phone. It was nearly midday and she was still in her pyjamas. She dialled a number. 'Morning, are you up yet?' Susan switched the call to Facetime so the friends could see each other.

Sabrina Clarke was older than Susan, but the girls' matching tans and heavy Russian lashes made them look more like sisters than friends.

'I've got to clean up here then I'll come and meet you if you want,' Susan said as she pouted at herself in the phone camera. 'My mam has been pecking my head all morning, telling me I'm grounded. Like that will ever happen again. I'll be straight out of the bedroom window if they think they are locking me in like last time.'

Sabrina burst out laughing. The Clarkes were well known in these parts. Most of them had been served with ASBOs over the years and she had about as much faith in following the rules as did the rest of her family. 'I've told you before, you can do what you want, you're not a kid. Come and live here with me. My mam said it's sweet. I've already asked her. But you'll have to pay rent, she won't let you live here for nothing. We all have to pay our way.'

Susan let the thought sink in. She wouldn't mind getting closer to the Clarkes. Scully, Sabrina's older brother, was someone Susan had had her eye on from the moment she'd met him. Proper eye candy he was, right up her street. But he'd never given her a second look, probably had loads of girls on the go anyway. That would change if they were under one roof, she would make sure of it. Plus Sabrina would help her get some cash, she was convinced. Sab had had endless jobs, though none of them ever worked out.

'I might just do that,' Susan said with a smile. 'I can't see me sticking it out here much longer. My mam said she's heard the rumours about me, so God knows what people have been telling her.'

'Hurry up then, get ready and come over here. We can go into town and see what we can lift. I need some new clothes.'

Susan started playing with her long lashes, stroking the side of her finger along them. 'I need an infill on my lashes too, so I need cash and fast. If I lose anymore then she'll charge me for a full set.'

Sabrina touched her set too and fluttered them. 'So, let's get grafting. If we can nick enough of the decent stuff we'll get us a couple of nice outfits and we'll have enough left over to flog. Get off the phone and get sorted.'

'Alright. I'm coming. See you soon.' Susan ended the call, lay back on her bed and looked around her bedroom. It was nicely decorated; modern furniture, velvet curtains. Her wardrobe was bursting too. She thought how furious her folks would be if they knew Sabrina was teaching her how to shoplift. Still, there were a lot of things her parents didn't know. And she wanted it to stay that way. She just had to keep them sweet until she could move out. She reached over and touched her speaker to turn it on and connected her playlist. D Block started playing – just what she needed to give her the motivation to start cleaning up. Surely, once she'd done all her chores her mother wouldn't be on her back. Susan walked along the landing and spotted Emma sitting on her bed with her laptop open. As soon as she walked in, her sister slammed the computer shut.

'What do you want?' Emma asked.

Susan stood at the bedroom door. 'Why aren't you at work?'

'Got a day off to do some online training, haven't I, so clear off.' Her sister looked towards the hall.

Susan ignored her, edging further inside the bedroom, and sat on the end of her sister's bed. She looked around and clocked a new outfit hung on the wardrobe door. 'That's smart, can I have a borrow of it when you've worn it?'

Emma scoffed. 'No way is your scatty arse wearing my clothes. Get a job and buy your own like I have to.'

'Duh, I would if I could.'

'Unlucky then. You should have been a good girl and not got yourself expelled from school. I told you that big mouth of yours would end up getting you in trouble.'

Susan rolled her eyes and fell back onto the bed. 'Blah de blah. Heard it all before. We can't all be brown nosers like you are, can we?'

'I'm not a brown noser, I just know what I want in life. And lying in bed with no job and no money is not on the agenda for me.' Emma prodded her sister to make her point.

'Why are you so prim and proper? Honest, that's all I hear from Mam and Dad: Emma this, Emma that, it does my head in.'

Emma flicked her long honey-blonde hair over her shoulders and licked her pearly-white teeth. 'Some of us have got it and some of us haven't, Sis.'

Susan rolled on her side and admired her sister's lips. 'You said you would take me for some filler, what happened to that?'

Emma stroked her single finger along her own heart-shaped lips. 'I know I did. I'm due to have mine topped up next week, maybe if you sort yourself out, I might take you.'

'Would you really? Go on then, tell me what I need to do to get some filler and I will do it.'

Emma looked around her bedroom and smiled. 'You can do my share of the housework for me. I'm going to be busy studying all week, so I need peace and quiet in here, don't be bothering me.'

'Consider it done.' Susan grinned. 'Oh my God, I can't wait to tell Sabrina I'm having my lips done, she'll be so jealous.' She jumped up from the bed and started to pick up the dirty clothes scattered about the floor. She picked up an underwear set and held it out in front of her. She smirked and shot a look over at her sister. 'I didn't have you down for wearing stuff like this, I thought you wore them passion-killer knickers.'

Emma went beetroot and made no eye contact. 'Bloody hell, just put them in the washing basket. You weirdo.'

Susan burst out laughing and started to shove the red knickers in her sister's face. They were both screaming howling.

'Move them away from me! Oh my God, Susan, if you don't shift away from me with them then say goodbye to getting those lips done.'

Susan backed off and smiled at Emma. 'So come on, who's getting to see these kinky knickers?'

Emma was on the defensive and Susan could see she was getting angry. She was like that, Emma, one minute she would be laughing and joking and the next she would bite your head off.

'I just bought them to go with my new dress. I'm not wearing skanky knickers when I'm wearing a mint dress, am I?'

'Hurry up and get out of bed then if you want me to clean your room.' Emma shooed her out instead. 'You can clean later when I'm up. Turn that music down too because how on earth am I supposed to study with that crap blaring. You know next door will be straight onto Mam about the music being loud if you don't turn it down, don't you?'

Susan hurried back to her own bedroom and quickly turned her music off. Emma was right, with nosey neighbours like theirs, any loud music coming from the house would be reported to her parents and that was the last thing she needed when she was already in the bad books.

Chapter Two

Brooke McQueen sat in the corner of the bedroom with her knees pulled up to her chest. Long strands of dark hair stuck to the side of her cheek. She'd not slept all night, just dozed fitfully huddled against the wall. She was glad it was morning at long last, the birds tweeting outside her bedroom window, singing a song of freedom that she envied. Why was she still in a relationship with this guy when every time he had a few beers he would become abusive and kick ten tonnes of shit out of her? Every day she had to tread on eggshells, scared he would turn on her if she put one foot out of line. Time and time again, he'd promised her he would never raise his hands to her again, but it was all lies, pure bullshit. Every time it happened he held her past against her – and it felt like a noose around her neck. The more she struggled, the tighter it got.

She'd known it was going to be one of 'those' nights when she'd heard the scraping at the lock which signalled her husband was too boozed up to let himself in.

Vincent had finally got his key into the front door and lurched inside the house, falling into the walls, knocking over Brooke's vase on the hall-stand. He gripped the banister and made his way straight upstairs, falling over and mumbling to himself. Once he was at the top, he kicked his shoes off and stared at the bedroom door, a look in his eyes that said nothing good. He pushed the bedroom door open slowly with the flat of his hand and stood looking over at the bed. He moved closer into the room and sneered as he looked down at his wife. 'Look at you laying there thinking you're all that. I could have had any woman out there tonight and I chose to come home to you like a prick. Gorgeous women too, big tits, long legs. All over me they were, flirting, fluttering their eyelashes.'

Brooke had rolled over onto her side and pulled the duvet over her shoulder, sick of her drunken husband's voice, she'd heard it all before. Her eyes closed and she tried going back to sleep again. 'Just go to sleep, Vincent, have you seen the time? I have to be up early in the morning, I'm in work and so are you.'

Vincent stood over her, a tank of a man, chiselled chin, roughly shaven, tanned arms that stretched his shirt with their muscles. His teeth clenched together tightly as he bent his body down, his warm, drunken breath made her flinch. 'Like I'm arsed if you have work or not. You'll have to let all your clients down, like you let me down. You make me sick, Brooke; they say there is a lot of truth spoken when you're drunk and I'm saying it – you are the lowest of the low. What a plank I am for sticking by you, right til the fucking bitter end. Maybe I should clear out.

For once and for all.' He met her eyes with his and ran his tongue over his gums.

Brooke knew then there would be no sleep that night and rolled on her back so she could see his full face. She folded her arms tightly and snarled up at him. 'Oh give it a rest, will you? You say this all the time and yet the next day there are flowers and sorry notes all around the house. If that's what you want, then pack your stuff and be done with me. I'm sick of hearing it, change the bleeding record. But,' she paused, 'Don't expect me to be on my own for long. If you're moving on, then so am I. If it's good enough for you, then it's good enough for me.' As the words left her mouth she asked herself why she didn't just keep her mouth shut and let him have his say, she knew what he was like when he was pissed, knew he would kick off. Rule number one: never argue with a drunken man, her mother had always told her – but there was only so much of his crap she could take.

Vincent's nostrils flared and his chest expanded, she'd rattled his cage for sure. 'You're a slapper, why did I expect anything more from you? From the moment we met you were easy, so I guess it's my own fault for being with a dirty bitch. An unfaithful one at that. And I'm the daft bastard who put a ring on you. More fool me, aye?'

Brooke sat up and tucked the duvet under her arms tightly. There was no way she was listening to this anymore, sick of it she was, sick to death of hearing the same old story. Brooke had always been a pretty thing, long raven-black hair and big blue eyes, but she knew she looked haunted now. It came of a life of listening to abuse like this. Well, even a broken woman had her limits. 'You shouldn't drink if it makes you like this. You might not care about my work but you've got a shift tomorrow or are you missing it again? It's been twice this week; you'll end up losing your job. You've got a drink problem, just admit it and get some help and do us both a bleeding favour. Because I can't carry on like this.'

His head tilted to the side as he replied. 'I go out and drink so I don't have to look at your ugly mush every evening, drink to forget what you did, him and you, the whole sordid affair.'

Brooke swallowed hard and watched him from the corner of her eyes as he staggered around to the other side of the bed. Silence as he slumped onto the bed next to her, her heartbeat doubling, aware what would come next. She was a sitting target, and she knew it. Brooke slid one long tanned leg out of the bed, ready to make a dash for it into the other bedroom, the colour from her face draining with every second that passed. But as she inched away, his heavy hand reached over and gripped her tightly, dragging her back onto the bed. His voice louder.

'No you don't, you're staying here. What, you think you can just clear off when I have to relive you shagging that prick every night when I close my eyes? You're staying put, listening to what I have to say. Hearing the truth about yourself.'

'Just leave me alone, Vincent, we've been through this time and time again. It was a mistake, a daft mistake, are you going to make me pay for this every second of my life? I'm sick of the paranoia, the checking on me all day.

Just be done with me if that's how you feel. I can't take it anymore, it's torture. And keep your voice down, the neighbours will hear you.' Brooke was dicing with death, but she'd spent too long keeping her mouth shut – the words spewing out like lava now.

His voice roared and his eyes danced with madness as he ran his fingers through his hair. 'Do you think I give a flying fuck if the neighbours can hear me or not. I'll tell them all should I, tell them all about you and your dirty antics. I was never like this, it's you who has made me like this. Just because you couldn't keep your knickers on, you ruined everything, ruined us. I should have kept a closer tab on you, not trusted you like I did. Once bitten twice shy. I won't make that mistake again, trust me. You'll be by my side all the time. You're my wife, don't forget that, and you will act like it and give me some fucking respect. Til death do us part remember, shag-bag.' He dragged her across the bed and smashed his curled fist into her face, once, twice, three times.

'No, Vincent!' she screamed out.

'You're a dirty slag, say it, say you're a dirty slag.' Bright-red blood pumped from Brooke's nose and already her eyes were swelling up. She fought for her life, scratching at his eyes, punching, kicking, anything to get his huge body from hers. Finally, she wriggled free. Brooke was gasping for her breath. She ran to the corner of the room and looked around for something to defend herself. Anything she could find to belt him over his head with, a candlestick, a shoe, anything that would put him on his arse or even just buy her a precious few seconds. But it seemed like, for now, he was done. He turned away without another word.

Brooke could hear her husband's breathing from where she was sitting now; there she was, shivering in the corner while he was snoring, not a care in the world. She peeped over the side of the bed and stared over at him. Dare she move? She lifted her head up slowly and held her breath for a few seconds. Slowly, she got on all fours and crawled to the bedroom door. There was no way she could go into the salon first thing; she'd have to hide away from the world again until her bruises were covered. Tell lies, make something up. She was sick of it, sick of living in this hellhole. So why didn't she leave, pack her stuff up and leave his sorry arse to rot? Brooke asked herself this exact question after every bruise, every punch and she still didn't know the answer. Maybe it was the guilt, the affair.

Vincent would be on *his* hands and knees when he woke and realised what he'd done to her, crying like a baby and begging her not to tell anyone. Then the gifts would come; flowers, clothes, anything to stop her from telling the world and his wife he was a wife-beater. She'd threatened to tell his mother what was going on too, tell her all about her abusive son. But time and again she'd listened to him and believed he would change. Plus, he told her if she ever breathed a word to his mother, he would tell her all about her sordid secret, her cheating. A hot flush of shame always gripped her when she thought about what she'd done. But more than the guilt and the shame, it was fear that tied her to her vows.

Brooke edged into the bathroom and locked the door behind her with shaking hands. Her back was pressed against the door firmly, her body trembling from top to toe like she'd just stepped out of a freezer. She took some deep breaths and looked over at the silver mirror hung on the wall and cringed as she looked at her reflection. This was not the woman she was five years ago; where had her smile gone, her happy eyes, her perfect figure? She looked haggard, as though she'd aged in double-speed. She pressed her index finger gently against her eyes to test the swelling, a deeper-purple colour appearing with every second that passed. Her nose looked swollen too. Her throbbing hand twisted the tap on and slowly she started to wash the dried blood from her face. The water turned red in the sink as she sluiced her finger around in it, just staring. To the world outside they looked like a happy couple, but the truth was eating away at everything just under the surface. But he was right about one thing though, it was she who crossed the line first, made him lose trust in her. Was this what she deserved for her infidelity? She asked herself.

Before the affair, they were going through a bad patch where all they seemed to be doing every day was arguing. They had bickered over anything and everything. If he left the toilet seat up, she'd moan at him and if she left hair in the sink, he would have the house up in arms. Brooke had reached the point where she hated being in the same room as her husband then, almost living separate lives under one roof. So, on a night out with her friends in the local boozer, she'd met Lee Jakes for the first time, and he had been just what she needed to make her smile again. Lee was Jack the lad and from the moment she met him he had her in stitches laughing. Jake was married himself and never hid the fact away from her, said he was happy at home and loved his wife with all his heart so at first it seemed like a bit of harmless flirting. The perfect gentleman. For weeks Lee was always in the pub when she went, and though the temptation was always there, it seemed safe enough when it was look-but-don't-touch. If only it had stayed that way. But the way he looked at her, the compliments he gave her, the way he made her feel inside, giddy – she knew she was playing with fire. Brooke wanted him from the start, if she was being honest with herself and even though she denied it, he was fair game in her eyes. So what if he was married, so was she. It meant things wouldn't get out of hand, she told herself – a little fling that could maybe save both their marriages. It was just a bit of fun, nobody would get hurt, would they – they both had something to lose. The affair started with a drunken kiss, nothing more, nothing less. But as time went on, they both wanted more of the forbidden fruit. All she thought about was him, every day, every hour, couldn't wait for the weekend to come so she could see him again. Then the texts messages started to each other, words that made her heart skip a beat. Words that took her away from her stale marriage. Lee suggested they should spend more time together and booked a hotel room for them both. She was more than up for it and never batted an eyelid when she told her husband a pack of lies about her going away for the weekend with the girls. She went and bought new underwear, the full works to impress the new man in her life. The affair had lasted over six months, and she had been in deep danger of falling in love with Lee. They spoke about a life together and holidays in the future. But they were words spoken when they were drunk and not living in the real world. Brooke would have been one of the first people to tell her clients not to listen to anything a married man was telling them and there she was, lost in Lee's come-to-bed eyes listening to what he wanted her to hear, believing his lies.

It had all come crashing down one Saturday night when Lee's wife followed her husband and found him in the hotel room with Brooke after a tip-off from one of her friends. It was the night the car crash of her life finally burst into flames. She knew she deserved her fury but Lee's mrs was a nutter, had tried to scratch her eyes out, to scar her. When Lee had finally separated the women, his wife stood in front of him and asked if Brooke was what he really wanted. She remembered the day as if it was yesterday. She stood looking at Lee, remembering the sex they had shared, the excitement, and more than anything the night they said they loved each other. Lee had shot a look over at her and dropped his head low, he swallowed hard and took his wife's hand and walked away with her. He never looked back once either, never said goodbye. It had all been just a bit of fun for him, a leg-over – make-believe. Brooke promised herself after that day that she would never, ever let herself slip again. Patch things up at home. And that was her plan until Lee's wife turned up at her house and told Vincent everything about the affair.

Brooke had had a hard day's graft in the salon and couldn't wait to get home and snuggle up on the sofa and chill out. But as she let herself in through her front door, Gemma walked out from the kitchen and smirked at Brooke. A look in her eye that told her she wasn't getting away with anything after wrecking her marriage. Vincent made Brooke sit down and listen to what Gemma had to say.

'Did you think you could just walk away from this and go back to your own marriage without anyone finding out? You've destroyed my life and I'm making sure your husband knows exactly what he's sleeping with every single night. A lying, cheating whore. Lee has been bin-bagged and I told him I never wanted to see his sorry arse again, so, if sloppy seconds is your thing, go and get him because now I know he's had it shoved up you, I wouldn't touch him with a bargepole, love.'

Brooke tried to say something – the apology turning to ash in her mouth – but Vincent shut her up straight away with a cold stare. The look in his eyes was something she would never forget. As Gemma continued telling Vincent about all the hotels her husband had paid for on his credit card, the gifts, the underwear, Brooke was sobbing her heart out. She knew this wasn't going to end well. 'Babes, it was a mistake. A daft, stupid mistake. You're the one I love, nobody else. He meant nothing to me. We were arguing all the time and you said yourself that our marriage was pointless.'

Vincent told Gemma to leave the house after she'd filled him in on all the gory details. But after she'd left all hell broke loose. He smashed the house up, slapped her about and left her regretting each choice that had led her to this sorry state. He'd pissed off down to the pub to drown his sorrows and she was left behind, broken and bruised in the silence, realising at that moment that she'd been an idiot, that neither of these men were any good for her.

The trouble was, Vince wasn't the kind of man who you could leave easily. That first week he told her straight that he'd kill her sooner than let her leave him.

The days after the affair was revealed were hard, more tears from her while Vincent hit the bottle hard and hardly spoke a word to her. In the mood he was in, Brooke knew he'd come good on his threat if she tried to leave, so for months she bent over backward for him – cooking, cleaning and making sure he didn't have to lift a finger; she took him away on weekends, bought him clothes and anything else she could do to make him love her again. Determined to paper over the cracks, she remembered her mother always told her that time was a good healer and as the months passed, she thought perhaps so had the danger. Occasionally he'd hold her hand or ask about her day. Once, after a few beers, he even told her he loved her again. But the drinking never stopped; the brandy, the late nights coming home, and she was sure she sometimes smelled perfume on him when he fell into bed next to her. Maybe he had another woman, she wasn't sure – but she knew she'd lost her ability to say anything without enraging him. Even on good days, their relationship felt like a grenade. Vincent had spent many years in the military service, and he'd seen things no man was supposed to see, had friends dying in his arms. Brooke even tried to get him some help for PTSD, but he never took her up on her offer, always told her he was a big man and he would sort his shit out himself. He never did and so she'd learned to live a narrow life around his moods. Most of the time she could bite her tongue, but sometimes even a beaten dog will bite back. And look at where it had got her.

She'd spent the night on the bathroom floor but could see the dawn breaking thought the obscured glass of the window. Brooke stood up gingerly and scraped her hair back and tied it into a ponytail. She patted some witch hazel onto a cotton wool pad and pressed it softly against her eyes. At least she knew how to treat her injuries, by now she had lots of potions and lotions at hand to disguise the bruises. Brooke sat on the toilet and dropped her head low. What would she tell her clients today if they noticed the shiner showing through her make-up? How could she look at them in the mirror when she couldn't look at herself? Maybe she'd have to call in sick. Brooke rubbed at her arms as the hairs stood on end, a chill running up her spine as she heard her name being shouted from outside the bathroom.

'Brooke, what are you doing in there? Hurry up and get your arse back in bed where I can see you.' Her fists curled into two tight balls at the side of her legs and she banged them on the toilet seat.

'Piss off, will you? I'll be out when I'm out.'

There was a booting sound at the bottom of the door. 'I said: hurry up and get back where I can see you.' Brooke covered her mouth with her hands to stop the crying. She needed to be strong, go back into the bedroom and wait until he was fully sober. She was telling him then, telling him she couldn't take it anymore. Or maybe he'd meant it last night when he said he was moving on. She shivered as she imagined a life not in his shadow.

Brooke lay staring at the ceiling. She'd called the salon with an excuse, then crept back to bed to face her husband, only to find him snoring again. But Vincent was stirring now and she knew any second soon he would open his eyes and look at her. The same shit, different day. 'Babes, get me a drink of water, will you? My head feels like it's going to fall off. On my life, I'm never drinking again.'

Brooke remained silent. He rummaged about in the bed, found her hand and held it. Turning to face her, his eyes were wide open and his jaw dropped low. Brooke nodded. 'Yes, it was you who did this to me before you ask.'

Vincent sat up and scratched at his head. Here it was: the usual performance, denial. 'On my life, I don't remember a thing. You must have been winding me up or something because why would I do something like this to you?'

Brooke knew this was her time now, a chance for her to tell him she was leaving him. These brief moments where he was sorry would be her only chance to say something without him beating her to hell and back. She sat on the edge of the bed. 'Vincent, I told you last time that if you ever raised your hands at me again then we were over. It's the same old story; me and the affair and how much of a slut I am. I can't take it anymore. As sad as it is, it happened and I can't change it, but I can change how you are treating me.'

Vincent gulped, reached over and put his arms around her tightly, kissing her cheek, her face. 'I'm sorry, honest, I don't remember a thing. It's the PTSD – I just blackout, you know that. It was just the booze talking. I'll make it up to you.'

'Not this time. I'm packing my things and I'm going. You need to sort your head out and get some help.'

He was on the defensive now, blaming her for his behaviour. 'No, you're not going anywhere. We'll sit down and work it out, just like we did when you fucked up. You owe me that, Brooke, let me fix everything, make it right.' He started crying and dropped his head low. 'Without you, I'm nothing. I admit I've been drinking a lot lately, but I'll sort it. You just watch, starting from now I'll only have a few cans when the footy is on.'

'No, Vincent. I've made my mind up. I can't do this anymore. Look at my face, my arms, my legs. Do you think it's normal to beat your wife like this?'

'Any red-blooded man would do what I've done if they found out their wife was cheating.'

There it was again, old crimes she could never serve her sentence for. She softened her voice and turned to face him. 'How many times do I have to tell you that I know I fucked up. It was years ago yet you go on like it was yesterday. We can both move on, be happy. What's the point in living in this crappy relationship? We can let each

other go or we can do it the hard way – you telling everyone what I did and me having you up on an assault
charge.' The mention of the police frightened him.

'You would never be a grass, would you? Imagine if I
told everyone you were a snitch, you know as much as me
that it wouldn't sit right with anyone around here.'

'Do you think I'm arsed what people say about me?
You should be the one who is more worried when I tell
everyone you're a wife-beater. Maybe I'll start with your
mam, aye?'

Vincent switched, gripped her face in his hand and
squeezed it. 'I've said I'm sorry, what more do you want?
Tell you what, I'll go and get you that new perfume you
wanted, that should show you I mean it. Gucci, wasn't it?
Floral?'

Brooke shook her head and fell back down onto the
bed, exhausted. No perfume could cover the rot in their
relationship. 'Just leave me alone, Vincent. Leave me
alone.'

Chapter Three

Sabrina Clarke was dressed in her usual gear – an over-sized grey Nike tracksuit, big gold hoop earrings, a dodgy tan and pencilled-in brows that looked like boomerangs. Susan crossed the road to where her friend stood outside the corner shop. 'I need some fags, let's nip into Sav's and see if he will give them us on tick until we come back from town.'

They walked into the small shop and headed for the till. Sav smiled when he spotted the girls, who often came into the shop to chill with him when the shop was quiet. Sav had always had an eye for the ladies, and even though he had twenty years on Susan, she knew he was starting to notice her. There were plenty of rumours about him and a few of the women from the estate but nothing had ever been proved, maybe it was just gossip. Susan knew how quickly rumours spread around here. As the girls rounded the narrow aisle, Angela Towen appeared and snarled at Sabrina. Angela wasn't that much older than them but she'd worked here for what seemed like forever and once had caught Sabrina shoplifting. Ever since then she wouldn't take her eyes from her. She was on high alert now that she'd spotted Sabrina and Susan.

'Alright, Sav, how's it going?' Sabrina hollered over.

The shopkeeper smiled and stood up from his seat behind the counter. 'All the better for seeing your two pretty faces.'

Sabrina turned to face Susan and winked. Sav was in a good mood; it was a good time to ask the question. But hold on, bloody hell, Angela was weaving her way behind the counter. 'Can I help you, ladies?' she asked.

'No, I've not decided what I want yet,' Sabrina hissed.

Sav could see this wasn't going to end well. 'Ange, do me a favour, can you get those drinks in the back out and put them on the shelf. I'll serve these two.'

Angela stomped from behind the counter and headed into the back of the shop. Sabrina watched her and once she was gone, she whispered over at Sav. 'Why do you even have her working here with you? Look at the state of her, a slobby mess. You should give Susan here a job and cart that rottweiler.'

Sav kept his voice low. 'You're joking, aren't you? I'm petrified of her, she tells me what to do.'

They all started laughing. Sav looked over at Susan and scanned her up and down. 'But I do need a weekend girl for stacking shelves and all that if you're interested. Pay's not that good, I admit, but there are perks...'

Susan moved closer, excited at the thought of earning a quid at something that didn't look too much like hard yards. 'Yeah, defo. It will get my mam off my case. I'll start this weekend if you want? Tell you what, I'll rock up tomorrow and you can show me what's what.'

Angela was back near the counter and she'd clearly heard what was being said, her face like a smacked arse. 'Sav, I thought we were going to let Jeanette have the weekend job, she's been asking for ages and we know she's reliable.'

Susan was right back at her. 'I'm reliable too and if it's Jeanette Parker you are on about, she's only 14 years old. I've got way more nous than her.'

Angela shook her head and shot a look over at Sav. 'It's your shop, I'm just saying, that's all.' Angela stalked away.

Susan grinned. 'I've got a job; I've only gone and landed myself a job.'

Sabrina seized the moment. 'Now I've helped you out in recruiting this fine young lady here, I need a favour from you in return, Sav. Can you do me twenty Bensons and Hedges silver on tick until later?'

Sav craned his neck to see where Angela was and quickly passed Sabrina the ciggies. 'I know you're good for them. I'll write it down in my book. Make sure you come back and pay me though, because if at the end of the week they haven't been paid for then it'll show up on stocktake and you'll never get tick again.'

Sabrina snatched the cigarettes from his hand and rammed them into her pocket before Angela clocked them. 'Come on, Sav, I always cough up what I owe.'

As the girls started to walk out of the shop, Susan shouted back to the shopkeeper. 'See you Friday, Sav. I'll be here on time, don't worry about that. I'm a career girl now.'

Sabrina and Susan stood waiting for the bus to take them into town, chain-smoking. 'You can box that shop right off when you've been there a few weeks, Sue. We will always have cigs and beer now, won't we?'

Susan stood back. 'No way I'm nicking from the shop where I work. I'll get done – and I'll lose my first decent job.'

'Stop being a wet wipe, girl. I would have never suggested you work there if I knew you were going to be like this.'

Susan didn't know what to say and stood chugging hard on her fag. She faced the oncoming traffic and quickly flicked her cigarette. This was just step one. She knew if she wanted to get off the Manor, she needed cash. Once she had some dough, she'd show everyone she was no baby anymore.

Chapter Four

10 Manor Road was busier than usual. Bronwen Murphy was getting ready for her son's eighteenth birthday party at The Griffin, and even though she was holding it at the local pub rather than at home, she was stressed as could be. For weeks now she'd been planning her son's surprise do and now it had landed on her doorstep she was a bag of nerves. Cake: check; presents: check; guests arriving on time: check; the list was endless. Time and time again she went through her to-do list thinking she'd missed something. Everything was covered, but she still felt something was not right. Maybe it was just because she knew her little boy was an adult now. Old enough to leave the nest.

Bronwen's partner Anthony walked into the kitchen and looked around at the different boxes. 'Is that the cake?'

Bronwen twisted her head and clocked the large white cardboard box sat on the table. 'Yes, oh bloody hell. That needs dropping off at the pub before we get there. Is there any chance you can shove it in the car and whizz it over before Matthew gets home. He thinks we're just going for a few drinks. If he sees the cake, he'll put two and two together and realise we've done him a party. You know what he's like. Bloody hell, I think it'll be a relief when it's over – you know how I hate surprises.'

Anthony had been with Bronwen now for over eight years. They'd met online and while they'd both known from the moment they started talking that they had loads in common, Bronwen's son had only been a kid at the time, protective of his mum. Matthew hadn't warmed to his mother's new boyfriend at first and it was only over the last few years that he would even give him the time of the day. In his eyes it had just been him and his mam, nobody else, when he was little – they didn't need anyone else to be a family. Bronwen had always doted on her son, had done everything she could for him. Even now, when they rowed, Anthony said she treated him like a baby. According to him, the lad needed to grow a set and go and live his life instead of relying on his mother for everything. Anthony had tried telling the lad a few home truths – told him the moment *he'd* turned eighteen he'd moved out and got a job and stood on his own two feet. Like a real man. Whereas Matthew never had to do anything for himself. Even now Bronwen ran his bath, ironed his clothes, cooked all of his meals. Whenever Ant argued with his missus over it she never listened to a word, she just smiled and said he was her boy and that was the end of it. More or less, like it or lump it. But he knew she'd never change her mind, never encourage the kid to move out.

'I'll just put a clean shirt on and take the cake, is there anything else that needs taking because I'm not doing loads of trips. I've not sat down all day, knackered I am.'

Bronwen stood thinking for a few seconds. 'Oh yes, bloody hell, the balloons. Gaynor said she will sort them out for me when they get there so that saves me a job.' She checked her watch and raised her eyebrows. 'Hurry up then, love. By the time you come back he'll be due home from work.'

Anthony sighed. 'And we wouldn't want Sonny boy to be disappointed, would we?' Bronwen was on her high horse and gunning for him, ready to defend her boy as she always did. 'And you mean what by that?'

'You know what I mean, the kid is 18 years old today and yet you still treat him like a baby. It winds me up. I only ask you to make me a drink and I get carted.'

'I've told you, our Matthew has had it hard and I'm his mother, so I'll do what I have to do to make him smile each day. Jealousy is a bad trait, you know?'

He let out a sarcastic laugh. 'Had it hard, are you having a laugh or what, woman? It's me who has it hard running around after him every bleeding day.'

'He was bullied, Anthony; those bastards made his life a misery for years and we knew nothing about it. If it wasn't for our Malc chinning them, it would probably still be going on.'

'Kids fight, it's part of growing up. He should have listened to me when I told him to knock the fuckers out instead of running crying to you. That's what my dad did with me. Told me to stop crying, get back outside and stand up to them.'

Bronwen was furious now. 'He's not a fighter, he's not like you – brute force isn't his way. Using your fists isn't always the answer, you know.'

'Well, maybe he should be more like me instead, bleeding fairy.'

Bronwen slammed her hand on the kitchen table, eyes wide open. She was a small woman but seemed to grow with her fierce anger. 'Don't you ever use those vile names about my boy. That attitude went out with the Neanderthals. Just go and drop the cake off before we end up falling out. In future, keep your remarks about Matthew to yourself. If you haven't got anything nice to say, then be quiet.'

'I'm going, don't you worry about that. You can rely on me to get things done – that's what a real bloke does.' Anthony hefted the boxes and left the tiny kitchen.

Bronwen walked into the living room and smiled as she looked at all the gifts she'd wrapped for her son's birthday. Bright-golden ribbons, sparkling blue wrapping paper. They were arranged across the floor near the television, all ready for her son to open. Every year since he was a tot she'd done the same – determined her boy would never go without, even the years when she didn't know where the money was coming from. Bronwen had been a single parent since Matthew was six months old and she would have walked over hot coals to make sure he never felt the lack of having a dad around. He wasn't missing much, she figured. Matthew's dad was an arse-hole and although she'd been in a relationship with him on and off for a few years before Matthew came along, she knew from day one he was never going to stick around once the baby was born. Selfish he was, not a fatherly bone in his body. Norris was a workaholic, and he'd never bonded with his son, just told her to shut the kid up from crying. It had been a relief when he'd walked out, she admitted to herself. And it had been enough – just mother and son for the next ten years. She'd had a few dates, been set up by a few friends, but they'd not gone anywhere. Anthony was the only man she'd let move in with her and her son.

Anthony was back before Matthew got home, just like he'd promised. Bronwen stood at the window waiting for her son to arrive, anxiously walking one way then the other. He'd left for work early that morning so this was her first chance to make a fuss of him. Her voice was high-pitched as she clocked him walking down the garden path. 'Quick, Anthony, he's here.'

Matthew walked through the front door and Bronwen started singing at the top of her lungs. 'Happy birthday to you, happy birthday to you…' She turned and urged Anthony to join in too.

Matthew went bright red, he'd always hated fuss, but he knew his mum liked to mark the day. He kicked his black shoes off and hung his coat up on the peg in the hallway. Bronwen flung her arms around his neck and squeezed him tightly, kissing his cheeks, his head. Anthony stood back and made his way into the living room, he couldn't watch it any longer. Bronwen covered her son's eyes with both hands and guided him further into the room. 'Keep those eyes closed, I know you're a peeper. Come on, careful you don't trip.' Once she had brought her son into the living room, she dropped her hands from his eyes. 'Surprise!' She pointed to all the gifts and quickly turned to look at her son's reaction, was he happy? She wasn't sure.

'Thanks, Mam, you didn't have to do all this. Where have all these presents come from?'

'Me and Anthony, Son. My boy is only eighteen once and we wanted to make it special for you. You can open your presents then we are going down to The Griffin for a few drinks. I've invited Nana and Grandad and a few of the neighbours.'

Matthew settled down on the sofa. 'Mam, you know I didn't want a big deal. I said I would go out with Ben and Malc tonight. I wish you would ask me before you arrange stuff.'

'They can come to the pub with us for a bit surely? They'll understand you want to spend your eighteenth with family, I bet. Anyway, Gaynor has got a DJ on tonight so it should be fun. But never mind that now, open your presents.'

Matthew got down on the floor like he was still a little kid and started to open his gifts. Bronwen was on the floor next to him, passing him the presents. He opened the first gift and smiled over at his mother. 'Hugo Boss aftershave. Mint that, Mam.'

Bronwen's eyes flooded with tears and she placed a single hand on her chest to stop the emotions from rising. How had her baby gone from boy to man? 'I saw you looking at it when we were out shopping.'

Anthony looked over at the bottle of aftershave and huffed. It looked like the real thing. If he remembered rightly, for his birthday, he'd only got a Lynx set. He shouldn't be jealous of a mother and son's bond, he knew that. But the kid was a brat in his eyes, a mummy's boy, and it would do both of them good to cut the apron strings. Maybe they just needed a bit of help to make that happen.

Bronwen watched her son open all his presents and waited for the cuddle at the end of it, the cuddle that told her he was happy.

'Thanks, Mam, you shouldn't have got me all these presents though! I bet you spent an arm and a leg?'

'Don't you worry what I spent. This is the big one-eight. Now, come on, hurry up and go and get a shower. We need to be in the pub for half seven. I've ironed your clothes and hung them up in your wardrobe.'

Matthew climbed to his feet and went over to shake Anthony's hand. 'Cheers for the presents, mate.'

You could have cut the atmosphere with a knife – Anthony nodded in acknowledgement but nobody was speaking. To escape the awkward silence, Matthew picked up his gifts and left the room.

Bronwen gasped. 'Bleeding hell, you could have been a bit more enthusiastic.'

'What for? I sat here and watched him open his presents, didn't I? Did you want me doing the bleeding conga around the front room?'

'No, I just wanted you to be happy like I am.'

Anthony stood up and walked to the front window, gazing outside. 'I'll never be enough, will I. If it's not being happy enough then it's something else, isn't it? You've always made it quite clear that Matthew is your son and not mine, so I don't know what else you want from me?'

Bronwen dropped her head low, aware that she had always been clear that Matthew was her son, and she didn't need any man to step in and become his father. She was all he needed. When she started dating she always said it was because she wanted a partner, not because her boy needed a dad. And she'd have done it all again if she could have – it wasn't her fault that Anthony was unable to father a child, was it? Bronwen stood up and walked behind him and hugged him. 'Let's not fall out. Today's a big day for Matthew. We have to look happy when we walk into the pub and see all the family, don't we?'

Anthony closed his eyes for a few seconds and turned to face her. 'We sure do, don't we? Always put a smile on our faces and pretend to everyone that everything is rosy in the garden?'

———

'Surprise!' all the guests shouted as Matthew Murphy walked into The Griffin. He blushed bright red and didn't know where to look as he spotted members of his family scattered about the boozer crowded with friends and locals. Bronwen was standing in front of him, now taking photographs on her phone. 'Smile, birthday boy!' she yelled as she encouraged members of her family to get in the photo too.

Anthony went straight to the bar and ordered himself a drink. Partly because he wanted a beer, and partly as an excuse to avoid all the fuss and photos. Dane, the land-lord, was behind the bar tonight and he smiled when he spotted Anthony. Dane loved talking to his regulars and he would chat for hours given the chance. There was a new barmaid tonight behind the bar and the doe-eyed blonde looked like she was rushed off her feet. She'd done a few shifts earlier in the week, but up until now Anthony had not really spoken to her.

Dane stood facing Anthony and shot a look over at Alison, the new girl.

'A bit of alright, isn't she? A bit clumsy though. She's already dropped two pints. I'm going to see how she does tonight, then make a decision on whether or not she's staying or going.'

Anthony hung over the bar to get a better look at her and smiled over at Dane. 'I'd keep her on to look at. Nice arse.' They both started laughing, checking that nobody had heard them. Dane's wife, Gaynor, would have decked him if she'd have heard him and Anthony was still stung that Bronwen had called him a neanderthal earlier – and just because he wasn't ashamed to be an old-fashioned bloke.

'A pint is it, mate?' asked Dane.

'Yeah, I'll be on the whisky later on no doubt, but a pint is fine for now.' The barmaid was smiling at him now. He checked over his shoulder to make sure it was him she was looking at and nobody else. He swallowed and pulled his shoulders back. 'How are you finding it, love?'

Alison rested her elbows on the bar as she spoke to him. His gaze shot to her low-cut blouse, eyes already wandering.

'I'm trying my best, but I keep messing up. I thought it would be easy, but I keep forgetting what people are ordering and spilling stuff.'

Anthony quickly checked where Bronwen was and carried on talking. 'It will all become second nature to a bright girl like you soon enough. Practice makes perfect. If I'm at the bar I will try and help you remember what people are ordering.'

Alison blushed. 'That would be so nice. I just need to get used to it, I think. Dane said everyone's like this when they first start but I can't see it, I'm bobbins.'

Anthony winked at Dane as he passed over his pint. 'You've got a good one here, Dane, best in a long time.'

Alison playfully nudged his arm and went to serve another customer on the other side of him. Anthony listened carefully to the long order and once she started to pull the first pint, mouthed over to her. 'A double vodka next and a pint of cider.'

She was flustered as she tried to stop the frothy head on the first pint slopping over, and kept looking over at him for support.

Matthew sat with Ben and Malcolm across the pub. Malc had been his closest friend for years and they were hardly ever apart. They both knew they looked like an odd pair – Malcolm was built like a fridge while Matthew could have hidden behind a lamppost. But their friendship went way back and Malc would protect Matthew if any aggro even looked like starting. Many a time he'd stepped in and chinned someone for having a go at him.

'Give it another half an hour and we're out of here. Sorry, lads, I didn't know they were throwing a party for me. You know what my mam's like, don't you?'

Ben looked around the pub. 'Mate, you're eighteen now, not a fucking pensioner. Your mam's invited a bunch of old farts. We're out for some decent pussy tonight and looking around this pub I don't think we will find it here.'

Matthew chuckled. 'Well it's not what I'm looking for!' He turned to Malc. 'Are you out for a bit of fun tonight too?'

Malcolm shrugged. 'I'll have a look who's out. That lass last week was a right nutter. I went back to her house, and she woke her mam and dad up she was that loud.'

'Did you get a shag though?' Ben asked.

'Yes, but still, it's not the point. Her dad was pissed off, but her mam was ready to go into the kitchen to make us all something to eat until I refused and told them I had to leave. On my life, a bunch of weirdos. I'm staying single me, can't be arsed with women.'

Matthew clocked his mam heading his way, just as the music changed. 'Ah, for fuck's sake, here comes the dance-with-me moment.' He dropped his head low and all he could feel was his mother dragging him up from his seat.

'Come on birthday boy, let's have a boogie.'

Ben and Malc sniggered to each other and found it hard to keep their faces straight. What a nightmare for Matthew's street cred. Bronwen twisted and spun her son around the dance floor, aware people were watching them. Matthew shook his head, knowing his mum well enough to know what was coming. And there was no stopping her once she got on a dancefloor. As the beat took over, Bronwen slut-dropped to the floor.

'Wow, Mam, sort it out, will you? Stop making a show of me, my mates are here. Are you forgetting that?'

Bronwen had had a few too many and didn't listen to a word he said. 'Oh lighten up, mard-arse. I'm having a good time. This is what I do when I let my hair down. It might be your entry into adulthood, sunshine, but I'm also celebrating eighteen years of being a mum. And I've still got it...'

Matthew shook his head and couldn't wait for the song to stop. Why couldn't he have had a normal mum like all his mates? Bronwen was still going for gold; snake-hips, fast feet, dancing her heart out. At last, the song finished, and she ran over, grinning, and took her son in her arms again. 'See, miserable arse, it's over with now.' She shot a look over at the bar at Anthony and saw he wasn't missing her. Another song came on and she was straight back on the dancefloor, arms held high in the air.

Matthew plonked down next to his mates and sighed. 'Get me out of here Ben, ring a Uber and let's get into town.'

Ben reached into his back pocket and pulled his iPhone out. 'Thank fuck for that, I thought we'd be here all night.'

Malc patted Matthew's shoulder. 'Brace yourself, it looks like your nana is on her way over to bust some moves, too.'

Matthew cringed, but by the time he'd spotted her it was too late to avoid her, as she beckoned him up to join her. It might have been mortifying, but he couldn't say no to his nan on his birthday. One more song and then he was out of there.

Matthew was almost trapped on the dancefloor between his grandmother and mother. They sandwiched him, spinning him, jiving, practically breakdancing. They were funny to watch, Matthew thought – funny if you weren't related to them. Bronwen was trying to teach her mother some moves and all her son could do was watch in horror. At last, Ben came up behind him and tapped him on the shoulder. 'Taxi's outside. Meet you out there.'

Bronwen was busy showing her mother how to slut drop and it wasn't going well. Matthew saw his chance and took it. He was gone.

———

The Gay Village was alive with music pumping from every pub, punters everywhere, bright clothes, wigs, high-heeled shoes tall enough to give anyone a nosebleed. The boys had hit all their favourite bars across town before ending up on Canal Street. Malc looked uneasy, out of his comfort zone. 'Why have we ended up here, we should have stayed where we were, the music was mint too.'

Ben patted the top of Malc's shoulder and kissed his cheek. 'Aw, are you scared that you might get picked up, lad.'

'Shut it, you prick,' Malc hissed.

Matthew was in his element though, singing his head off, necking mouthfuls of the champagne that Ben had bought him.

'Do you think he's bent or what then?' Ben asked Malc as they both looked over at their friend.

Malcolm was too busy checking out a new gaggle of girls that had walked in. 'I don't know, ask him.'

Ben watched Matthew in the distance dancing and turned to face Malc. 'Nah, I would rather not know if he's not ready to talk about it. Leave him to it. I'm happy if he's happy. Anyway, leaves more women to go around for you and me.'

The night was coming to an end and Ben and Malc could barely stand up as the lights started to flicker back on in the final bar. They'd copped off with a couple of birds with a plan to go back to their house and continue the party there. Although by now, Malc wasn't up for it, but Ben was pecking his head telling him not to be a misery.

Ben craned his neck, staggering as he stood up. 'I don't know where Matthew has got to, do you think he's pulled and gone somewhere or what?'

Malc was well gone and could hardly speak, his words were slurred. 'Leave him, he'll be fine. He's eighteen now, a big man.'

Ben nodded his head and held his hand out to the girl who was sat next to him. 'Come on, you, let's go and make some babies,' he chuckled.

Malc wobbled as he stood up too, leaning on the girl who was with him to hold him up. Ben shot another look around the pub to see if Matthew was anywhere to be found, but there was no sign of the birthday boy.

As the lights came up, Matthew scanned the emptying room for his mates. He could usually spot Malc's huge figure and Ben's bright-ginger hair anywhere. He'd been dancing the night away with a new gang of friends that he'd met; every time he tried to go back to his friends, they'd dragged him back to the dancefloor as another epic tune came on. They'd told him it was a crime to leave when Kylie was playing. But he'd assumed he'd see the lads outside. Yet he stood on the pavement now, looked one way then the other. The streets were still filled with drunken people, dancing and singing, but he couldn't spot Ben or Malc. The night air tickled his skin, and he started to cool down. Bloody hell, where were his friends? It was his birthday and it looked like they'd done one and left him on his own. He would never have left them on their tod.

Matthew grabbed himself a doner kebab from a takeaway and started to walk along the canal, still singing. He loved it down here and, when the weather was nice, he'd often walk this way to clear his head. He stood still for a moment, trying to get his bearings. If he followed it all the way, he wouldn't have far to walk to his house. Though he wasn't looking forward to getting home – his mum would be ready to read him the riot act for bailing on The Griffin earlier.

Red sauce dripped down the front of his shirt, but he didn't care as he munched his food. Between mouthfuls, he was still humming tunes. He saw a bench only a few steps from where he was and headed towards it, unsteady on his feet, trying to send a message on his phone. He plonked down on the old metal bench and looked around him. He could still hear the sounds of partying from other clubbers who'd been kicked out but didn't want the fun to stop and he smiled to himself as he took another bite from his kebab. It had been a good night. One to remember. Noises behind him of branches crunching disturbed his thoughts.

'Yo, bro, you got a ciggie I can have?'

Matthew turned his head and tried to focus on where the voice was coming from. As he blinked, his vision got clearer and he could see a man, although he smelled him first, even over the oil and garlic tang of his kebab. Scruffy the guy was, and, as he stumbled nearer, Matthew caught the reek of bin-juice on him. 'Have you got a cig or what?' The voice asked again.

'Sorry, I don't smoke.'

The man came closer and stood right in front of Matthew and eyeballed him. 'Are you one of them fags from over there or what?'

The last thing he wanted now was a drunken argument with some kind of scummy bigot, but Matthew hated anyone being homophobic and decided he'd have to give this idiot a piece of his mind. 'For crying out loud, it's the 2020s, not the bloody 1960s. *Fag* is not a nice word. And, if I am or not, it's none of your bleeding business. Why would you even ask someone that?'

Matthew's head flicked to the side as the first punch landed, he was dragged from the bench along the ground being booted and punched as he tried to fight back. Soon, his body lay still, strange hands rummaging through his pockets, his shoes dragged from his feet in the ruckus. 'You gay twat,' the voice said from above him as he felt another kick to his face. Footsteps were running away in the distance as he lost consciousness.

Bronwen swayed about at the window, holding the blinds back to get a better look. 'Anthony, he texted me over an hour ago saying he was still in the Village, and he was coming home soon. It's a friendly part of the city, he should have been home by now. Please go and have a walk down there and see if you can see him. He will be walking up the canal, I know what he's like. You know I won't rest if he's not home in his bed.'

Anthony shook his head and reached over and grabbed his ciggies from the table. This was normal behaviour for Bronwen – she was a born worrier – and this wouldn't be the first time he'd been walking the streets at night looking for her son. Still, he could do with the break from her; she was pecking his head. Anything for a quiet life. 'Have a look on his locations and see where he is.'

'I checked it before, and he was on the canal. It's been switched off now and I can't find out where he is,' Bronwen answered without moving her eyes from the window.

'He's probably got a bird or something. Bloody hell, how many times do I have to tell you that he's not a kid anymore? Let him live his bleeding life, for crying out loud, without you stalking him all the time.'

Bronwen turned on the spot, ready to give him a mouthful, but he was too quick for her. He'd grabbed his keys and was gone.

———

Anthony walked along the road that led to the canal. There was an eerie silence tonight and the roads seemed to be empty in this part of town. Just as he crossed the road, he spotted Alison the new barmaid coming out of the pub and his pace quickened. 'Oi, what are you doing out this late hour on your own? It's bloody dangerous for someone as pretty as you.'

Alison swung her long blonde hair over her shoulder and squinted to get a better look at who was shouting at her. 'Oh it's you. Thank God for that, I thought you were some weirdo,' she chuckled.

'Cheeky cow,' he replied.

'What are you doing out at this time, you left the pub ages ago. I thought you would have been tucked in your bed by now.'

'I was but birthday boy is on the missing list and I'm the daft bastard who has to go out in the midnight hour looking for him. Where you off to anyway?'

'I'll come part of the way with you to keep you company if you want. I've got nothing to hurry home for and it would be nice to get some exercise and clear my mind. This job is stressing me out and I need to unwind.'

Anthony stuttered as he answered her. 'Er, yes, come on then, the company would be nice. It can be scary walking down that canal on your Jacks you know.'

'Yeah, I always go by the main road normally but I feel safe with you.' Alison zipped her coat up and smiled at him as they headed towards the canal.

The two were soon getting on like a house on fire and Anthony was in his element, cracking all his best jokes, complimenting her all the time. He sparked a cigarette up and chugged hard on it. 'So, have you not got a fella or what?'

Alison shook her head. 'No, I'm as single as it comes for now. All the guys I meet are pricks, they don't know how to treat a woman. They're just after getting their end away and that's it.'

'We're not all like that. I respect women.'

She smiled. 'I know you're not, I can tell. That's why I liked talking to you tonight. Most blokes wouldn't have helped me out like that. But I've got to ask, are you married?'

Anthony hesitated. 'No, but I'm in with someone. Long-term, like.'

'Shame,' Alison purred. 'I was hoping you were single, and I was going to ask you to come back to my flat for a drink.'

Anthony could have kicked himself. Why didn't he just lie and play the game? This girl was top notch, a dream come true for him. He'd forgotten what it was like to be around someone new, who still saw the best in him. He must be old enough to be her dad, and had thought earlier was just a bit of banter – that he was way too old for her, but he guessed some women appreciated an older man.

'I would have loved to come back to yours, but I've got to go and find Matthew. Maybe another time . . .'

Alison fluttered her eyelashes and pouted her glossy lips seductively. 'That would be nice. I only live over there in those flats, number 24.' She stopped and looked to her left. 'Right, this is me. If you change your mind, you know where I am.' She winked.

Anthony was lost for words. He couldn't believe he actually had a chance with her. She walked over to him and kissed him on the cheek. 'Bye then, nice talking to you.' Her heels started to clip off in the distance and Anthony carried on walking down the canal with a face like thunder. He kept turning back around and watching her until she was out of sight. He booted a can on the floor and picked up speed down the canal towards the city centre. He'd been walking for ten minutes when he stopped dead in his tracks. There had been no sign of Matthew, or anyone for that matter. 'Fuck this,' he whispered under his breath. He turned around and started jogging back up the canal towpath.

Anthony was gasping for breath when he rang the bell. The door opened slowly and Alison looked down at him. 'Are you alright?'

Still trying to get his breath, he stood up tall. 'I changed my mind and ran all the way here. Note to self, get my arse back in the gym next week.'

Alison guided him inside and purred over at him. 'I'll keep you fit, don't you worry about that.'

It was five in the morning when Anthony sneaked back into his house. He stood at the living room door and saw Bronwen fast asleep on the chair. She must have been trying to stay awake waiting for Matthew. But once she'd had a skinful, she was dead to the world the moment she closed her eyes. Anthony eased his shoes off. For the second time that night, he headed up the stairs to bed.

Chapter Five

Bridie stood at her front window the next morning, her eyes wide. 'Bert, there is a police car at number 10. I wonder what they want?'

Bert was sat in his armchair reading his newspaper and dropped it onto his lap as he answered her. 'They should be here investigating where my cup of tea is. Ten minutes ago you said you was making me one and I'm still waiting,' he whined.

'Oh stop bloody moaning, will you. You're more than capable of making me a brew you know. It would be a nice change if you actually got up from that chair and did something instead of having me running about after you all day.'

'Get away from the window, will you. Honest, you're such a nosey cow, you don't miss a trick.'

'I'm *vigilant*, Bert. You've seen the news lately – people getting robbed when they're asleep in their beds at night. You know I like to keep a watch for any strangers on the street. I'm just doing my bit to be neighbourly. You could learn a thing or two about that.'

Bert went back to reading his newspaper – hunched over the horseracing page, studying the form. Bert had always thought of himself as having a lucky streak, liking a flutter. But a few years back it had got out of hand – Bridie had only realised when she tried to use her bank card in Asda one morning and had it declined. After that, she'd had the house up, searching for receipts, betting slips, anything. She'd even marched into the bank and demanded statements for their joint account. He'd always run their account; she'd never asked to see the details before – just trusted her husband when he told her about what they'd saved for a rainy day.

That day it hadn't just rained – it had poured. Bridie was heartbroken at first when she found out that her husband had gambled all the money they had saved up after a lifetime of scrimping and going without. Then in true Bridie-style, she dried her eyes and got mad instead. She'd swung at him with a frying pan, launched shoes at him and told him he had to move out before she told all the family exactly what he'd done. Twenty thousand pound he'd spent on his addiction. This was every penny she'd ever saved, money she'd saved up for a dream holiday, money to make sure they would be comfortable as they got older. And it was all gone – every last pound and penny fed to the slot machines or the bookies.

Bert hit an all-time low; he'd had to sleep at his pal's from the allotment, but he'd been determined to show Bridie he'd learned the error of his ways. He had phoned

Bridie every single night after she'd bin-bagged him, he'd even sent her flowers, letters, anything he could do to get his wife to forgive him. Bridie was a proud woman – and a stubborn one too, and it was weeks before she would even answer his calls. When she finally did, and agreed to see him, he fell to his knees and begged for forgiveness, telling her how sorry he was.

Bridie had a heart of gold and she would help anyone who needed help, but with her husband she had toughened up and stuck to her guns for over two months. When she eventually let him back into the family home, it was only on her rules. From that day, she ran the finances and gave him any money he needed. He wasn't even allowed a bank card of his own. Daydreaming over the racing pages was as close as he got to his old ways.

Bridie stood away from the window now and glanced over at Bert. She started to walk towards him. He quickly closed the newspaper.

'Do you fancy a walk to the shops, Bert? They'll know in there what the police are doing at number 10. That Angela is a right nosey parker. On my life there isn't anything that gets past that woman. *News of the Bloody World* she is.'

Bert stood up and stretched. 'Come on then. Bloody hell, Bridie, I know you won't rest until you know what's going on.'

Bridie went out of the living room and came back holding their coats. 'Here you go, love. Come on, hurry up.'

Bridie walked into the corner shop and smiled as she spotted Sav. 'Good morning, it's a lovely day out there today.'

Susan popped her head out from the store room and shouted over to her. 'Morning, Bridie. You two are up early this morning, what's got into you?'

Bridie chuckled, just tapped the side of her nose. She turned to face Sav. 'How long has Susan been working here?'

'She's only just started. She's surprised me, you know, she's a grafter.' Bert raised his eyebrows and sighed. He knew Susan and he'd had his dealings with her in the past when she'd given him a mouthful stood outside his garden. Littering was a pet hate of Bert's and once he spotted her dropping a crisp bag in his lovely garden, he was down on her like a ton of bricks. The backchat she'd given him could have turned the air blue; she called him an old git, told him he was just a bored old man who needed to get a life and she would drop worse in his garden when he wasn't looking. Bert had gone straight round to her parents' house, told them every detail of their daughter's rancid behaviour. Later that night, when he was watching the soaps, Susan knocked on his door and apologised. Bert accepted the apology, but he knew the girl had been forced to come and say she was sorry by her parents. He didn't trust her an inch. He walked away now and started looking at the magazines, rifling through the copies to try and get a glimpse of the *Racing Post*.

Bridie stood at the till and smiled as Angela joined them. Gossip time. Bridie folded her arms and kept her voice low. 'Hey, I've just seen the police at number 10, I wonder what's going on there. Bronwen and Anthony are hard-working people, good morals and all that, so God knows what's gone on.'

Angela lifted her hot cup of tea up and sipped, ready to tell them everything she knew. This was her moment. She matched Bridie's confidential tone and began to speak. 'They have been there since the early hours this morning. I walked past around seven o'clock this morning and I saw two cars outside there. I don't know what they are there for though, but I bet it's big if they've been there that long.'

Bridie was deflated at her wasted journey – she'd been sure Ange would have some decent gossip. She didn't hide her sour expression and sucked at her gums. 'Well they're not doing door to door or anything like that. We've just walked past and they're still inside. I might just pop in on the way back and see if she needs anything.'

Bert was back at her side now and he chirped in. 'You bloody won't. Just leave them alone, if they need anything they will ask us.'

Bridie pulled her shoulders back and growled at him. 'Shut up, Bert. I'll do what I deem fit. Bronwen is a close friend of mine and if she needs anything I will be there helping her out.'

Bert rolled his eyes. 'A close friend since when?' he replied in a sarcastic tone. 'You only say hello to her in the morning when she is going to work.'

Bridie was bright red, fuming that her husband had belittled her in front of everyone. She held her head high. 'Piss off, Bert, I know her better than you do, I've spoken with her for hours out on the front.'

Bert could tell he'd rattled her cage and knew to keep it zipped. That was all he needed; his wife going off on one. There would be no tea made, no washing done, if he'd put her nose out of joint. Oh yes, he'd be in the doghouse for days if he got on the wrong side of her.

'Right, I'm off for my fag break,' Angela said. 'I might wander down the street – see if I can scope out what's going on with the dibble.'

She'd barely been gone two minutes when she came storming back in, the shop door clanging open like it was a Wild West saloon. Angela couldn't keep the excitement out of her voice – she lived for a good bit of gossip. Usually she made do with second-hand information from the customers, so she was almost glowing with pride at having something first-hand to share. 'Oh my days, it's Anthony.' She paused to get her breath back.

'What, is he hurt? An accident?' Bridie's imagination had gone into overdrive.

'No, they're arresting him, I swear. Honest to God. Go look for yourself if you don't believe me – you'll be able to see from here. The coppers have got him out in the road.' Angela pointed to a small patch of the shop window not covered in adverts and fliers. 'Look, two of them have got him handcuffed taking him to the car.'

Bridie nearly fell over the stacked boxes of crisps trying to get to the window to have a better look. She squashed her face against the cold glass, eyes squinting to focus on the hive of activity at the end of the street. 'Bert, get over here and have a gander. I've not got my glasses on. You be my eyes.'

Bert knew he had a chance here to get back into his wife's good books. 'Move over then, let me have a look.'

Bridie moved back from the window and let her husband in. 'You're right, Bridie, they've got Anthony. Bronwen is at the front door crying.' Before her husband could give her any more detail, Bridie motored out of the shop and walked at speed towards number 10.

Bert shook his head at Sav and sighed. 'Bloody women, aye?' He left his magazine on the counter and followed his wife. There were more important things to tend to now.

Bronwen was bent over as if she was in physical pain as Bridie hurried past the patrol cars and down the garden path. 'Oh, sweetheart, what on earth is going on?'

The policewoman at Bronwen's side was escorting her back into the house. Bridie edged her way into the house. 'I'm her friend, her neighbour, is she alright?'

The officer asked Bronwen if she wanted this woman to be allowed to stay. Bronwen nodded her head and they all trooped into the front room. The police officer's radio beeped and crackled and she left the two neighbours alone.

Bridie sat beside Bronwen and gently rubbed her arm. 'Now what's gone on – is your Anthony in some kind of bother?'

Bronwen dabbed a crumpled white tissue into the corner of her eyes. 'It's Matthew, they've found him in the canal.'

Bridie swallowed hard, not sure if she'd heard her right. 'Is he in hospital?'

Bronwen looked at her directly, eyes wide open. 'He's dead, Bridie. The police found his body in the early hours of this morning.'

Bridie covered her mouth with her hands, shocked, the hairs on the back of her neck standing on end. For once she couldn't find any words to say.

'And they've took Anthony because he was seen on CCTV running away from near where Matthew's body was found.' Bronwen continued.

'What, they think your Anthony has done him in?'

Bronwen sobbed as she spoke. 'I don't know what's going on. It's like a nightmare – none of this feels real, Bridie. They are taking Ant for questioning, that's what they said. He was out on the canal last night, I know that for a fact. I sent him down there looking for Matthew and, well, I fell asleep and didn't even know what time he got back in.'

Bridie reached over and held Bronwen in her arms. 'Come on, love. Anthony is a good man; they must have got it wrong.'

Bronwen was a mess. 'What will I do without my boy, Bridie? My baby, he is my world, my everything.'

Bridie just patted her softly and stared into space. No words seemed big enough for the shock of the moment. The policewoman came back into the room and spoke directly to Bronwen. 'We need to check your doorbell footage, Mrs Murphy, do you have access to that?'

Bronwen reached for her mobile phone and opened the app for the officer. Bridie leaned over and peered at the tiny screen as the constable scrolled through clips. There was silence as the three women all tried to make sense of what they saw.

Bronwen broke the quiet first. 'Oh my God, that's at five in the morning, where the hell was he for all that time, and why is he looking so shifty?' she said as she watched the video of Anthony looking over his shoulder furtively as he let himself into the quiet house.

The policewoman looked serious. 'We may need to seize your phone as evidence. But for now, I'm going to have to review the footage in greater depth, can you send it to me?'

Bronwen's hands were trembling as she stabbed and swiped at the screen to send a copy of the clips to the officer. Once it was sent, she sat down again and pinched the bridge of her nose. 'He left here about half past twelve, and he comes back in at five in the morning. It just doesn't add up, does it?'

Bridie had turned pale, this kind of thing wasn't meant to happen on Manor Road. Sure there was Bert's obsession with kids dropping rubbish, the occasional boy racer or drunken teenagers – but a murderer on her watch, living on her street?

Bridie stayed at number 10 until Bronwen's sister and her husband arrived. All these years she'd spent looking for gossip and now she'd heard the biggest bombshell she could have imagined, all she wanted to do was get home. She stood up. 'Bronwen, if you need anything then you know where I am. I'll leave you with your family. But remember, you're never alone – we're all watching out for you, you can come and knock day or night if you need us.'

Bert was just as shocked when Bridie told him the news. 'I'm not having that, Anthony is a sound fella. No, there must be some kind of a mix-up.'

Bridie shrugged. 'Why on earth would they take him if he's innocent?'

'I bet it will be all over the news on the TV tonight, there will be camera crews all over the street. It won't do anything for house prices around here with a killer living on the street, will it?' Bert shook his head.

'Trust you to say something like that, Bert. A young boy has lost his life, maybe even been murdered and all you can think about is bloody house prices. That woman has just lost a son, where is your heart?'

Bert knew he should have kept his thoughts to himself, but it was too late now, he'd said it. He got up out of his seat and tried to smooth things over. 'I'll make us a cuppa, you sit there, you look a bit pasty.' He hadn't seen his wife this rattled in a long time. As he headed for the kitchen he looked back. She was just staring into space rubbing at her arms, talking to herself. 'That poor young lad, shocking it is. Life can be very cruel sometimes, very cruel.'

Bridie stayed in the front room all day. Even when, as predicted, the camera crews arrived and set up their equipment, Bridie didn't dash to the window or make up a reason why she suddenly needed to be in the front garden. The sun faded from the sky and the reporters left again and still Bridie had sat with her back to the window.

She'd spent years watching the goings-on of the street but couldn't stomach it today. Instead she let the TV play its endless quiz shows and soaps, all with the sound muted, just casting patterns onto the wall in silence.

Finally, the news came onto the television that night and Bert turned the sound up.

'Bridie, Bridie, didn't I tell you it would be on the news. Bloody hell, look, they've filmed our house too, the cheeky bleeders.'

Bridie sat up a little as a photo of Matthew Murphy came up on the television. She caught the words 'suspicious circumstances' and 'ongoing investigations' and her eyes flooded with tears. 'Terrible it is, bloody terrible that someone could hurt another human being like that. He was only a kid. Snuffed out like a light and on his birthday too.'

Bert agreed and reached over to make a roll-up, his go-to habit whenever times got tough. This news had shaken the neighbourhood. He knew the whole Manor estate would be filled with journalists and camera crews for days. There was a phone number flashing across the bottom of the screen for anyone with information regarding the murder of Matthew Murphy. The reporters hadn't named the suspect in custody, but anyone on the estate already knew it was Anthony being held. And Bert knew one thing for certain – guilty or innocent, there was every chance the residents of the Manor would decide their verdict way before the police did.

Chapter Six

B rooke stood looking out of the window. Her bruises were nearly gone now and just a yellow tone lay underneath her eye. Vincent sat watching her and spoke. 'Scary shit all that on the news, isn't it? I've spoken with Anthony loads of times down the boozer and had a few pints with him, just a normal guy in my eyes. I never had him down for being a murderer.'

Brooke turned around and sat back on the sofa. 'Nobody knows what happens behind closed doors, do they? All you guys sit down the pub laughing and joking with your mates and once you come in through the door any one of you could turn psycho.'

Vincent knew she was having a pop at him. 'I've not had a drink for over two weeks now. I told you that was the end of it, and it is. I was thinking we could go out tonight for a curry or something, celebrate the new me and all that.'

'The new you,' she stressed. 'It should be the new me. Don't think the girls in work haven't asked me about my bruises because they have. But I'm the daft cow who has lied to cover up what is really going on.'

Vincent narrowed his eyes. 'I told you I was sorry. Fucking hell, Brooke, what more do you want from me? I've not touched a drink and I've been doing everything to make you happy. Sometimes I can't do right for doing wrong, woman. You know what, tell me you don't love me and I'll go upstairs right now, pack my shit up and be gone. Go on, just say it.'

Brooke knew he was just testing her, taunting her with the offer of freedom. She'd played this game before and when she first told him it was over and gave him his marching orders, he had flipped and dived on top of her, punching and kicking at her. No, lesson learned, she kept her mouth shut. His eyes never moved from hers. His voice softer, sitting next to her, stroking her hair, making her skin crawl. 'Everything is going to be fine, Brooke. I understand that you're still angry with me, but I've changed. Go on, tell me I've not changed.'

Once again, she knew the drill and told him what he wanted to hear. He sat smiling at her as she agreed with him. 'I wasn't going to tell you until tonight but fuck it, I'm going to tell you what I've planned. Hopefully it might bring a smile to that miserable face of yours.' He took a deep breath and blurted it out. 'I've only gone and booked us a week in the sun. We're off next week to sunny Benidorm, all-inclusive in a smart hotel.'

The colour drained from her face. Nightmare. How on earth could she cope with him when she was in another country and he was pissed up on all the happy hour drinks. Benidorm was a party place. How could she imagine he'd be able to sit there at the side of the pool or in a beach bar without a drink. And that kind of drinking came with a high price to pay. 'I can't get the time off work at that short notice, you know that, love. I have clients booked in and I don't have any holidays left. Can you move it to later in the year?'

Vincent looked like thunder. He was on one now and she knew any second he could snap. 'I do nice things like this and you throw it back in my face, you ungrateful bitch. Do you know how much it cost me and you think I'm just going to cancel it? I'd rather go on my own – or find some other bird who wants to come. I am going on this holiday – end-of.'

'Couldn't you have asked me first? That's what normal couples do. We are a team or so you keep telling me. For your information, there is no "I" in team.' Brooke folded her arms tightly across her chest. She was relieved he'd not walloped her for what she'd said and didn't want to push her luck saying more.

Ten minutes passed before Vincent broke the silence. 'Are we going for a curry or what? Or is that another thing I should have discussed with you first?'

He was bitter, and she knew it. But this felt like a safe option, at least. He might still be fuming but she would be out in the real world and seeing people instead of being stuck behind four walls at his mercy. 'I'll get ready,' she said.

Vincent looked pacified and nodded his head slowly. That's what he liked; a woman who listened to him, one who jumped every time he spoke.

Sitting in the mellow light of the curry house, Brooke looked stunning. She was wearing a faded pair of ripped jeans and a lime-green fitted top with shoes to match. Her hair was big and bouncy and her make-up was on point.

Vincent sat looking at her from across the table, inhaling her floral perfume. 'You look mint tonight, babes. I'm so lucky you are mine. I know I've been a prick lately but honest, on my life, it's all going to change. We'll be back to how we used to be in no time at all.'

Brooke sipped on her red wine. She knew in her heart that all Vincent wanted was a woman who didn't answer back unless it was to agree with him. The wine caught in her throat but she forced herself to smile back.

'Can you think about the holiday, Brooke? And I promise on my life I will discuss with you anything I'm planning in the future.'

As the meal went on, Brooke felt the wine hit her veins. Soon she was a little bit tipsy and singing softly to the song that was playing in the restaurant, swaying to the beat. She felt like herself for the first time in a long while. She'd thought her old self, the happy-go-lucky woman she used to be, had been beaten out of her – but maybe she could be that woman again.

Vincent reached for her glass and smiled. 'Can I have a little sip of that? Come on, I've not touched a drop in weeks. You can't be that tight on me. Look at you all dancing and singing and I feel like I'm not on the same wavelength as you.'

Brooke knew it wasn't the kind of question she could say no to. She'd been surprised when he'd ordered her a glass in the first place. Maybe he'd been planning it all along. A few mouthfuls weren't going to hurt anyone, were they, she told herself. In all fairness the night had been going better than she'd imagined, they were getting on and she hadn't flinched when he'd leaned in and given her a kiss. She passed him her glass and watched as he necked most of it. Brooke stood up and flicked her hair over her shoulder. 'Just going to the loo.'

As she walked off she heard him call over to their waiter. 'Bring us a bottle of red over, pal.'

Brooke was just about to go into the loo when she heard someone say her name. She twisted her head and briefly looked at the man tucked away at the table in the corner. She tried not to react and carried straight on. As soon as she was in the cubicle, she stood with her back up against a wall. She put a hand on her chest and felt her heart galloping. She blew out long, hard breaths through her mouth. 'Fuck, fuck,' she whispered.

Once she was finished, she went and looked into the mirror. The colour had drained from her face, but her make-up was on point. More deep breaths before she stepped back into the restaurant. Brooke froze on the spot; he was there, waiting for her, staring right at her.

The man shoved a piece of paper in her hand. 'Ring me, please, we have so much to talk about, please ring me.'

Brooke's feet seemed glued to the spot. The man walked away and left Brooke feeling flustered. She swallowed hard and tried to casually check out if anyone had seen them.

Brooke sat back down at the table and clocked the bottle of wine, already half gone. She lifted it up in her hands and examined it further. 'Have you drunk all that?'

Vincent started laughing out loud and sat back in his seat. 'Relax, woman, I had a few glasses to catch up with you. You've been ages.'

But instead of fearing the consequences, a part of Brooke was relieved. A few glasses in, Vincent would be too buzzed to notice how flustered she was by her brief encounter. She knew there would be hell to pay later but she sat quietly while Vince ordered more drinks when his food came. Brooke was glad he didn't ask why she was pushing hers around her plate, barely eating, always looking around the room. The piece of paper was shoved deep in her bra and she regretted she hadn't taken the chance to read what was said on it. Vincent seemed to be getting louder and louder now. He started throwing chips about the restaurant and being a complete dickhead. The waiter came over and asked if he wanted the bill. Vincent stared at him, and Brooke could see a familiar look in his eyes that told her he was ready to kick off. He snarled at the waiter, and she could see his fist curling into two tight balls. 'Do I fucking want the bill? Are you trying to get rid of us or what. Oh yes, that's what it is, had our money and now you want us gone, cheeky bastard. That's all your sort—'

Brooke cringed as she knew some racist rubbish was about to spill out of his mouth. She leaped in. 'Please bring us the bill. I'm sorry, he's drunk.'

The waiter walked off in silence. Brooke hissed at her husband. 'Stop being an arse, Vincent. Bloody hell, there was no need for that. He is only doing his job, sort your head out, will you? And cut those racist remarks, no need whatsoever.'

Vincent leaned forward. His words were chilling. 'Shut the fuck up, woman, and keep quiet. That prick wants us out of here and you can't see it. Well I want him out of my country. I'm sick of these spongers coming to our country and thinking they own it. I fought in the army to live in a good country and these wasters are ruining it.'

Brooke stood up and scraped her chair back. 'I'm going to pay. I'm not staying here with you when you're acting like this. Embarrassment you are. Listen to you banging on about your army time like you were some kind of hero. Instead of getting kicked out. And as for these guys – they're working all hours, making something of themselves. And I bet they don't go home and beat their wives.'

That was it. Vincent flipped the table and roared at the top of his voice. 'Fuck you, fuck them all. Come on then, who wants it?'

Brooke knew she needed to get away – and fast. She grabbed her coat and flung some notes at the waiter. Her husband was still trashing the place and didn't even notice his wife leaving. Once outside, Brooke ran and ran. She didn't know where she was going, just that she needed to get away – and fast.

The rain hammered the pavement and she was soaking wet by the time she ducked into a bus shelter for cover. Brooke stood back and wiped the rain from her face. Her green top was plastered to her, her chest was heaving and tears were running down her cheeks, mingling with the rain. What now? Where would she go? Nobody would have her at their house knowing Vincent was on the rampage looking for her. In the past, when she'd got her head down at her friends' houses, Vincent had come booming the door down looking for her. He'd told all her friends not to get involved and once they'd seen that, in the end, Brooke always got back with him, they'd stopped trying. Slowly, those friendships had fizzled out – she couldn't blame them. Brooke shoved her hand down the front of her top and searched for the piece of paper she'd stashed there. Now it was in her hand she slowly opened it. She read the phone number over and over again. Maybe she should screw it back up and chuck it in the bin, she thought, but right now it felt like a lifeline. Brooke peeped outside the bus shelter and once the coast was clear she was on her toes again.

When the rain finally let up, Brooke found a place that was dry enough to perch and sat on a cold brick wall looking out onto the main road. Slowly, she pulled her mobile phone out from her jacket pocket and just stared at it. The phone started ringing, Vincent's name was flashing across the screen. 'Fuck off, Vincent, just fuck off!' she yelled at the phone, letting it ring out. Whether he was calling to rant and rage or to apologise, she didn't care. Her hands were shaking as slowly she typed in the phone number and held the phone to her ear.

'It's me,' she stuttered. Brooke listened to the voice at the other end of the phone and big, fat tears started to roll down the sides of her cheeks. 'I need help, I need to get away from him, far, far, far away as possible.' Brooke was sobbing by now. 'I don't know where I am. He's just kicked off in the restaurant and I've run off. I can't do this anymore. On my life I can't.' She sat listening for a few seconds to the voice at the other end of the phone. She stepped out onto the pavement to look for where she was. She walked a couple of steps and tried to read the street name. 'I'm on Walker Road, it can't be far from the restaurant.' She scuttled back to where she'd been sitting, hidden in the shadows, and ended the call. In the distance she could hear yelling and as it got nearer she could tell it was Vince, roaring her name at the top of his voice. She leaned back further into the gloom, wishing the dark would swallow her.

Brooke kept her eyes on the traffic, looking one way then the other. A black car was moving towards her slowly. Was this him? She stepped out from the shadows and waved her hand. The car stopped a few metres from where she was and Brooke yanked at the door in panic and jumped inside. 'Please drive, just get me away from here and quick.' Brooke slumped low in the seat and kept her eyes on the road. 'He's been screaming for me. I heard him, he won't rest until he finds me. He'll be at all my friends' houses banging on their doors, waking them up. He's a nutter, a screw loose in the head the bastard has.'

Lee Jakes smiled over at her. 'You're all right now. Breathe.'

Brooke lit up a fag and passed one to Lee. 'Thanks for coming for me.'

'It's the least I can do for you. I've spotted you a few times when I'm out and about but I've never had the courage to come over and speak to you. I mean, there is bad blood between us, isn't there? I saw you once down the shops – even behind your sunglasses I could see you had a shiner. It was him who did that, wasn't it? And it's all because of what we did, what my Gemma told him, too.'

Brooke closed her eyes and that night when he'd walked away with his wife came flooding back into her mind. The tears she'd shed, the beatings from her husband, the way he left without a backward glance. Her voice was sad. 'You were an arse-hole, Lee. I'm not going to lie, I'd fallen for you and once your wife was there in front of us, I thought you were going to tell her it was me you loved and not her, but you folded, didn't you?'

Lee panicked. 'Brooke, for fuck's sake, my head was all over the place. My life was wrecked just the same as yours was and, looking back, I should have told the mrs that it was you that I loved. What we did was wrong, I know – but once it was done, there was no saving either of our marriages. You're right, I fucked up big time.'

Brooke opened her window and blew the smoke out from her mouth. She looked over to examine him. He looked older than she remembered, strands of grey threading through his hair, cheeks sunken. 'You sure did mess up, and you're right, I should have left Vincent after he found out about us. My life has been a living hell since then. He's been drinking and…' She paused. 'Well, it's not your problem what has been going on, that's for me to sort out. Now please, I'm freezing to death, my clothes are soaking wet and I've snapped a heel.'

'My house is just up the road from here, do you want to go and get dried off?' It could have been an innocent offer but both of them knew they were far from innocent.

Lee pulled up outside his house and turned the engine off. 'I've lived on my own ever since I got divorced. I get to see the kids when she feels like it, but apart from that I'm living the single life.'

'And how are you finding that then?' Brooke thought of all the times she'd dreamed of a life on her own terms, her own rules.

'It's shite, if I'm being honest with you. Sometimes you have to be careful what you wish for, don't you? But sometimes life gives you a second chance. I've never stopped thinking about you, Brooke. I want you back, I don't think I ever stopped loving you.'

Brooke let out a sarcastic laugh and pressed the button for the window to close. 'Bullshit, Lee. I'm older and wiser than I used to be. I was just a bit of fun for you. I realise that now.'

'No you wasn't. You meant a lot to me. I loved you with all of my fucking heart.'

'Fuck off, Lee. If you loved me then why did you never try and contact me after we got found out. If I loved someone like you say you loved me, I would have climbed mountains to be with them, never give up. Go on, tell me what you did to try and see me after the affair was uncovered. Because I'll answer that for you, shall I?' She leaned over and spoke into his face. 'Fuck all.'

This was all getting heated, and Brooke was getting ready to get out of the car when Lee gripped her by the shoulder. 'I know you're angry, Brooke, and this is what I've been dreading but seeing you tonight has made me realise just how much I loved you. I'll throw my hand up and say, yes, I fucked up. I should have been banging your front door down telling you that it was you that I loved but I folded, I had children to think about.'

Brooke sat back in her seat and stopped him dead in his tracks. 'You weren't thinking about the kids when you were screwing me, were you? You weren't thinking about them when you told me you and I had a future.'

Lee sat back in his seat too, shaking his head. 'Come in for a bit and get dried. Just let me say all the things I've had bottled up to say to you then you can leave if you want to. You owe me nothing and I'm just happy that I'm finally here with you. It's been a long time coming, Brooke. Go on, tell me you have never thought about me and what could have been.'

Brooke swallowed hard and closed her eyes for a few seconds. She was calming down now, her heartbeat slowing. 'I'll come inside with you for a bit. My head is mashed, and I need time to think about everything.'

Lee opened his door and got out of the car. Brooke walked behind him slowly. She had to hide her surprise that his house was nicely decorated inside. It almost had a woman's touch about it; nice curtains, matching décor. She'd expected dirty floors and takeaway boxes.

'You go into the front room and I'll get us a drink. I've got a t-shirt you can throw on if you want, and I'll put your clothes in the dryer.'

She nodded her head and started to take her jacket off. Lee was behind her now and passed her a grey t-shirt. Bloody hell, it didn't look that long, it would barely cover her bum. Brooke held it up in front of her and smirked over at Lee. 'Have you got anything bigger than this?'

'I'll get you my dressing gown to put on over it. Pass me your clothes when you've changed, and I'll get them drying.'

Brooke waited for him to leave the room and started to strip off. You could see all the faded bruises on her body and she quickly yanked the t-shirt over her head and pulled it down as far as she could, not relaxing until Lee walked back in with a fleecy grey robe and lobbed it to her.

Lee looked at Brooke wearing his dressing gown and smiled at her. 'You'd look good in a paper bag. You look amazing, Brooke.'

'I don't feel it, I can tell you.'

Lee went to the sideboard and pulled out a bottle of wine, pouring generous glasses for them both. 'So why have you never left Vincent? When we were together you kept saying you were unhappy and yet the years have passed and you're still with the guy.'

'It's complicated, Lee. I think I feel guilty. I broke his heart, Lee, *we* broke his heart. Like you broke my heart. And two wrongs don't make a right, so I thought maybe I could fix it. But then this started...' Brooke pulled up the robe sleeve to show a fading set of bruises that were still clearly recognisable as fingermarks. '...and then I got scared. He said he'd kill me if I left. I mean he always says sorry the morning after, but when he's had a few and the Devil is in his eyes, I don't know what he's capable of.'

'Brooke, you should listen to yourself. I mean if tonight is anything to go by, I don't know why you would stay a second longer than you had to.'

Brooke sipped at her drink. 'I have nowhere to go, Lee. He'll find where I am and torment me until I go back home. It's always been the same old story.'

'Do you still love him?'

Brooke fidgeted; the question was not what she was expecting to be asked. She sat playing with her fingers before she answered, 'No, not no more. The man is delusional and when he drinks, I detest every bone in his body. I'm not saying I'm a saint, and I don't know when to button it, sometimes, but in my heart, I know I don't deserve the shit he gives me. On my life he knocks me sick to the pit of my stomach.'

Lee moved in closer to her and stroked his finger down the side of her face. 'Leave him then, Brooke, come and live your life with me. We can be happy together, finish what we started.'

Brooke scoffed. 'And what, do you think he will just leave us to it when he finds out where I am and who with? Trust me, you don't know him like I know him; the guy is tapped in the head. He would never leave us alone.'

Lee squared his shoulders. 'And do you think I would let that happen. I know people who will deal with him, make sure he never comes near you again. Like I said, Brooke, I missed the boat with you, and I would do anything for us to try again.' He stared at her for longer than he needed to and slowly brought his lips to meet hers. Her eyes looked deep into his and, slowly but surely, she kissed him back.

Brooke opened her eyes and looked over at Lee, lying next to her in the bed. They'd only had a few hours' sleep and most of the night they were catching up on the years gone by. There was still a spark there, she could tell. A dangerous chemistry between them both. But the butterflies in her stomach were more than attraction. She could recognise the lurch of fear that curled inside her too. What was she doing? Talk about going from frying pan to fire. She was burning her whole life down if she carried on like this.

Lee cuddled in closer to her and kissed the side of her cheek. 'Brooke, I promise that I will never hurt you again. You've got to believe me. Give us both a chance at happiness. Why don't you go and get your belongings today and come and move in with me?'

Brooke shuddered at the thought of going back home to face Vincent. He would never let her leave without a fight, never let her leave the house again once she was inside. She swallowed hard and looked deep into Lee's eyes. 'Just let me think for a minute, just let me think.'

Lee held her hand and kissed her fingertips softly. 'I'm not going anywhere this time, I'm with you all the way. I'll fight for you if I have to, do whatever it takes.'

Chapter Seven

Susan sat twiddling her thumbs. There was no shift at the shop today and she was sitting in her bedroom chilling listening to music. As the track ended, she walked out of her bedroom and stopped dead in her tracks when she heard giggling coming from her sister's bedroom. She smirked and crept further towards the door. Her sister was speaking in a sexy voice. Had she got a man in there? The house rules were no boys in the bedrooms, always had been. Her parents were strict like that – had raised them that while they were under their roof, there was no sex before marriage.

Susan stood listening a little bit longer before she gripped the door handle and pressed it down slowly until she felt the latch click free. Catching her out would make great ammo. It would be the perfect threat if her sister pissed her off. Yes, once she'd caught her with a guy in her bedroom, she would threaten to tell her parents every time she was doing her head in.

'Captured!' she shouted as she pushed the bedroom door open with force. Susan stood there, her jaw nearly hitting the floor. Her sister was standing there – alone – in only the skimpiest of thongs and a cutaway bra. Emma froze for a second then slammed her laptop with speed and grabbed her dressing gown from the chair beside her.

'What the hell are you doing, you idiot?'

Susan was still lost for words, her mouth moving but no words coming out.

Emma went to open her curtains, kicking a pair of towering platform patent heels out of her way.

'What were you doing, stood there dressed like a bleeding brass in stockings and suspenders?'

'I was just trying them on to see what they look like; I've got a nice dress to wear and I wanted some underwear to go underneath it. I do wear nice underwear, you know. I like to take care of myself – unlike you.'

Susan was having none of it and as Emma turned her back to grab a make-up wipe she moved closer to the bed and sat down. As her sister started to wipe away the heavy make-up she was plastered in, Susan lunged for the laptop and pressed the screen. The OnlyFans page lit up the display.

'Emma, what the hell are you doing, you dirty cow? I've heard all the stories about slags on there showing their fannies off for money. You dark horse, you.'

'I'm not showing my fanny to nobody, Susan.' Emma knew she'd been uncovered and sat down on the bed too and hung her head low, ashamed. 'If you must know, I lost my job and I didn't know what else to do. Mam and Dad always sing my praises about how well I'm doing, and I just couldn't face telling them.'

'So you sell your body then? Give strangers a good look at your kitty for cash?'

'Stop saying I'm selling my cooch. I just talk to people and, yes, I send them pictures for money but it's tasteful, my choice. At first I was a bit apprehensive but after a few times and I started to earn some proper money it was a no-brainer. Susan, I've earned six hundred pound this week and it's not even Friday. I'm smashing about a grand in a good week. Trust me, there are loads more people doing it than you know. I just wear nice underwear and get in different poses, and people send me money for it. I'm not arsed what you think about me. Check my bank balance, then judge me.' Emma went on her mobile banking app and got her balance up. Eight thousand pounds she had stashed in her savings.

Susan's eyes were stretched open now, mouth opened wide. 'Are you for real? All you do is pose and send pictures to them?'

Emma smiled and nodded her head. 'My body, my choice. It's easy money.'

'I want in, I want to do it.' Susan was scrolling through loads of pictures. She could do this – a few pics and she'd be minted.

'Not a chance, you're not even eighteen yet. It's illegal at your age and if Mam and Dad found out they would go sick. No way, wait until you're older and if you still want to do it then, well, fine.'

Susan had a cunning smile on her face and licked her bottom lip slowly. 'If you don't help me do this then I'll grass you up. Simple.'

Emma went bright red, reached over and gripped her sister by the scruff of the neck. 'You won't do shit, you daft cow. I swear if you breathe a word then I'll tell them about you drinking and smoking and having sex. Don't think I don't know about that Duffy lad on the fields.'

Susan went white. How the hell did Emma know about that? But it was true, she was steaming drunk a few months back and ended up having sex with one of the local lads. He wasn't her boyfriend, he was just there at the right time. He wasn't even her first. Duffy was her number 4, or that's what she told Sabrina. But she couldn't let Emma know she was rattled. 'I'm not arsed, I'll just deny it, whereas you won't be able to deny your dirty pics – a few clicks and I can show Mam.'

Emma knew she was backed into a corner. If she didn't give her sister a piece of the action then her cash flow would stop, she'd be skint again and back to square one. She sat thinking, twiddling her hair. 'OK. You can try it just once and I need to be with you, so you don't end up with some creepy guy blackmailing you. Because, let me tell you, you have to be careful on there. There are lots of scammers; people who won't pay you. I know the ropes, so I'll set you up.'

One day was better than nothing, Susan thought. She rubbed her hands together. 'Right, what do I need to do?'

Emma looked her up and down. 'What, with that greasy hair? I don't think so. You need to be in top condition; hair washed, make-up done, all your bits shaved.'

Susan went beetroot. 'You said I didn't have to show my kitty.'

Emma shook her head. 'No, but you don't want hairy legs and pubes sticking out from your knickers, do you?'

Susan felt her confidence draining, not really sure now if this was for her. She'd heard a few stories about girls on this website and until now they'd been a joke, dirty slags. But there was big money to be earned and, even if she was just getting a fraction of what her sister did, it would mean the kind of money that would buy her the new Nike Air Jordans that she'd had her eye on. She was working in Sav's for pennies, she thought, wasn't that exploitation too? She needed any extra money she could get if she was going to keep up with Sabrina, maybe even move in with her. Susan stood up. 'I'll have to borrow some of your underwear. I've got nothing like that stuff you're wearing. All my knickers are from Primark,' she giggled.

Emma grimaced. 'Not a chance. You're not having that sweaty motty in my knickers. I'll see what I have in my collection that I've not worn yet, but you can buy it off me. You're not having it for nothing.'

'Wow, stop being tight. I'll buy my own when I get up and running. Gizza loan for now, you know I'm good for it.'

Emma lay back flat on the bed and stared at the ceiling. Her voice was low. 'You tell nobody about this, do you hear me, no one.'

'I'll just tell Mam and Dad that Sav has given me extra shifts at the shop. They won't know anything. My lips are sealed. When do I start?'

Emma stretched her arms over her head and yawned. 'Tomorrow. I'll tell Mam I am going to help with your studies or something, tell them you're thinking about enrolling in college when you can. They will love that.'

Susan took a deep breath. This was getting real. 'They'll both go for a few drinks down at The Griffin or go to the bingo tomorrow night, so we will have the house to ourselves. I'll do my tan tonight and shave my legs and that. Can you do my make-up for me, I'm shite at it compared to you. You've seen the last time I tried to do my eyebrows, you said it looked like I'd drawn them on with a Sharpie.'

Emma chuckled. 'I told you not to go out with them like that, but did you listen? Nice you can finally give your big sis some credit.'

Susan was sat thinking, chewing on the side of her fingernail. 'This could be the answer to all my prayers. If I get good at it, I'll be earning decent money in no time.'

Emma shook her head. 'It's still graft. I've been doing this a lot longer than you. You have to get followers, people interested in you before you start earning proper cash. You might even have to give away some pics first. But once you've got a name for yourself, there are easy pickings. I mean, when I'm bored, I take photos of my feet sometimes and, believe it or not, I still earn from showing them off too.'

Susan glanced down at her sister's feet and burst out laughing. 'Who the hell would pay to look at those trotters?'

'You'd be surprised what people will pay for. But, like I said, you can only go online when I'm with you. I'll teach you some good poses and hopefully then you can start earning. Pay me back for getting you set up.'

'Ready when you are.' Susan giggled and pouted.

'Not now, I need to go back online. A guy was just about to pay me fifty quid for a picture of my legs. Go on, piss off and let me see if he's still online.'

Susan watched her sister open her laptop again and slowly edged out from the bedroom. Already in her mind she was spending the money and as for her sister saying she could only be online when she was there, was she born yesterday? Susan needed nobody to make sure she was safe. She was more streetwise than her sister and she could spot a wrong un a mile away, couldn't she?

Chapter Eight

D ane leaned over the bar at The Griffin talking to Bert. The pair of them filled their time with the usual blokey chat – mostly the footy and how United needed to sort their front row out and start winning more matches. The regulars at The Griffin were all the same – each one of them thought they could have done a better job picking a squad than the manager. It didn't occur to them there was a reason they were propping up a bar not sat in the dug-out or on *Match of the Day*. Dane's wife, Gaynor, had made it worse when she'd bought him a bench-coat for his birthday last month – it had made him all the more convinced he was a manager-in-waiting. Dane loved football; always told his wife he should have made it big when he was younger. But every second guy in Manchester had the same bullshit – a story about being scouted, or a promising amateur league career cut off by injury. In truth, Dane had been just an average player, nothing special; Sunday league. He hadn't so much as kicked a ball in years – all he did now was chat shit and pretend he knew better.

It was only half past twelve and there were just a few punters in the pub scattered about, mostly staring up in silence at the muted TVs with their rolling sports and headlines. Bert folded his newspaper and lifted his head up. 'Load of donkeys I picked yesterday. Not one bleeding winner. I definitely thought the favourite would have won. I studied the form, and the other horses didn't stand a chance in my eyes. I can't bleeding pick my nose lately, never mind a winner. The missus will give me the boot if she realises.'

Dane shook his head. 'There's only ever one winner, Bert, and that's the bookies. It's a fool's game gambling and in all the time I've listened to your tales of woe, you never win back the money you've put on. I admit I was a bit of a gambler back in the day and I was forever chasing my bleeding money. Honest, there was a time when I got my wages and went straight into the bookies every Friday after work and, before I knew it, I'd blown every bleeding penny. The times I had to go home and make up excuses for her indoors was unbelievable. I owed everybody too; robbing Peter to pay Paul every week. But I saw the road it was leading me down. I just play poker with the lads now, and only bet what I can lose.'

Bert gulped a mouthful of his pint and placed it back on the bar. He knew Dane's story well, wished he had the strength to walk away from it too. But, he never got out, never really quit. Even when Bridie cut off his cash he was still gambling any way he could – he'd bet on anything he could – heads or tails, flipping beermats – he could never resist a wager. Bridie would have gone berserk if she knew the half of it. Then he'd got clever. He'd applied for credit cards using pals' addresses, got loans from the kind of websites that didn't ask too many questions and sold old pieces of jewellery he had knocking about. At first, he set himself a limit of how much he would spend each week but that didn't last long. He maxxed the thousand-pound limit on his credit card and a couple of hundred from the other ones he'd applied for. Soon even the payday loan places wouldn't give him anything. That was when Bert first met Isaac Parker in The Griffin. Everyone knew if you had fallen on hard times he was the man to go to, but Bert had never seen himself as desperate before. Isaac was a loan shark; he didn't hide it, but what other option did he have when he was up shit creek without a paddle? Even now, when he was up to his neck in debt, he was sure he was just one big win from getting all square. When you owed proper money, you had to gamble big to win big. Made sense really. He just had to keep his nerve. That and dodge Isaac.

Bert twisted his head over his shoulder looking for him now. It was payday today and every Tuesday he met him here at this time to pay some of what he owed him. But today was different; Bert couldn't meet the payment. That last daft nag had let him down. Isaac was not a man that he wanted to upset; he'd heard the stories about non-payers and what this man would do to make sure he got every penny back that he was owed. Dane walked off to serve another customer and Bert was left staring at his pint. Someone squeezed his shoulder, causing him to cringe.

'Are you alright, Bertie lad?'

Bert didn't have to turn round to see who it was. He felt his pulse race – even his head was sweating, and he found it hard to raise a smile to cover his fear. He was too old for this lark, he thought as he shifted to face his creditor. 'I'm not that good actually, pal. My legs have been playing up and some days I can't bloody move them at all,' he lied in the hope that Isaac would feel sorry for him.

The loan shark sat at his side and tilted his head as if weighing the situation. Then he got straight to the point, no messing about, 'Payday. Forty quid it is today, my old mucker.'

Bert swallowed hard. His voice was low, stuttering. 'I'm a bit short this week as it happens. I had to pay for the brakes on the car and I didn't expect it to be as much as it was.'

Isaac sat back, used to people making every excuse under the sun as to why they were not paying him. He shrugged. 'Not my problem, pal, still forty smackers to pay. You know what they say: you can't pay, I take it away,' he sniggered.

'I'll pay a bit more next week to make up for it. You know I've never missed a payment before, don't you?'

'Listen, Bertie, we have an agreement, don't we?'

Bert nodded his head slowly and gulped. 'Yes.'

'So, I'll ask again, have you got the money you owe today, not fucking next week, not in a day's time, I mean today.'

Isaac's voice was raised now, and Dane was listening in. He walked back over towards them both and stood in front of the pair. He clocked Bert's distress. 'Are you alright there, Bert?' Isaac knew Dane and didn't hide anything away from him.

'He's not got the money to pay me, Dane. You know me. I'm a fair guy, simple rules. But one of those rules is "Don't take the piss". And being late counts as taking the piss. I can't go making exceptions, even for old codgers like our mate Bertie, here. It wouldn't be fair on my other customers. Wouldn't be good for my rep-u-tation.' He dragged out the last word while cracking his knuckles.

Bert was going paler by the second and his hands were fumbling as he pulled a crumpled ten-pound note from his old brown wallet. 'I'll pay an extra thirty pound next week, but that's all I've got. Honest. I've only got this pint here because one of my mates was getting a round in and…'

Isaac was just about to snap when Dane dug his hand in his back pocket and held out a wad of cash in his hand. 'Here, I'll settle up what he owes. For fuck's sake, Isaac, how many times do I have to remind you that people are up against hard times around here? One surprise bill, one bit of bad luck and you're tanked.'

'Like I told Bertie-boy, not my problem. Forty quid he owes in total. I'm not arsed who pays it as long as some-body does.'

Dane gripped the ten-pound note from Bert's hand and added another thirty pounds to it before he gave it to Isaac. 'Here, piss off back to whichever rock you crawled from now and leave people alone to have a quiet pint.'

Isaac tucked the money in his jacket pocket and smiled as he stood up. He went nose to nose with Bert. 'Same time next week and, just for the record, if you don't have the money bang on time then I'll be asking your mrs for it. Do you get me?'

Dane snarled over at Isaac and that was enough for him to leave Bert's side. Once he'd gone, Dane let out a laboured breath. 'What the fuck, Bert? You know that guy is an out and out tool. What the hell are you lending money from him for? He's for the really desperate – I'm not being rude, but you're too old to be messing with geezers like him.'

Bert hung his head in shame and his voice was low. 'But I was desperate, had nowhere else to turn. Please keep this just between us. If the wife found out, then she'd go ballistic.'

Dane studied Bert and leaned further over the bar, speaking in a hushed voice. 'I've got a poker game on tonight if you want to join us – not to play, yet, but you could come along and see the set-up, see if you might be interested in buying yourself a seat at the table. You could sack off the horses and try your luck around the table with the lads. You've got no control when you're betting on the nags, but with cards, that's skill. We have some great kitties; five, six hundred quid, some of them.'

Bert's eyes were wide, he was listening now. 'I used to play poker when I was younger; wasn't too shabby at it either.'

'There you go then. This might be the way to get some money in your back pocket and pay that prick off.'

Bert smiled. 'You're a gent, Dane. I'll pay you that thirty quid back as soon as I get paid, mate. You bailed me out and I won't forget that. And yes, I'd love to come along and have a gander at your game. And, in the meantime, anything you need, pal, just give me a shout and if I can help I will.'

Dane thought for a minute. 'I'll tell you what you can do. I need someone serving the drinks tonight if you're up for it. Gaynor usually does it, but she's pulling her face at the minute. I think she's on the rag or something. And then you won't owe me anything, we'll call it straight.'

Bert nodded his head. 'What time do you need me?'

'It's going to be a late one, Bert, probably start after I've locked up here tonight, so about twelvish.'

Bert rubbed his chin. 'Bridie always goes up to bed about ten and she's usually out for the count, so yes, I'll be here.'

There was fire in Bert's blood at the thought. His lucky streak started now, he knew it.

Chapter Nine

Brooke looked at her wristwatch, it was nearly eleven o'clock.

Lee was sitting next to her and could see she was thinking about something. 'Are you alright?'

'Yeah, just dreading what lies ahead when I do go home. He'll probably still be pissed, laying in bed. He never goes to work when he's been on a bender.'

'You don't have to go today. Stay here for a few days and just chill. Like you said, it's just going to be drama when you tell him you're leaving.'

Brooke scratched at her arms, causing bright-red marks to spring up. 'If I don't go now I will never do it. My head is strong, and I don't care what he says or what he does, it's over. I need my stuff and I need to tell him what's what. You've given me somewhere to go, given me some backbone. I can't hide from him forever – and I'd rather have it out with him now than have him come and find me at work screaming the odds.'

Lee nodded. 'That's my girl. It must have been awful feeling trapped like that. But you've got me now and it's probably not the right time to say it, but I would love to make my life with you. Properly, like. You know, you shouldn't just stop here while you find your feet, you should move in properly. A real couple.'

Brooke stood up and her cheeks blushed. 'Lee, like I said last night, please don't rush me. It's not that I'm not grateful, I just need to concentrate on me for now, nobody else.'

'Yeah, I know that. I'm just saying… I'm here, you know, to look after you.' Brooke was sick of men calling the shots. She pulled her shoulders back and turned to face Lee. 'I mean it when I say thanks for helping me out last night. But I'm making no promises to nobody. If I can stay here with you until I sort things out that would be great. But don't ask me for more than that.'

Lee nodded his head. 'Of course, no pressure. I would rather just be here for you, that's the least I can do to make up for how I treated you.'

Brooke managed a gentle smile. She didn't want to dig over the past right now – she needed to sort her future out. She reached over and started to put her coat on. 'I'm going to ring a taxi now. If you've not heard from me by seven o'clock at the latest, then ring the police and tell them everything, where I am; who I'm with.'

Lee swallowed hard, not sure if he even should be letting her go back home on her own. He'd told her he would go with her, but she'd said straight this was something she wanted to do on her own. Lee reached out towards Brooke. 'Come here and give me a cuddle before you go. Just remember, this will all be over soon, and you will be happy again. Abuse it and lose it is what I always say, and the guy fucked everything up by treating you the way he has been doing. Remember that when he's on his hands and knees begging you to stay.'

'You don't need to remind me how I've been treated, Lee, the bruises on my body do that. He can say what he wants to me today because his words will fall on deaf ears. Been there, wore the t-shirt and all that.' Brooke rang her taxi and stood looking out of the front window.

'I didn't put you down as the green-fingered type.'

'Nor did I. It started with a few bedding plants when I moved into this place and I kind of got into it from there. It helps with my anxiety.'

Brooke looked back at him. 'You have anxiety?'

'Yes, since my marriage broke up it just came over me.'

'Me too,' Brooke replied. 'I think everyone's messed up, aren't they, in some way? Who gets through adult life without a few scars?'

'None of us,' he replied, as the cab pulled up. This was it.

Brooke twisted the silver key in the lock and took a deep breath. It was now or never. She opened the front door and stepped inside. She stormed into the living room before her courage failed her, ready to tell her prick of a husband that she was done with him. Her eyes darted one way then the other, nothing. She was right – the lazy sod must still be in bed. She marched up the stairs, shouting, 'Vincent, it's me. We need to talk.' She booted the bedroom door open, her heartbeat doubling as she readied herself for a fight.

The room was empty. She froze, listening for a reply, nothing. With speed she dragged the suitcase from under the bed and started to empty her wardrobe. She was flinging everything she owned into her old black suitcase, looking over her shoulder. She might not have had it out with him, but at least she could get what she wanted and be gone before he came home.

Less than fifteen minutes later, Brooke rang the taxi and dragged her suitcase down the stairs, banging it against the walls and nearly dropping it. Once she was stood at the bottom of the stairs, she placed her hand on her chest and exhaled. 'Come on. Calm down, you're nearly there now. Just breathe, woman. Breathe.'

The taxi honked its horn outside, and Brooke was ready to leave. She looked around the living room one last time and headed into the hallway. Maybe this way was for the best. If all her stuff was gone then Vince would have to get the message. She stopped suddenly and bolted back up the stairs. Brooke opened her bedside drawer and searched for her passport. At last, there it was. She popped it into her jacket pocket and ran back down the stairs.

Outside, Bridie was out in her garden picking up litter that had blown into the neat hedge that ran along the front edge of her garden. As soon as she spotted Brooke, she went to her garden gate. Bridie clocked the suitcase. 'Oh, are you off on holiday, love?'

Brooke was hot and flustered; she'd caught her off guard. 'Yes, you could say that. My friend is having a bit of a bad time so I'm going to stay with her for a while.'

'That's lovely, is Vincent going with you too?'

Brooke was dragging her suitcase to the back of the taxi, and it was clear she didn't want to have this conversation. 'No, he's going to stay here, Bridie.'

Bridie frowned; she knew all was not what it seemed. If Brooke was going anywhere, she usually gave her the heads-up weeks before and asked to keep an eye on the house. And Vincent staying at home, on his own. It wasn't adding up. No, this wasn't right. She delved deeper. 'And how long are you going to be away for, any ideas?'

Brooke had her hand on the taxi door now, it was clear she was in a rush. 'No, Bridie, but I have your phone number and I'll give you a ring when I know more.'

Bridie walked closer to Brooke, noticing her red eyes. 'Yes, give me a ring. It would be nice to have a catch-up. I feel like I've not seen you for ages.'

Brooke was in the back of the taxi now, couldn't wait to get away. She waved through the window, leaving Bridie stood there with a puzzled look on her face.

Bridie walked straight back down her garden path and into the house. 'Bert, Bert, where are you?' Her husband popped his head round the kitchen door. 'I'm here, what's up?'

Bridie stood with her hand placed firmly on her hips. 'There is something going on in that house. First it was the shouting late at night, then Vince weaving home drunk as a lord, and now Brooke's just rushed out with a big suitcase, saying she's staying with her friend. Didn't I tell you those two were having troubles?'

Bert started to go back into the kitchen. He didn't thrive on local gossip like his wife. Yes, he listened to all she had to tell him about their neighbours, but it wasn't as important to him as it was to Bridie. He'd told her time and time again to keep her beak out of everyone's business, but she never listened, never would.

Bridie walked into the kitchen after him and flicked the kettle on. 'I'm going to have a quick cuppa and go over to see Bronwen. I saw the police there again earlier this morning and I'm sure they still have Anthony locked up.'

Bert was in a world of his own. He was stood at the kitchen sink washing a few pots with his shirt sleeves rolled up as his wife spoke to him again. If he didn't care about his neighbours, he cared about his stomach. 'I was thinking we could have liver and onions tonight for tea. I'll do a few potatoes with it and a bit of white cabbage.'

'You know me, I'll eat anything you put in front of me.' Bridie stood watching the kettle boil, thinking. 'Maybe I'll put Vincent some tea out tonight too.'

Bert shook his head and gasped. 'You're such a nosey cow. Don't think your "good neighbour" act washes with me. You'd do anything to find out what's bloody going on.' Bridie raised her eyebrows. She knew her husband was right, but she would never admit it to him. Bert walked back into the living room and spotted his wife's handbag. A quick look behind him and he dipped his hand inside it and opened her brown leather purse. He pulled out a twenty-pound note and stashed it in his back pocket, then sat down and grabbed the newspaper.

Chapter Ten

Anthony sat in his cell and stared at the walls. He looked rough, purplish dark circles under his eyes. The police had already had him in for endless interviews, but up to now they'd not charged him. Every time he closed his eyes the dibble was back in wanting to talk to him again, never letting him rest. Anthony stuck to his guns and told them he walked up and down the canal and back home again. He was innocent, this was just a mix-up and hopefully once they knew he was telling the truth he would be released from here and allowed back home. He repeated it time after time.

An hour later, Anthony sat with his solicitor facing two police officers. Another interview, more questions asked over and over again. He dragged his hands through his hair, wondering if this was breaking point. He'd heard stories about people confessing to crimes they hadn't committed – were they trying to frame him? He'd been so sure they'd release him after the first interview, but he could feel his spirit breaking now. These bastards knew exactly what they were doing, and they clearly were hoping for a full confession.

'How many times do you want me to fucking tell you. I'll tell you again. Bronwen asked me to go and look for Matthew on the canal because that was the way he was most likely walking home and so I did. Where is the fucking crime there, go on, tell me. I'm devoed the kid is dead – for my sake, but even more so for his mam. She'll never recover from this. But I can't tell you what happened to him because I never bleeding saw him after he left The Griffin that night.'

The police officer sat unmoved. Another officer entered, and the interview was paused. Anthony was used to that – all tactics to mess with his head, he figured. It must be easier for the police to break him than bother going out and finding the real killer. If there even was a killer – he still wondered if the poor lad had just gone in the canal after one too many. A tragedy maybe, but not a crime.

Before he could think on it more, the officer was back – this time with a buzz about him. He was clicking his pen and had opened his eyes wide as if he had a bombshell to drop. 'So, you left the house around midnight and the canal is about ten, fifteen minutes from where you live?'

'Yeah, about that, I'm not one hundred per cent sure.'

'So, you agree you went out of the house around midnight?'

'For crying out loud, yes, for the hundredth time.'

Here it was, the moment the investigating officers had been waiting for. 'So can you tell me where you were until five o'clock in the morning because we have doorbell footage showing you coming back at exactly two minutes past five.'

Anthony swallowed hard, wriggling about in his seat, his mouth suddenly becoming dry. His solicitor sat up straight and shot a look at his client. You could have heard a pin drop. Anthony dropped his head onto the table. He'd been so busy trying to hide his night with Alison that he'd gone and put himself in the frame for Matthew's murder. He'd thought he'd been doing the right thing – he couldn't imagine what it would do to her to know he'd been cheating on her while her son was fighting for his life. But it was time to face the truth – he had to come clean. The facts might prove he was a scum-bag – but they'd also prove he wasn't a killer.

Anthony lifted his head up slowly and look directly at the officer. 'I was with a woman. Alison, the barmaid from The Griffin pub. I met her on her way home when I was heading to look for Matthew on the canal, and she asked to walk with me because it was late.'

The officer looked at him and urged him to continue.

Anthony sat playing with his hands and, as he spoke, he closed his eyes for a few seconds. 'I walked with her for a bit, and when we got near her place she asked me to come back to her house for a drink. I said no at first, carried on the way I was going, but there was no sign of the kid anywhere, and I'm ashamed to admit it but I changed my mind. I figured Matthew was just out getting pissed some-where, and there I was turning down an offer from a gorgeous woman. I'd had a few drinks earlier, and I guess I let them go to my head. I'm not proud of what I did, but most red-blooded men would do the same in my shoes. We had a bit of a fun, me and Alison, then, when it was nearly morning, I went home, creeping in, expecting Matthew to be there, but all I found was Bron asleep in the chair. She'd waited up as long as she could. I never told you any of this before because if my girlfriend found out then I would be in a lot of trouble. Come on, lads, you know the score.'

'If I was sat there where you are, accused of murder, I would have told the truth from the start of my interview.' The detective leaned back in his chair – the satisfaction of getting the truth out of Anthony clearly mingling with the knowledge that their suspect had potentially just ruled himself out of the investigation.

Anthony's solicitor stopped the interview and asked to speak with his client. The two investigating officers left the room and Mr Conal turned to face Anthony. 'This doesn't look good, Anthony. You should have disclosed this from the start. Now it looks like you could be hiding other things. If she backs your alibi then you might be in the clear but if she doesn't, then your word is worthless now.'

Anthony looked defeated. 'I would have told you, but, come on, I've been caught with my pants down and who in their right mind would admit to that?'

'Well, the truth is out now and your other half will know sooner or later. So, let's go through it again, the whole truth, not leaving anything out.'

Anthony sipped on his lukewarm glass of water. He was going to have to face everything sooner or later.

Across town, two police officers knocked at Alison's front door and stood back waiting for her to answer. When she opened the front door to the police they could see they were the last people she expected to see.

'Can I help you?'

'Alison Grailey?' the lead officer replied.

This knocked her for six; she stepped back from the door and replied with a shaky voice, 'Yes, that's me.' She'd clearly assumed they'd come to the wrong house or were just knocking at every door. But the fact they knew her name meant it had to be serious.

'Can we come in and have a chat with you? There has been a murder and we hope you can help with our enquiries.'

Alison blinked trying to take in the words. 'Me, how on earth can I help?' She invited the officers inside her house and showed them to the living room. 'So, how can I help?'

The junior officer pulled out his notes and sat twiddling his black Biro. 'We have arrested Anthony Sands in connection with the murder of Matthew Murphy, and he's given us your details relating to the investigation.'

Alison inhaled deeply, but still her chest felt tight. The officer continued. 'Mr Sands has told us he was with you that night. He told us you invited him back here after he walked you home down the canal?'

Alison sat biting on the edge of her fingernail. It had been a spur-of-the-minute thing – and now she was part of a murder investigation. Still there was no point making a bad situation worse. 'Yes, he walked me home down the canal and I did ask him if he fancied a nightcap. He refused and carried on walking down the canal.'

'Can you tell us what happened afterwards please, Ms Grailey?'

Alison was flushed and it was obvious she was embarrassed. 'He came back. Not straight away, probably about twenty, thirty minutes after I left him.'

'I see. He said in his interview he changed his mind and came back here with you. Would you say that's a fair description of events?'

'I suppose so.' Alison fiddled with a ring she wore. 'I was getting into bed when he knocked on my door, out of breath he was, couldn't breathe, said he'd ran all the way here and had a change of mind.'

The officers looked at each other and carried on with the questions. 'How did he seem in himself?'

'He was panting, I told you, it took him about ten minutes to get his breath back. But I took it as a compliment – like he was in that much of a hurry to see if he was still in with a chance with me. I don't mind telling you what happened. I have nothing to hide, and I've not committed any crime. Do you mind if I smoke?'

The officers shook their heads. Alison sparked a ciggie up and sat on the edge of her seat with her legs crossed. 'He came back here, we had a few drinks and we ended up having sex. Just two consenting adults. He was riddled with guilt after though, I could tell all he wanted to do was leave. Despite the fact it was him who made all the moves, not me, you know?'

The lead officer nodded his head, keen for her to continue. 'He left here about four o'clock in the morning I think, but I'm not sure. It is what it is, isn't it?' Alison sucked hard on her cigarette and just sat staring at the floor, aware she was being judged. Yes, she knew he had a girlfriend, but she was lonely, just after a bit of fun, where was the crime in that, and the bloke had been kind to her earlier that night. He seemed like a nice guy – but what he'd done in that missing twenty or thirty minutes, who knew?

Chapter Eleven

B ronwen squeezed her hands into tight fists when the
officer told her the news that her husband had been
with another woman the night her son was killed. She still
couldn't even bring herself to use the word 'murdered'.
She held it together while the Family Liaison officer told
her the news, but, as the young officer finished speaking,
Bronwen couldn't contain herself any longer. She bit down
on her knuckles and howled like an injured animal. 'The
lying, cheating bastard. And with that tart from behind the
bar, what the hell was he thinking? That girl is like a
bloody bike; everyone's had a ride on her, and she's only
been there five minutes. I'll rip her to shreds when I get
my hands on that slut. How long has he been seeing her,
do we know that?'

The female officer could see how distressed the woman
was and used the voice she'd had to practice in training. 'I
can understand this is extremely distressing for you, but
our investigation is focused only on the night of your son's

death. We can't confirm anything beyond that timescale.' As she looked at Bronwen's ashen face, she took pity on her. 'Look, I'm speaking out of turn here, but from what I've read, it was only one night.'

'I appreciate that, pet. But it doesn't stop the pain. My boy is gone and the man I should be leaning on to help me through it turns out to be no better than a sewer rat.' Bronwen's grief was cooling into an icy rage. 'So now you know where he was that night, is he being released? Because if he is, tell him not to bother stepping foot near my door because I'll drop the fucker faster than shit off a shovel.'

'No, he is still under investigation. Again, in confidence, there are a few things that don't add up. Times are not matching up, unaccounted gaps – that sort of thing.'

Bronwen covered her mouth with both hands and the tears steamed from her eyes. 'Please, don't tell me anymore. I can't take it. Can you leave me be now, please, I'm not in a good place and want to spend some time alone.'

'Do you want me to get somebody to sit in with you, a neighbour or someone else? I can't leave you upset like this?'

Bronwen was sobbing her heart out. 'Yes, get Bridie from number 8.'

Ben Walker stood behind the counter in Cash Generator and clocked Bobby Owen coming in through the main entrance. Bobby was an addict, always in flogging bent stuff. Not that Ben cared much – he always got a good bargain from him. When he could, he cut him off before the counter and met him outside to buy the goods from him for himself. Bobby was so desperate for his next fix he'd take any price, and Ben walked away with nicked stuff that was usually the real deal at half the price he'd pay for knock-off stuff from anyone else. He'd had all sorts in the past: gold chains, bracelets, watches, all nice stuff, mostly untraceable, that he could make a few quid on when he re-sold them.

Bobby eyeballed Ben, knew the score. He kept his voice low. 'I've got an iPhone, top of the range one too, I want fifty quid for it.'

Ben nodded his head and spoke in a low voice. 'Meet me around the corner in five minutes. I'll have it from you if it's decent.' He watched Bobby leave and walked back behind the counter. This was his first week back in work after being on the sick for over a week. He'd taken the news about Matthew badly and blamed himself for leaving him behind. Malc was the same too, both of them couldn't get their heads around it. They should have been planning their next session with Matthew, not planning his funeral.

Most nights Malc could be found on the canal smoking a spliff, just looking at the murky water. He always sat near the place his best mate's body was found floating, trying to figure out what had happened the night his best friend was murdered. He'd put the word out, and a friend of a friend had a sister who worked on the civilian side for the police. She'd been the one who'd been able to tell them the post-mortem suggested the death was no accident. Ben joined Malc on the canal some nights and they'd sometimes have a drink there, a few cans, just chatting about the good old days, feeling close to their mate in the only way they had left.

Ben told his co-worker he was nipping out for a ciggie, and hot-footed it round the corner. Bobby was walking like he had a penny squeezed between the cheeks of his arse, pacing one way then the other, sweat pouring from his forehead. Ben walked up closer to him and checked that nobody was watching. That was the last thing that he needed; losing his job. Ben's nostrils flared as the smell of this guy attacked his airways; putrid. He stood back from the junkie and looked him up and down. Bobby was a down and out, for sure. He looked like a walking anti-drugs advert: a few black pegs as teeth, dirty grey skin, clothes that hadn't been washed in forever.

Bobby pulled the phone from his filthy black leather jacket and bounced about on the spot. 'Fifty quid I want, bro. It's a top phone, looks like new.'

Ben examined the phone further and nodded his head. It was flat but if it worked, this was a bargain for sure; he could more than double his money and he knew it. 'Where's it from, Bobby, I don't want any comeback from it.'

Bobby was rubbing his hands together; grubby finger-nails, tobacco-stained fingers. 'Nah, bro, one of them fucking fairies from down the gay village dropped it. It needs charging, unlocking, resetting and all that. You know I don't know how to do all that shit. But you're not robbing no one with this thing – some drunken fag dropped it, their own fault for being so fucking careless.'

Since the night Matthew had died, Ben had found himself noticing how many people around were happy to drop casual slurs – racist or homophobic shit that in the past he might have laughed along with. But losing a mate like Matthew – seemed he was ready to come out – had been a wake-up call. He wasn't going to change the mind of a junkie like Bobby, but his shitty attitude made Ben even less guilty about cheating the addict out of cash. He'd have got twice the money if he'd taken it inside the shop. He had another look at the phone and checked for any scratches or damage. Ben dug his hand in his trouser pocket and counted out five ten-pound notes. Bobby was always eager to get the cash and get gone, looked like he was going into withdrawal and had to score some drugs as soon as possible.

'There you go, Bobby lad. Remember, anything decent always come and see me first. Now go and spend some of that on a fucking shower. You need that more than you need the skag.' But the baghead had already turned and was on his toes as he shouted back to him, 'Yeah, will do. Nice one, bro.'

Ben stashed the phone in his pocket and went back into work. He'd reboot the phone when he got a mo, nick a box from the stockroom to make it look kosher, and flog it again before the weekend. Dirty money sure, but easy money too.

Chapter Twelve

Susan stood in front of the mirror and looked at herself. With her sister's help she didn't look like a school girl any more, she looked like a woman. She figured she could pass for early twenties in all this get-up. Her boobs were pushed together in a tighter bra, her hair was curled, her make-up was on point, and she was wearing a black and red lacy underwear set that she'd 'borrowed' from her sister.

Emma came into the bedroom and locked the bedroom door behind her, flustered. 'Right, that's Mam and Dad gone. I thought they would never go; it was Dad pissing about looking for his house keys. Anyway, let's have a look then.'

Susan dropped her dressing gown to the floor and paraded around the bedroom in her high-heeled shoes, only wobbling slightly. 'I look mint, don't I?'

Emma looked her up and down and nodded her head, slowly. As her big sister she still had an apprehensive look in her eyes, not sure if she was doing the right thing letting her baby sister into this world, but knowing that if she didn't, her own chance of coining it in would be lost too. Emma sat down on the bed and fanned out her long candy-pink nails. 'You have to remember the rules. You never do this when I'm not here, ever, do you understand me?'

Susan was eager to get started and was already positioning herself on the bed. She flicked her hair back over her shoulders. 'Just get me on and let me start earning some cash. Just remind me one last time what I need to do.'

'When you're on camera, you speak in a sexy voice and your aim is to get them to part with as much cash as possible. You can use my account; it's better that way, nobody will ask any questions. Get some more lip-gloss on and, remember, sexy voice.'

Susan's heart was pounding inside her chest, hands shaking slightly as she adjusted her position on the bed. Emma shot a look over at her kid sister and spoke. 'Right, once I press this button you will be live and that's when you need to be on the ball. No matter how ugly or creepy they are, just remember it's all about the money. They can't touch you, but make them feel like they can. If they want photos sending, then they pay the cash first. Want a certain pose, a blimp of a nipple, anything, they pay the cash first. Do you get where I'm coming from?'

Susan felt the colour draining from her by the second and was glad of the extra layer of tan she'd applied last night. Suddenly it felt more like armour. Was she even ready to get involved with this world? She was no longer sure.

Emma sensed she was crumbling and reached over to give her a great big hug. 'Once you've done the first one the rest will be easy. I was like this on my first go, but once the money starts coming in you won't be arsed. Right, three, two, one.' Emma pressed the button and Susan laid on the bed looking at the screen. A middle-aged man was on camera, zoomed out enough to tell he was sitting in a pair of shorts, bare-chested.

Emma whispered from the side. 'Talk to him then, sexy voice – tease them, seduce them.'

'Hi there, what's your name?' Susan could hear the tremor in her own voice.

The man didn't seem to notice. 'I'm Tommy and I'm ready for a squeeze if you are?' Emma was showing her sister what to do next, tracing one finger across her collar-bone, licking at her lips. Susan copied her and kept her eyes focused on her sister, tried not to look shocked when she saw Emma lie on the floor and position her legs so there was more on show. Just inch by inch, an extra glimpse of inner thigh, higher and higher. Emma had told her she had to get this guy horny, make him want to see more, but she hadn't expected it would be so full-on, so fast. But she was in too deep now. Susan copied and that was the money shot; the more poses she did, the more the guy sent her money. Emma looked on, tracking how much money this bloke was shelling out. She knew more from experience that after the punter had enough for his wank bank he would be gone; sixty quid she'd got out of him so far – not bad for a first go.

The chat ended and Susan was bright red.

'Did I do all right, did he send the cash?'

Emma checked her online banking and smiled over at her sister. 'You've just earned forty pounds with a little wave of your legs.'

Susan clapped her hands with excitement. Emma smirked at her sister. This could be a good set-up for her too, taking a bit of commission from her sister's chats. The kid would never know.

Susan composed herself. 'Come on, let's get as many as we can chatting. I'll tell you what, I could do this all day long. I don't know why you made it sound so difficult.'

Emma snapped. 'There's a lot you don't know. I say when and where you do it. How many times do you have to be told that there are a lot of messed-up people who go on these sites. You never go online without me. Honest, Susan, let me get one whiff that you're doing it on your own and I'll lock you out of this faster than you can drop your knickers.'

'Yeah, whatever, Em. Now let's get on with it. I want to get as much dough as possible while I'm all done up.'

Susan took a deep breath and Emma hit LIVE once again. Susan oozed confidence this time, didn't need any prompts or poses from her sister to keep the conversation – and the cash – flowing.

It was ten o'clock now when Emma held her ear to the door as she heard noises. She mouthed over to her sister. 'Mam and Dad are back, knock him off, say goodbye.'

Susan was hesitant, still eager to get one last payment. Emma hurried over to the laptop as she heard the front door close and slammed it shut. 'Quick, get that dressing gown on and kick those shoes off. Get those books from over there and fling them on the bed.'

Susan hurried around the bedroom. With haste she wiped her make-up off and tied her hair back as she fastened her powder-blue dressing gown tightly around her body. Both girls jumped on the bed after Emma slid the lock from the door and gripped a book in her hands. The bedroom door opened slowly. Joanne smiled over at her girls and placed her hand over her heart.

'Oh, this is so nice, seeing you two studying together. Frank!' she shouted behind her. 'Come and see our girls.'

Emma gave a warm smile to her mother and ruffled her sister's hair. 'Our Susan is not as thick as I first thought, Mam. She's pretty clever when she puts her mind to it.'

Joanne came further into the room and plonked down on the edge of the bed. 'Oi, don't talk about your little sister like that. I know she's a smart cookie; we just need her to get her head down, and if she follows in your footsteps, she'll get into college.'

Susan smiled too. 'Yep, following right in Em's footsteps, that's what I'm doing.' Her sister dug her in the ribs but Susan was loving making Emma squirm.

'I'm learning from the best, Mam, so you can stop pecking my head. I don't know about college. I think I might like to get working. I mean, look at Emma – she's a proper good example. Earn some money, you know. I bet you wouldn't say no to me paying a bit of board if I get some more money than the pittance the shop pays me.'

Joanne nodded. 'Well we won diddly shit down at the bingo, so we're not getting rich that way. I needed one bleeding number to win five hundred pounds and I was waiting ages for it before someone else shouted house. I swear to you, I wanted to run over and slap her silly. That money would have done for me and your dad to go away for a weekend. It's our anniversary next Friday and it would have been nice just to get away for a few days.'

Susan shut the book she held in her hands and looked over at her mother. 'I'll see if I can get any extra shifts down at the shop. Sav said I'm doing really well. He said in a few more weeks he might even let me have a go at serving some customers.'

Joanne was so proud of Susan's new attitude, the girls could see it in her eyes. 'I know you've messed up in school, Susie-sue, but I just want a better life for you. I left school with nothing and look at the shitty jobs I've had to do all my life. I've been a cleaner for over twenty years now. I want you to have the choices I never did. You can do more than scrubbing shit out of office lavs – both of you.'

Susan squirmed. 'Mam, you should report them to your boss. It's not fair that you're expected to clean other lazy people's crap from the loo. If it was me, I would be straight into the office to name and shame them all.'

Emma started laughing and jumped into the conversation. 'Me too, I would launch the toilet brush straight at their head and tell them to clean it themselves.'

Joanne laughed and Frank appeared at the bedroom door and rested his hand on the doorframe. He was a big, strapping man – he'd been a looker in his day, that was clear – bright-blue piercing eyes, dark hair with strands of silver running through it. The girls could tell their dad had

had more than a few drinks at the bingo as he jiggled into the bedroom and pulled Joanne up from the bed. 'Come on, love, have a dance with your hubby. They used to call me snake-hips back in the day and I'm not blowing my own trumpet, but I would dance the pants off that bleeding Magic Mike you watched on the box the other week. Look at my hips move, love.'

The girls giggled, and Joanne fell back laughing on the bed. 'I don't think you're a *Magic Mike*, love, more like frozen Frank.'

He scoffed and dropped to the floor, trying to do the caterpillar, though it looked more like a slug according to Susan. Emma shook her head. 'Dad, don't even dream of trying that when you're out. I thought you were having a stroke. Wow, how embarrassing.'

Frank laughed, then rolled onto his side and held the side of his stomach, his expression changed. 'Bloody hell, Joanne, you might have to help me up, I think I've pulled a muscle or something.'

His wife shoved him with one foot. 'Well, I've told you hundreds of times that we are not no spring chickens anymore.'

Frank chuckled, wincing slightly. 'Oi, there's a good tune played on an old piano, or so they say.'

Joanne was right back at him. 'Well, this pianist won't be playing tonight for sure. Come on, let's get in bed and watch a film. I might watch *Magic Mike* again if you're out of action.'

Susan waved them out of the room and shouted over to them both. 'Oh my God! Get a bloody room, you two.'

Frank hauled himself up from the floor and limped out.

'Note to self, no more dancing,' he chuckled. 'Night, girls, sleep tight.' Susan sat up straight as soon as their parents were gone from the bedroom. 'So, add it up and tell me how much I earned tonight. I spoke with five guys so the money should be decent.'

Emma scrolled through her phone, looking at her banking app. She was adding up in her head, counting on her fingers. 'You've earned the grand total of one hundred and fifty pounds tonight, not bad is it for lying on a bed chatting to guys.'

Susan held her head to the side, trying to do the maths. 'Is that it, I thought I would have had at least two hundred quid.'

Emma kept her eyes on her phone. 'Some guys only pay twenty pound or send you tenners. Not all of them are as quick to splash the cash as the first bloke you got. Listen, you've earned decent money so don't be pulling a face. How long would it take you to make that stacking shelves?'

Susan suspected her sister was having her over, but she kept her gob shut; she knew not to bite the hand that fed her. Emma had always had a snidey streak. Even when they were growing up, she would stash her sweets away and eat all of Susan's. But she knew if she called her out there would be no chance of getting back on camera. Until she was old enough to do it legally, she was stuck with her sister's rules.

But in the meantime, she was going to reap the benefits. She was eager to get her hands on her money; there were trainers she had her eye on, maybe some proper nice undies of her own, and she could have spent the remains of the cash twice over on the nails and lashes she wanted. 'Will you go to the bank in the morning and draw it out for me? Oh my God, Sabrina is going to be so jealous when she sees I've got top dollar to spend. I'm working in Sav's in the morning so just drop it off for me and I can whizz to town after work.'

'Relax, will you. I'll sort the money out, don't worry. I won't be getting up early though, so I'll go to the cash-point once I'm up and ready. Right, go on, piss off and let me earn my money now. I'm doing the night shift; I have two regular guys who log on around this time, so off you go and let your big sister earn her wage too.'

Susan lay in bed staring out of her window. It was windy tonight and it had just started raining. She snuggled under her duvet and gripped her mobile phone from the bedside cabinet. She messaged her best friend.

'Be ready to go shopping tomorrow after I've been to work. I've got a good way of earning us some decent money. I will tell you all about it tomorrow.'

As she hit Send, Susan had an idea. What if she didn't need Emma anymore? She and Sabrina could set this up on their own, couldn't they? Her best mate was old enough to pass all the ID checks, and if she was the one showing Sabrina the ropes there'd be no way she'd be creaming money off the top. Susan rolled on her side and snuggled down even deeper. She'd have sweet dreams tonight, of that she was sure.

Chapter Thirteen

Bronwen sat in her front room with Ben and Malc. She had all the old photographs out on the floor and the lads could see she'd had a drink, not that they judged her. She passed a photo over to Malc. 'Look at you and my Matthew there, how old were you both? You both look so young.'

Malcolm held the photograph in his hand as if he was holding something fragile. 'I think we were fifteen, this was taken before our school prom.'

Bronwen snatched the photo back and examined every inch of it. Her eyes were flooding with tears. 'He was such a lovely lad, had such a big heart and I don't know what I will do without him.'

Ben hesitated and then joined Bronwen on the floor and gave her a hug. 'We all miss him; I don't know how you are coping, it must be so hard for you. My head has been mashed for weeks. I just can't get my head around it. I should never have left him to come home on his own.'

Bronwen lifted her head up slowly and gripped Ben's face in her warm hands. 'Don't you blame yourself. It wasn't your fault. I know the police have interviewed you both and even they've said it's nothing to do with any of you.'

Malc picked at his dry, cracked lips, his emotions getting the better of him. Bronwen pulled herself up from the floor finally and sat on the sofa. She reached over and took a large mouthful from her drink. 'But you can still help me, boys. There must be something you saw, or someone, that stuck out. On that night, who was he with when you left him?'

Ben hunched his shoulders. 'The last place was wild. Me and Malc had copped off with these two girls and Matthew was flying about the bar talking to everyone. You know how much he loved dancing and every time I looked for him, he was on the dancefloor dancing with someone new.'

Bronwen spoke in a soft voice. 'So he looked happy?'

Ben nodded. 'He was as drunk as a skunk, but having the time of his life. He came back to the table a few times, talking to Malc and me, but we were all steaming drunk and I didn't really pay attention to who he was with. The bird I was with was mithering me to get off to her place and every time I asked Matthew if he was ready, he said yeah give me another ten minutes.'

Bronwen swallowed hard. 'Do you think my son was gay?' Ben looked at the floor and Malc started fidgeting about in his chair. She was waiting on an answer and directed her stare at Malc. 'You were his best mate; did he ever tell you he swung the other way?'

Malc was bright red, wished she would have asked Ben the question – not him. Malc shook his head slowly. 'I dunno. I mean, not that I know of.'

Ben jumped into the conversation. 'I'm going to be honest here, I've thought it. We probably all have. Come on, Malc, Matty never had a girlfriend and whenever we tried to hook him up, he always made excuses.'

Malc glared over at Ben. Bleeding hell, he wasn't shutting up. 'I mean, look at Fat Donna. She worshipped the ground he walked on, and he would never go near her even though she promised him everything if you know what I mean.' Ben realised he might have said too much and back-pedalled. 'What I mean is, none of us knew. But none of us cared. He was just Matthew and that was fine by us.'

Bronwen's eyes filled up again, tears soon rolling down the side of her cheeks. 'Thanks, Ben. I needed to hear that. Everyone's been walking on eggshells around me, like I didn't know my own son, or that I'd give a shit if he was gay, straight or the Queen of Sheba. I just want to know who laid hands on him, who took him from me and why? He was a pure soul, wouldn't hurt a fly. But me? I'll make sure someone swings for this.'

Bronwen took another long swig of wine. 'Anthony is still claiming he's innocent and the police said he will probably be released on bail. That dirty cow Alison from behind the bar in The Griffin has said he was with her, so they don't have much else to go on; only that he was out of breath when he got to her.'

Ben sat back on the sofa and dug his hand into the bag of crisps he was eating. 'I can't believe you're dealing with all that at the same time, Bronwen. My mam said she always thought he was a shady fucker, but I never expected him to cheat on you, no way on this earth.'

Bronwen reached over for her fags and sparked one up. She looked over at the lads and spoke through clenched teeth. 'Just let me see him around here, I'll yank every bleeding hair out of his head. Innocent or guilty, he never had a good word to say about him; jealous he was that he wasn't my priority. And he told me that too, always said Matthew should grow a set and stand on his own two feet. So he had the motive, didn't he?'

Ben and Malc just sat listening and let her vent her anger. When the fire of her rage had burnt out, Malc looked over at Bronwen and asked in a soft voice, 'Have you got any idea when the funeral will be?'

'The police are releasing his body in the next few days, so I'll start making plans then. I want you two to carry him, along with some of my brothers and nephews, if you will?'

Ben choked up and his bottom lip trembled as he replied, 'I would be honoured. We were side by side in life, and this is best we can do by him in death. Isn't that right, Malc?'

Malc was away with the fairies, looking stoned. He'd been on way too much weed since Matthew's death. Ben knocked him with his hand to bring him back to the present moment. 'Malc, for fuck's sake, mate, we were talking to you.'

'Sorry, I've not been sleeping well. What did you say again?'

'Bronwen has asked us to carry the coffin and I said we would be honoured. That's right, isn't it?'

'Yeah, course we will,' he said. How could a mother ever bury a child, he was thinking, how would a parent say goodbye to them, not be able to see them ever again, it must be heart-breaking.

Ben reached over and touched her hand. 'We're here to support you. No matter what you need, just let us know.'

Bronwen broke, her words hard to understand. 'My boy, my precious son. My life will never be the same again without him.' Ben and Malc dropped their heads low. No words would ever take away the hurt this woman was feeling. There had to be something they could do.

Ben and Malc were walking home. There was an icy Northerly wind tonight and it was bitter cold. Ben dipped his head as they walked along the busy main road. 'I can't wait to get in my bed tonight, my head is fucked up with all of this. Every time I close my eyes, I just see his face, laughing and dancing. Do you really think Anthony did him in or what?'

Malc had his hood up and you could only see the side of his face. 'Fuck knows, but somebody did and he's in the frame for it. He was there at the scene of the crime and his story doesn't fit in my eyes. Yes, he was screwing that barmaid but come on, it's all a bit suss, isn't it? How do we know that she's not covering up for him? Matthew told me all about him too, he was a fucking weirdo. I think he was jealous of Matty and the attention he got from his mam, so he got rid of him.'

'The police have had him locked up for ages. If they had enough evidence, they would have charged him by now. And he and Matthew had their rows, I know, but mostly Anthony got on with Matthew. He took him every-where, all those football matches, picked him up from late nights from yours, and he was always bunging him money when he was skint. I think we're all missing something here. Surely someone must have seen something.'

'That's why I sit on the canal most nights until late and see who's lurking. I've spoken with lots of passersby about the night Matthew was murdered and up to now nobody's seen nothing. But there is that a gang of homeless people who doss near the canal and when I get the chance I'm going to see if they remember anything about that night. I just don't want to do it solo, they look dodgy as hell. I'm going down that way tonight if you want to come. I'll have a spliff down there and see if I can see anything new. Are you coming or what?'

'Nah, mate. I've got work in the morning. You're mad if you keep going down there anyway, it spooks me out just thinking about it. Go home and get in bed.'

'Go home to what, my old man kicking off and making me skivvy for him? No, I'll go and take my chances on the canal rather than listen to his crap again.'

Ben nodded his head, knew what Malc's old man was like. For years he'd slapped him about and some of the stories he'd told them would make your toes curl. Malc's dad was a functioning alcoholic for sure and since his mrs had walked out on him eight years ago, he took his anger out on his son, belittled him, woke him up from his sleep and made him cook and clean for him. You never knew what shit people were going through at home, he thought.

Malc sat on his usual cold metal bench and popped his spliff into the corner of his mouth. He could hear the homeless people behind him settling down for the night in a sheltered area. He'd often thought about joining them just to get away from his dad, but the reality of setting up camp in one of the tent cities was bleak. If you didn't freeze to death or get your few possessions robbed, pissed on or lobbed in the canal, then you had to be on something just to take the edge off life. Malc lit his spliff and instead turned his eyes in the direction of the gay village, he could hear music and people laughing. But it just reminded him of what he'd lost. Instead he looked at the canal in front of him and stared at the dark muddy water, hoping he would find the answers to his questions in there.

Chapter Fourteen

Brooke looked over at Lee, noticing things about him that she hadn't before; his button nose, his perfect white teeth. She still felt guilt over how they'd got together, but she wondered whether if they'd met when they were both single they'd have still had a spark. Was he right for her or was it just the lure of the forbidden that had drawn them to each other? This time round she couldn't fault him though. He'd welcomed her into his home and not judged her for her past. Even if he kept pushing for more than she was ready to give.

'Shall we go away for the weekend? Maybe go to the Lakes?'

Brooke smiled. She really did appreciate his help, but this was too much, too soon. She just needed time to sort herself out, get some headspace, without him giving her the ick. 'I need to go back to work, Lee. The girls have been good enough to cover my clients for me, so I need to get back in the mix and get some normality back in my life.'

Lee could see he was fighting a losing battle and nodded. He'd just made them a coffee and he sat down next to Brooke, snuggling in, invading her private space. 'Will you be OK at work? What about Vincent showing up? I can't understand how you would ever be attracted to someone like him.'

Brooke sipped on her drink. She closed her eyes and was carried right back to the first night she'd met Vincent. Her body felt a warmth rising up from her feet to her chest and the corners of her mouth started to rise as she remembered when she was head over heels in love with her husband. 'Vincent was on leave from the army when we first met. He was in the Special Forces you know, told me lots of stories about the missions he'd been on, some scary stuff – though he always said there was much stuff he was sworn to secrecy about. I was out with my friend in Manchester and he was on a stag night with the lads. I always say he made the first move, but he would always say it was me who came onto him. From the second I started talking to him I knew he was the one for me. My heartbeat quickened and I couldn't stop looking at him, he made me weak at the knees. Vincent was honest with me from the start; told me he was an army boy and had another year to serve his country. It never bothered me in the slightest and later he told me that impressed him – that I didn't sulk when he said his duty came before me. People talk about love at first sight, and I believe you can love someone from the first second you meet them.'

Lee looked pained as she continued.

'Vincent had some weird ways when he was discharged and we started to date each other. He always said he had PTSD from being in the forces, the things he'd seen and done during his service. It was like the cups in the cupboard; all the handles had to be facing one way, his shoes needed to be straight and touching each other when he took them off each night.'

'That's not normal behaviour, Brooke, you should have seen the warning signs.'

'I was in love, Lee. The man could do no wrong in my eyes and those little habits weren't harming anyone. At first I thought he was just being tidy. I just ignored his traits hoping they would subside.'

'And did they?'

'No, did they 'eck. They got worse. But it wasn't his habits that were the real problem. It was the way he'd kick off if things weren't just so. The towels in the bathroom had to be folded on the radiator and placed in the correct size order. He'd go berserk if they weren't left properly.'

'The guy sounds like a proper head the ball.' Lee was relieved Brooke had got through the love at first sight stuff and on to all the things that made her ex sound like the loony he clearly was.

'He had a kind heart though, and when he was good, he was really good. When he left the army it took a long time for him to adjust to the world outside. He took forever to get a job; said he wasn't ready to work, and I had to just go with it and make sure we had enough to live on from just my wages. When he finally got a job working on the roads I praised the Lord; at last he was bringing some money into the house and we could start getting on our feet. But then…' She paused and started twisting a piece of hair at the side of her face. 'He started having a few cans every night after work. He said he needed a drink to unwind. I never thought anything about it at first, but he started to drink more and more each night. I confronted him about his drinking and he told me he would sort it out, but he never did. Even when we went on holidays together, he would get steaming drunk most nights and make a show of us. Nightmare it was. And you know the next part. I met you when we were going through a bad patch; we hardly ever spoke anymore, and sex was a distant memory.'

Lee saw his chance and jumped in. 'I can't believe he neglected you like that. I mean, I knew you were special when I first set eyes on you. You took my breath away and I said to my mate that you should have been the one that I married.'

Brooke burst out laughing, immune to his bullshit. 'Yeah, whatever, Lee. You have to remember, I'm a lot older and wiser now. I take everything you say to me with a pinch of salt.'

He held her gaze. 'I would marry you tomorrow, Brooke. I hope you know that.' She changed the conversation. Here she was, just walked out of an abusive marriage and on her arse and this guy was talking about weddings, he needed to give her room to breathe, room to think.

Brooke chewed on the side of her fingernail, thinking. 'The girls at the salon have not seen anything of Vincent and none of my friends have rung me to say he's been hammering at their front door either. It's strange that is, he's normally a loose cannon when he's angry and me not being in his bed will send him crazy.'

'He might know it's finally over this time,' Lee said, in hope.

'Are you having a laugh or what? That man has told me if I ever leave him, he will hunt me to the ends of the earth.'

'He won't do anything while you're by my side, love. If he comes within an inch of you the police will be all over him and he'll be arrested. Did you ring the police and tell them what has been happening, because you can have a restraining order on him.'

'Do you think he would ever listen to the police, Lee? He's his own law and that's what he's drummed into me over the years. It's only now that I'm away from him that I can see the light at the end of the tunnel. I just want a divorce and to be done with the man and then I can start again mending my own life. Lee,' she paused. 'It's like I've had an awakening and I'm my own person again, the girl I remember being. The anxiety that I feel crippling my body every single day is leaving me, and I feel like me for the first time in a long time.'

'That's great news. I knew coming here for a few weeks would help you clear your head. And if you think you are strong enough to go back into work then do it. You're right, no man should stop you living your life and, like I said, if he comes near you just ring the police.'

Brooke stood up and stretched. 'That's settled then. I will ring the girls and tell them I'll be back in work tomorrow.

Come here, you, and give me a cuddle. I know I've resented you for a long time for what happened when we were found out, but I'm finally over it. Today is a new day and from now on I'm not going to let anyone, or anything, break my stride again. The world is my oyster and I'm going to do all the things I've wanted to do for years. I'm going to see what life is like beyond the estate, beyond Manchester. I want to go to Verona and see Juliet's Wall, I want to go to Rome and see the Vatican City and I want to go to Ireland and go into the country pubs and listen to the folk music.'

Lee laughed out loud. 'You've just been watching too many Hollywood versions of Ireland. Life isn't all *PS I Love You*. Though I loved that film too. I'll tell you what, fuck going to the Lake District, let's start that bucket list of yours and go to Ireland.'

Brooke jumped about on the spot. So this was what it was like to be happy and living her life! She ran at him and jumped on him with her legs tightly around his waist. 'Let's do it, let's go to bloody Ireland.' So what if she'd been all for swearing off men completely? You had to take your chances in life and maybe this was her only chance to see Ireland.

Lee swung her around the front room and fell onto the sofa with her. He looked deep into her eyes and slowly their warm lips met. They both shared a passionate kiss. Brooke opened her eyes and stared into his big blue eyes. 'Thank you for saving me, Lee, thank you.'

Vincent sat at the bar in The Griffin, nursing a drink. He looked as rough as a bear's arse, as Dane had told him went he sat down, unshaven, greasy hair, grubby hands. He smiled over at Dane as he slurped the last bit of beer from his pint glass. 'I'll have another one, Dane, when you're ready, lad. It's going to be a long night.'

Dane went to the pump and pulled another pint of lager. He placed it on the bar in front of Vincent and could see he was already well on his way to being pissed. The big guy stared into the pint like it was a crystal ball.

'How's the mrs, Vincent? I've not seen her in here for a while, is everything alright?'

Vincent lifted his head up slowly, his eyes were dancing with madness. 'Don't mention that slag's name to me. She's left me, pal, probably laid on her back getting shagged by some other guy now.'

Dane was used to acting as an agony aunt for his regulars and he always tried to offer advice rather than judgement when he could see they were struggling. He placed his elbows on the bar and leaned in. 'Mate, you're just going through a bad patch. I'll tell you something for nothing though, you won't find the answer at the bottom of a pint pot, will you?'

'I drink to forget, Dane. Forget what that bitch did to me.'

'Do you want to talk about it, pal, a problem shared and all that?' Dane heard all sorts from behind the bar and nothing tended to shock him any more.

'No thanks, I'll sort myself out. You know I'm a lone wolf and work alone.'

Dane looked puzzled; what on earth was this guy going on about? 'Anyway, the darts are on tonight if you fancy a game. You were a good chucker when you played for the team last time.'

Vincent tapped the side of his nose, then reached for his new pint. 'I always hit my target, Dane, always.'

Dane started to walk away to serve someone else at the other end of the bar. Vincent was talking in riddles and if he didn't want to open up, he was better left alone.

Vincent stumbled into the house at the end of the night and flung his keys onto the coffee table. He went straight into the kitchen and opened the fridge to grab a can of lager. He looked for something to eat, but there was nothing there he could just shove in his mouth. If his mrs had been here, he could have shouted her down to make him something proper to eat, but she wasn't here, and the house seemed to shout her absence. Vincent flicked the TV on and sat staring at the screen. After the last swig from his can of Stella he squeezed at the can with all his might and snarled. 'So, you think you can leave me, do you? We'll see about that, won't we? We'll see who's laughing then, won't we?' Vincent said to himself. 'Come out, come out, wherever you are, Brooke, because I'm coming to find you. Oh yes, I'm coming to find you. This wolf always finds his mate.'

Chapter Fifteen

B ridie stood at the front window and cradled her cup of tea in both hands. Bert was just getting up and already she had a list of jobs for him to do. She always felt their house set the standard for the street and just because they had police back and forth, reporters and just nosey folk coming to stare at the Murphys' house, it was no excuse to let their standards slip. In fact, she was pushing Bert more than ever to keep the place ship-shape, never knowing when their house might be in shot on a news report. The garden needed weeding again, the windows were mucky, and she could do with a hand with changing the duvet covers. She spent so much time at the windows watching the comings and goings that she was behind on so many of her usual little jobs. But she just couldn't take her eyes off the street for long.

She looked at the clock, it was nearly nine. Today was Tuesday which meant the market was on. Bridie and Bert would often have a walk round Harpurhey market and grab some bargains. They had been going to the market for years and loved that they would see lots of old friends. The chat was as important as the shopping for her. Bridie always stood gossiping with them for ages, catching up on the stories, finding out who was ill, who had left their partners, who'd had a run-in with the law.

Bert walked into the room, he looked knackered. 'I've made you a brew, love, it's on the side in the kitchen. I'm not making any scran this morning because it's Tuesday and we can grab a full English from the café on the market.'

Bert didn't reply, just went into the kitchen and got his drink. Chief Blackcloud she called him when he was like this. Bridie was still stood at the window. She pulled the blind back slowly. 'Hey, did you not hear that drunken git again last night. That's every night he's been out now for over two weeks. He put the music on loud too, so he'll be getting an earful from me when I speak to him.' Bridie knew some folk on the street wouldn't face up to Vincent, but she wouldn't let the size of the guy frighten her.

'He's just enjoying himself. If the wife has gone away to see her friend, then give the guy a break. Stop overreacting.'

Bridie frowned at him as she watched him sit down with the newspaper. 'Stop bloody sticking up for him, Bert. He's a drunk and there's no denying it. I think Brooke has had enough of him and she's pissed off. Good on her if she has. No woman should have to put up with a drunken arsehole every night. He's let himself go too; scruffy he is. The garden is looking wild too – I'm not having number 6 letting the side down.'

'You know I care about the street as much as anyone on the Manor. And yes, I'll grant you he could do with mowing the lawn. But beyond that, you've got to drop it, Bridie, quit interfering in other peoples' lives. Give it a bleeding rest, woman.'

Bridie stood with her hand on her hip. 'Listen, miserable arse. I just look after the community and make sure all our neighbours are all okay. You're normally just as bad as me so I don't know why you're chirping up today. How many times a day do you stand at that bloody window telling me who's walking past, who's let their dog mess everywhere, or which kids are standing on the corner vaping, so shove that in your pipe and smoke it.'

Bert knew when her cage was rattled and he opened the newspaper and held it up high so she couldn't see his face.

Bridie came and sat down on the sofa. He could hear her huffing and puffing at the side of him. He dropped the newspaper and shot a look over at her. 'What's up with you now?'

Bridie shook her head and stared out of the window. 'It's Matthew's funeral soon. I'll start collecting money from the neighbours for some flowers. It's going to be such a sad day, isn't it? A boy so young, his life left in front of him, taken just like that.' She rubbed at her arms as the hairs stood on end. 'I believe they've let Anthony out on bail too. I wonder if he'll turn up for the funeral.'

'I can't see why not. He's not been charged with anything so it's innocent until proven guilty, isn't it?'

'Bronwen won't have him there, surely. He's been messing about with that fancy piece from behind the bar

140

in The Griffin, hasn't he. As if that woman needed any more heartbreak. Losing a son is bad enough, let alone to find out your fella is cheating on you. It's not something I would ever bear thinking about.'

'Sad for all those who are involved, isn't it. But as long as we are good, Bridie, that's all that concerns me these days. Happy wife, happy life is what I always say.'

Bridie smiled over at her husband, his earlier comments already forgiven. Today was market day, a day to gossip, a day to shop.

Bridie stood in the kitchen with her purse open in her hands, thinking. She looked puzzled as Bert came into the kitchen behind her. 'I'm forty pounds short. I know how much I had so don't start saying I must have spent it like you usually do. It's been happening a lot lately, money just going missing.'

Bert dipped his head over her shoulder and looked into her purse too. 'Bridie, you're right. You are doing this a lot lately. I don't want to scare you, but your memory is not what it once was. How many times a day do you walk into a room and say you've forgot what you came in for?'

Her eyes widened. She turned to face him and shook her head. 'I've not been anywhere to spend it, so stop saying I'm going bloody loopy when my memory is perfectly fine. I know what I had, and the only money I've spent was paying the bloody window cleaner.'

Bert stepped back and rested his hand on the kitchen worktop. 'If you don't know where it's gone then how am I supposed to bloody know? Are we going shopping then or what?'

Bridie squeezed her purse shut and flung it into her tan shoulder bag. She zipped her coat up in a huff and growled over at husband. 'Well, something is fishy because I thought the same thing last week about money being missing. I'm not daft, you know.'

Bert was flushed. 'I hope you're not pointing the finger at me, Bridie?' He paused, waiting on her reaction, watching her every movement.

She pulled her shoulders back and her nostrils flared. 'I'm not pointing the finger at anyone, but there is only me and you who live in this house so if I've not had it then it only leaves you.'

Bert raised his voice, pacing about the kitchen. 'Search me then, check every pocket I have. I can't even believe you would say that. You're crazy, woman, you need that head of yours testing. If I was you, I would book into the doctor's tell him your memory is going and see if he can give you any medication for it.'

'Bastard,' she whispered under her breath as she turned to get a cold drink of water from the tap. The couple stood in the kitchen for a few minutes more before Bridie spoke. 'Come on then, if we're going to the market. There will be no steak tonight, for sure, you'll be on stew.'

As soon as Bridie walked out of her front door, she quickened her pace as she spotted Vincent. Bert hung back and locked the front door. Normally he'd have tried to intercept and stop his wife from poking her nose where it wasn't wanted, but it was too late; she'd already collared him.

'Good morning, Vincent. I'm glad I've caught you. We're doing a collection for flowers for Bronwen's son if you would like to make a donation.'

Vincent grunted as he shoved his hand into his pocket. Bridie was never one to miss a chance and couldn't help but delve deeper into his relationship. 'When is your Brooke back? She said two weeks.'

'I'm not arsed if she ever comes back, cheeky cow.' Vince looked unabashed.

Bridie wasn't used to such a direct response and clearly had to weigh up her next move. 'I'm not sticking my nose in, but I thought something must be up. I've heard you coming home late most nights and we can hear your loud music – I wondered if you were nursing a broken heart?'

Bert was stood behind her now. 'Morning, Vincent. How's it all going, pal?' Bridie could have strangled her husband right there and then. Here she was, getting down to the nitty gritty and her other half had stopped it.

'I'm getting there, Bert. You know me, ducking and diving, wheeling and dealing.' Vince immediately switched to the kind of matey chat that stopped anyone from getting to the heart of things.

'That's the best way, Vincent. Keep your chin up, lad.' Bridie was chomping at the bit to talk to her neighbour again and realised she'd have to get straight to the point. 'So, are you two splitting up?'

Vincent smirked. 'We'll always be together, Bridie, just a bit of a bad patch we're going through. Don't you worry, my girl will be back home before you know it.'

Bridie had no comeback so she quickly changed the subject as she took the five-pound note from Vincent's hand. 'I'll let you know when the funeral is. Bert was only saying before about what might happen if Anthony turns up.'

It was obvious Vincent couldn't be bothered with Bridie and her gossip today; he thought of himself as a man's man and liked to talk about straightforward stuff like the footy, or who had a new motor.

Vincent muttered and walked off and Bridie stood for a few seconds on the same spot watching him walk away. Bert nudged her. 'Come on then, motormouth, let's get to the market before it shuts.'

'Just let me nip into Sav's to grab some ciggies before we set off. I've only got a couple left and I can't run out while I'm having the kind of day that I've been having.'

Bridie smiled at Susan as she walked into the shop. 'It's nice to see you doing well, Susan. I bet your mam and dad are so proud of you getting a job. It's better than being sat on your arse all day doing nothing isn't it?'

'It sure is, Bridie. I like working, helps me save up for some new clothes and takes the pressure off my mam and my dad having to buy them for me.'

Bridie nodded her head. 'You keep it up and make your parents proud of you.' Bridie walked to the till and smiled at Angela. 'Can I have twenty Benson & Hedges silver, sweetheart?'

Angela turned around and grabbed the fags from the counter behind her. 'I thought you said you were giving up, Bridie. These are no good for you, you know.'

'I know, I know. I keep saying I'm going to try one of them vapes everyone is smoking, but I've not got around to it yet. Anyway, I've smoked for that long now it's pointless. The damage is already done.'

Angela took the money from Bridie and gave her the change. 'I've just served Anthony about five minutes ago. He's got a nerve showing his face around here, hasn't he?'

Bridie gasped and leaned over the counter, wanting to know more. 'The man has no shame. If Bronwen gets her hands on him he'll be a dead man walking.'

'For sure. I wouldn't like to be in his shoes anyway. Ben and Malc are gunning for him too. They told me they're going to do him in.' Angela's eyes sparkled with the illicit thrill of feeding the rumour mill.

Bridie picked up her fags and shoved them in her coat pocket. 'It's getting worse around here. I told my Bert that the other day; bloody murderers, drunks and God knows whoever else are all living under our noses, a stone's throw away. I know some folk think I'm a nosey parker, always keeping watch – but someone's got to do it or we'll be dead in our beds.'

Angela nodded. 'You keep safe, Bridie. I'll see you again and we'll have a proper catch-up when you have more time to chat.'

'Yes, I'll try and pop back later when I've done my shopping.' Bridie left the shop in a hurry.

Susan was bent over stacking some shelves when Angela came up behind her. 'New trainers?'

'Yes, I can afford new clobber now that I'm working here.'

'On the wages Sav pays, you can afford sneaks like them? I couldn't afford new laces on the amount he pays me. I'll be after a pay rise now.'

Susan got back to her work, no time for talking, she had a busy night tonight and the sooner she'd finished her shift the better.

Sav stood watching his staff from the doorway, his eyes never left Susan. He was onto a good thing here. A very good thing indeed.

Chapter Sixteen

Anthony had his cap pulled down low as he walked past his house. The place he'd lived and felt safe. For the last twenty minutes he'd been pacing up and down trying to find the courage to knock on the door. Five cigs he'd smoked, one after the other, trying to calm his speeding heart rate down. Balls to it, he thought. He flicked his cigarette butt and motored down the garden path like a man on a mission. It was do or die time. If Bron phoned the police then so be it, he would deal with that if it happened. His trembling hands lifted up the silver letterbox handle and he rapped on the door about five times. Anthony stood back from the window and jumped about on the spot trying to keep warm, blowing his hot breath into his cupped hands. It was freezing today, the cold wind biting at his face. The front door opened and Bronwen stood there gobsmacked, as white as a ghost. He knew time wasn't on his side and he blurted it out. 'Please, Bronwen, let me say my piece then I will go and leave you alone.'

There was no way she was letting him speak anything more than that; she'd imagined this moment time and time again in her mind. She knew exactly what she was going to say to this prick. He made her skin crawl, made her stomach churn like a washing machine on the spin cycle. She was as good as ready to attack him, scratch his eyes out. 'You dirty, no-good bastard. How dare you even darken my doorstep, have you no shame? I'll ring the police on you, get you flung back in a cell where you belong. Fucking vermin you are, a sneaky, murdering snake.'

Anthony knew he had to be quick before she slammed the front door shut on him. 'I would never have hurt a bone in Matthew's body, he was like a son to me no matter what I said about him. My heart is broken just like yours. I swear to you on anybody's life that I'm innocent. Please believe me. Come on, Bronwen, you know me better than anyone. You know, deep down, this is not me.'

Bronwen stepped out of the front door; she was ready to claw his eyes out. 'My son was murdered and you were shagging some tart. I hope your dick falls off.'

Anthony broke down, his legs melting from underneath him. He held his head in his hands and sobbed like a baby. 'I'm sorry, so sorry. I have no words to tell you how much you mean to me. I should be the one comforting you at an awful time like this, but I know you must hate me. You're my world. I fucked up big-time and I know that. She meant nothing to me, it was just a daft, stupid mistake, a great big mistake.'

She placed her hands on her hips, bent over slightly and spoke in a sarcastic tone. 'Forgetting to put the bins out is a bloody mistake, Anthony. Screwing some tart who's probably had more knob-ends than weekends is disgusting, not a mistake. Me and you are done. And...' She paused. 'Rot in hell and don't ever come near me again. Oh, and just for the record, tell that slut of yours that she's not off the hook either. Once I'm thinking straight, I'll be giving her a slap too. Cheeky bitch.' Bronwen marched back inside the house and slammed the door behind her, nearly taking the door from its hinges. Once she was inside, she slid to the ground and drew her legs up to her chest. She needed to breathe, but it felt like the air just caught in her throat. 'Bastard, no-good bastard,' she sobbed.

Outside, Anthony picked himself up from the floor and walked out from the garden. His life was in tatters and he had nowhere to go, nobody he could speak to – and no one to blame but himself. The residents here all stuck together and once Bronwen had blackened his name there was no going back. He might be able to prove he wasn't a killer – but to the residents of the Manor, he'd always be the man who cheated on the night his stepson died. Head low, he trudged down the street. Nowhere to go, no one to speak to, an outcast.

Vincent was steaming drunk when he saw Anthony. He spotted him sat on the floor near the shops and made his way towards him, weaving from side to side, slurring his words. Once he reached him, he steadied himself and tried to put a sentence together. 'Come on, lad, why don't you come home with me? We'll have a drink together and put the world to rights. I figure everyone's talking about me almost as much as they're bitching about you so we may as well stick together. It'll blow over in the end – nobody really gives a fuck at the end of the day what happens to anyone. It's all just gossip, so it's every man for themselves.'

Anthony lifted his head up and had to wipe the tears from his eyes to focus. He knew Vincent casually and many a night they'd shared a few beers down the local boozer, not because they were mates or actually planned it, more because there wasn't much else to do round here but have a drink at The Griffin. Anthony stood up, pleased that some-one had offered him a lifeline. 'Thanks, mate. I've got no home, nothing anymore. I made a mistake, that's all. I never laid a finger on Matthew. May God strike me down dead, I never touched that kid. Someone needs to believe me.'

Vincent started to walk off. 'I believe you, pal. Come on then, if you're coming,' he shouted behind him.

Inside number 6 Anthony had peeled his coat off and was sitting on the sofa; his hands were purple and no matter how much he rubbed at them, he couldn't get them warm. Vincent was sitting in the chair facing him, he was already on his second can.

'Go on then. What was Alison like in the bedroom? She looks like a right dirty cow. A few of the lads down the pub have been trying to get her knickers off since they heard you'd had a go, but she's having none of it.'

Anthony tried to smile knowing this kind of crude, man-to-man chat was what was expected of him, but his mouth seemed to have forgotten how to do it. He knew he should try a bit of banter, but it felt ugly now – he'd broken

Bron's heart, dragged Alison into a mess she didn't deserve and, worst of all, walked away from trying to find Matthew. No wonder he couldn't even force a fake grin. He'd not smiled for weeks, let alone had / experienced happiness flowing through his veins, and probably never would again. He changed the subject. 'I'm going to the funeral. I don't care what anyone says, I'm going. I brought Matthew up, virtually. He's my son in my eyes. Bronwen can kick up a fuss all she wants, love nor money won't stop me attending his funeral.'

'Do what you have to do, pal. Fuck women, I say. We're brothers in arms and all that. I'll stand with you. Let anyone say a word to you and I'll punch their lights out. That's the problem around here, folk all have too much to say about everybody's life. Fuck them, fuck them all, that's what I say.'

Anthony shot a look over at Vincent and knew this was going to be a long night. He knew Vince was trying to back him up, but he couldn't share his rage – nothing cut through the guilt and sorrow that seemed tied around him like a rope. At least he had a roof over his head for now, but tomorrow was another day and he'd have to find a place to stay. His world had fallen apart and at least the alcohol numbed his pain, temporarily blanking out the misery that was his life. And soon enough he didn't have to even try to force a reply back to Vincent. The big guy was hammered, ranting.

'My wife, she thinks she's got away with it. That she's had me over? Well I don't believe in "you don't get angry, you get even" – I do fucking both.' He let out a laugh and crumpled the can in his fist.

Chapter Seventeen

Bert was hunched over the card table, sweating. There was a big pot of cash in the middle of the table and if his luck kept on the way it had been all night, that money was coming home with him. He could go and buy back his wife's jewellery, sneak it into the house without her even missing it. Bridie had lots of jewellery; rings, necklaces, bracelets. Her mother had left her a lot of gold when she passed away and she always said that it was her back-up plan if they ever fell on hard times. She never wore it anyway, it had been stuck in a box for years, just sitting there doing nothing. So Bert had cashed in on them and now that he was sitting around the table holding what he knew was a cracking hand of cards, he was sure he'd made the right choice. You had to invest if you wanted to win big. And Bert figured it also helped that he had a bit more life behind him than some of these young pups. Dane had thrown his hand in minutes before and he'd spat his dummy out because he'd lost a lot of money.

Dane's pal Tommy was one to watch, though. Tommy was a cracking poker player and most nights when they played cards in the late hour he would always leave with a wad of cash. Bert had been watching these games for a few weeks now, but never playing before, he had just been there serving them sandwiches and snacks and making sure their glasses were full. Dane told him that he could lose everything he had around this table and told him time and time again that he shouldn't buy in unless he could afford to lose as much as he wanted to win, especially with his financial status at the moment. But Bert was headstrong; once a gambler always a gambler. He'd been dodging the loan man now for weeks and it was only a matter of time before Isaac came knocking on his door. But that could all change tonight; he'd win this hand and clear up, get his wife's jewellery back and no one would be any the wiser.

Tommy sucked on his Cuban cigar and blew a big cloud of grey smoke out towards Bert. He sat tapping his fingers and smiled at the older guy. This was a blagging game and you needed to keep a straight face when your opponents were studying you, make them think you had a good hand, make them think there was no way of winning. Bert was doing a good job, his eyes never leaving his cards in his hand. Dane broke the silence. 'Are you folding or what, Bert, or are you carrying on? It's going to cost you to see Tommy's hand. Have you got enough left in the kitty to continue?'

'Don't you worry about me, lad. I've got more than enough to see this out.' Dane turned to Tommy. 'The ball's in your court.' Tommy inhaled deeply, sure this old codger had nothing, he was ready to call him out. Tommy slowly spread his cards out on the table, like the cat that had got the cream: three kings and an ace of spades.

Bert swallowed hard, his jaw dropping. Tommy sat forward in his seat, eager to see Bert's hand. Bert's eyes were wide and he seemed to be struggling to breathe. His hand covered his heart and his head fell back.

Dane jumped up and went to his side. Running the bar at The Griffin meant he was a regular first aider, although he was more used to dealing with drunken injuries than shock. But this looked like it could be serious. Luckily, he knew exactly what to do. 'Tommy, ring an ambulance, quick. Fuck me, he might be having a heart attack.'

Bert dropped the playing cards and Tommy clocked them. The old guy had nothing, piss all, a crock of shit.

Bert's legs were shaking when Dane came to assist him. 'Fuck me, Tom, he's grey, the mrs will go mad if he josses it here.' He checked the old man's airways and loosened his collar.

Tommy was on the phone now, speaking to the emergency services. Bert's eyes were staring into space, a look of fear deep inside them. Dane reached over and held his hand. 'Come on, Bertie-boy, stick with us, the ambulance will be here soon, you stay with us.

Dane stood outside Bert's house and looked up at the window. It was three o'clock in the morning and he knew

Bridie would be fast asleep. He remembered Bert telling him that once his wife was asleep, she was dead to the world. Dane looked around the garden and found some small grey pebbles. He stood back, aiming the stones at the window. He flinched as they hit the glass – he'd nearly put the window in. It worked though – Bridie's angry face was at the window. Dane was relieved, he'd asked his wife Gaynor to come and tell Bridie the bad news, but she told him to go and take a run and a jump and do it himself. This was his mess, she said, and it was up to him to sort it out. Still, he'd been almost ready to give up when knocking on the door hadn't woken Bridie. But lights were being switched on in the house now, a shadow appearing in the hallway through the glass. Bridie opened the front door, clearly fuming.

'What the hell are you doing here at this time of the night?'

Dane stared at the ground, there was no easy way to say this. 'Bridie, it's Bert. I think he's had a heart attack; the ambulance has just taken him to hospital. If you want, I'll take you up there.'

Bridie blinked, still half asleep, nothing making sense. Dane knew he'd have to give her more details. 'Bert was having a game of poker with the lads. We do it all the time and I think the excitement got too much for him. On my life, Bridie, I thought he was a goner.'

'My Bert's in bed, you bloody nutter.' Bridie shook her head. 'He sleeps in the spare room most nights if you must know – cheeky blighter says I snore too much.'

Dane spoke in a softer tone. 'He's not, Bridie, he's on his way to hospital.'

Bridie turned on the spot and then ran up the stairs, shouting, 'Bert, Bert, get down here will you?'

The silence said more than words ever could.

Bridie sat outside in the waiting room at North Manchester General hospital. The doctors had been with Bert for a long time now and her head was all over, not knowing if her husband was dying or not. She turned to Dane. She wanted some answers now the initial shock had worn off.

'How long has he been gambling?'

Dane didn't know what to say. 'Bridie, I swear, tonight was the first game he's played with us, usually he just comes and watches, helps out a bit.'

'So, this has been going on for how long? Don't bloody lie to me because my husband is laying in there and might never see daylight again.'

Dane knew Bert had a gambling addiction, but even so there was no way he was selling him down the river. What happened on tour stayed on tour. Dane knew the code of honour he and his mates swore by and knew he would have to bend the truth. 'Bridie, on my life he's only had a few nights around the card table, said he missed the buzz and watching was the next best thing. But even tonight the most he's lost is a few quid. Me and the lads play for big money and Bert doesn't have that kind of money around him, does he?'

'No, he's not got a pot to piss in. I manage all the money in the house. We've been down this road with him before,

Dane, and he nearly lost me because of it. If he's gambling again then I don't know what I would do. He promised me it was over, promised me.'

'And it is, Bridie. Let's just concentrate on him being alright for now. This is a conversation you can have with him yourself when he gets through this, but for now, let's say a prayer that he pulls through.'

Bridie reached to her neck, found her silver cross and gripped it in her hands. Her eyes closed; she was praying. The next few hours were going to be hard and she knew she had to remain calm; she just wanted her husband to be alright, to pull through. Even if just so she could tan his hide if he was betting again.

Finally, the news came through. The doctors smiled as they told Bridie he was lucky to still be alive and that she could go and see him.

Bridie sat with Bert. She reached over and touched his familiar hand. His eyes flickered, he was starting to wake up. The heart monitors were stuck all over his chest and he looked smaller and older than the man she'd said good-night to earlier that evening. She squeezed at his fingers now, tears streaming down the side of her cheeks. 'Bert, you scared the bloody life out of me. The doctors said you had a massive heart attack and have to take it easy, eat healthy and change your lifestyle. And that means eating your greens, no more bloody cakes, quitting the booze, too.'

Bert opened his eyes and looked directly at his wife. 'Oh, love, I've never been so scared in my life. I thought I was going to meet my maker. Honest, Bridie, I saw the light.'

Bridie made the sign of the cross. 'Thank you, Lord. Thank you for not taking him.' Bert was clearly still tired and his eyes started to close again. Bridie kept her voice low and got ready to leave. 'I'll be back later. Just lie back, Bert, and try not to get up. Bed-rest, the doctor said, and that's exactly what you are going to do. We'll speak about everything else when you're up to it, but for now, get some rest.'

But Bert didn't even stir, already asleep again. Bridie stood at the door and looked back at her husband one last time before she left. 'Don't you leave me, Bert, don't you dare,' she whispered in a soft voice.

Chapter Eighteen

All of Manor Road was out for the funeral of Matthew Murphy. They'd always turn out for a send-off for one of their own, but a young lad taken too soon; that was a whole other level. The street was lined as the black funeral cars pulled up outside Bronwen's house, the oak coffin visible through the glass of the hearse. Everyone was there; workmates, old school friends, even folk who'd never met the kid but needed some way to share their shock and sadness, all huddled together, whispering to each other, talking about the horrendous way the boy met his death. Plenty of them had Anthony's name on their lips; he might have been released by the police but that carried little weight with the mourners – he was the only suspect in their eyes, and plenty of the crowd were quick to say he should rot in jail.

Malc and Ben sat with Bronwen in her front room with other family members. Bronwen's dad, Ernie, came to her side and patted the top of her shoulder softly. 'The cars are here, love.'

Malc looked away, his bottom lip trembling as the reality kicked in. Ben could see he was struggling and offered him some support. Malc had really taken his friend's death badly; they had been friends for a long time, chilled together most nights. At that age, you were meant to be invincible, not being buried. Life was going to be so different without him, everyone knew. 'Come on, Malc, we need to be strong here today, make Matthew proud of us,' Ben ventured.

Malc fiddled with the cuffs of his white shirt. He needed a few minutes to compose himself. But tears kept forcing themselves out from his eyes. The family all started to head to the front door. Bronwen stood up with help from her father. She closed her eyes as a dizzy spell hit her with full force. Every inch of her body was shaking, and she looked like she was choking. Malc and Ben came to her side and tried to assist her. But how could you help someone with a broken heart? There were no pills to take the pain away; the memories that would one day be a comfort to Bronwen clearly still cut her like a knife. For the two young friends, it was the first time they realised the real weight of grief, that this was a state of mind, a feeling that would never ever leave Bronwen's body. Death was final, they realised that much, they knew now as the funeral cars waited outside that none of them would ever see Matthew again – there was no punchline to this sad story. In this moment, they learned that grief breaks even the strongest of people, takes a piece of their heart that they will never get back. Looking at Bronwen, they saw that despite the depth of their pain, a mother's loss of a child had no comparison. They knew this woman would never be the same again.

The music played as Matthew's body was accepted into St Patrick's Church in Collyhurst. The two large oak wooden doors were open fully and Father John stood waiting for the service to begin. Mourners wept as the music started. Matthew always loved his music and to pick the songs that would be played at the service had been a job his friends knew they had to get right. Malc and Ben had sat with Bronwen for hours trying to find the songs that would be played throughout the service. Malc had come up with most of the songs, after all, he'd spent hours listening to music with his best friend in his bedroom most evenings when they were growing up.

Bronwen wanted certain songs, too, and picked 'I'll never love again' By Lady GaGa to be played as her son's body was brought into the church. She'd watched the film *A Star is Born* with Matthew and they both loved the song and always played it around the house. Bronwen heard the song now as she walked down the aisle behind her son's coffin. Her body was crippled with grief, every word from the song stabbing deep into her heart. You could have heard a pin drop as the music played. Bronwen's shoulders were shaking, and her father and her two brothers were supporting her as she made her way to the front row of the church. Malc and Ben carried the coffin along with other family members and once they had placed it at the front of the church, they sat down behind Bronwen and her family.

Malc twisted his fingers and kept his head down low, that way nobody would see the tears he'd cried, the pain in his eyes. His dad had always drummed into him that tears were for wimps and although he was struggling today, he was trying his best to hold it together. The priest spoke about the life of a young man that had been stolen from him, spoke about all the things Bronwen had told them about him. Where he wanted to travel, the bucket list he'd created that showed the kind of lad he was, the dreams he'd had; it was heart-wrenching that Matthew would never fulfil the list.

Ben nudged Malc and kept his voice low as he nodded his head towards the back of the church. 'I don't believe it. Anthony has turned up. Bronwen will go sick if she sees him.'

Malc twisted his head slowly and got a butcher's at Anthony too. He was at the back of the church, hidden away in the shadows. 'God help him if the family clock him,' he muttered. 'He needs to do himself a favour and piss off quickly before they hang, draw and quarter him.'

When the service moved outside to the burial, even around the graveside the music played. Malc had picked this song and although he used to rib his mate something chronic for liking what he said was 'utter shite', he knew it was a favourite of Matthew's. 'There's a place for us' from West Side Story rang out around the grave side. No one expected a young man to even have this song on his playlist, but Matthew had loved the theatre and songs like this that made the hairs on the back of his neck stand on end. The words from the song hit the mourners hard and yet the music somehow helped – something beautiful amid the pain of this final goodbye. Bronwen held a red rose in her hand and stepped forward towards the open grave. She stood for a few minutes, just looking down at the coffin and it was only when her father came to her side that she dropped the flower onto her son's coffin. As she turned to walk away, she lifted her head up and clocked Anthony, stood crying. It was like a spell was broken. Bronwen ran at him, across the thick brown mud, her fist ready made to pound into every inch of his body. He needed to feel pain, pain like she was feeling. 'How dare you come here today, do you have no shame?'

Bronwen was being dragged back now, but not before her hand swung back and she slapped Anthony with force. Ernie watched as Bronwen was guided back to the funeral car and once he knew she was gone, he went nose to nose with Anthony. 'Fuck off before you are six foot under too. I will tell you, once and once only. Have some bleeding respect.'

The other mourners circled Anthony and he knew his time here was up – he'd said his goodbye to Matthew like he said he would, but he couldn't resist stating his case. 'I'm innocent, the police have bailed me. Do you think if they thought I had murdered Matthew they would have let me out? Please listen to me, I'm innocent.'

But the mourners pressed forwards, pushing him away and he knew he was beaten. He walked off, watching his back all the time. Manchester wasn't a safe place for him anymore. He'd heard there was a price on his head and, for now, he had to go. He'd show them all he was innocent though, even if it took until his dying breath, he'd find out the truth.

Matthew and Ben stood looking down at the grave. This was it, the last words they would speak to their friend. Ben dropped his rose and nodded his head slowly. 'See you on the other side, bro. Look out for me, aye.'

Ben walked off and left Malc to have a few minutes on his own. He dropped his own flower onto the coffin and closed his eyes. Malc whispered his last goodbye and trudged back to meet Ben who was waiting for him. The days ahead would be strange without Matthew by their side. The Three Amigos were no more.

Ben clapped Malc on the shoulder. 'Goodnight, God Bless, Matthew, rest in peace.'

Chapter Nineteen

Susan set her laptop up and kept running to the front window, checking she and Sabrina were still alone in the house. Emma had gone out to see her friend and her mam and dad were at Asda doing the big shop. Sabrina was sitting watching her friend get ready to go online. Susan had been surprised that her older friend had been so shocked when she told her what she was doing. She still looked half-fascinated, half-appalled now. 'Are you going to show your motty if they ask you to? Because that's hanging if you're doing stuff like that.'

Susan shook her head and plonked down on the bed, still wearing her dressing gown. 'Wow, how many times do I have to tell you that you don't show anything you don't want to, especially your kitty; you tease them. Listen, I'm doing you a favour here and giving you a chance to earn some money like me. Our Emma would shit a brick if she found out I was doing this by myself, so just watch and then you can see if you want in or not.'

Sabrina sat back in the chair facing the bed and rolled her eyes, still not sure if this was something she wanted to watch.

'I've set up my own account now using your date of birth and all that so Emma will be none the wiser. Just watch and learn and when you see my bank account after this, then you can decide. I've done this a couple of times by myself already, so I've worked it out now. Right, shut up and let me get on with it.'

'You're the one still talking,' Sabrina said. Susan stood up, took her dressing gown off and got back on the bed. Sabrina was gobsmacked – she had never really noticed her friend had curves and a decent pair of knockers beneath the tracksuits they usually wore. She looked down at her own boobs and wondered if she'd get any interest if Susan did convince her to have a go at this. She watched as Susan logged on and it wasn't long before she was talking to a guy. Sabrina cringed as she listened to her friend. This felt seedy and she was sure no amount of money would get her speaking to these perverts like her friend was. She'd feel too embarrassed to come out with the sort of chat Susan was telling the person on the other end of the camera. Sabrina wasn't one to get embarrassed easily, but this was a whole new ball game. She nipped to the loo to avoid listening to her friend simpering and purring. She was talking to a guy she could barely see, his face covered with a mask. Susan had already told Sabrina he'd probably be on – apparently he'd been one of her 'regulars' and even in the last couple of weeks had spent some decent money with Susan. The conversation was flowing between these two and Susan was glad her friend wasn't in the room to hear the man's next question. He didn't speak online – just typed requests in the chat box.

'What about meeting up and I can take you for some nice food, maybe even buy you some gifts.'

Susan knew the rules her sister had drummed into her, but now she was flying solo she realised she could choose to ignore them. 'If I was to meet you then the money needs to be right. I wouldn't meet you for less than two hundred pounds.' She licked her lips and pouted at the man she could see on her laptop. She had to hide her shock when he agreed immediately, no messing about. Susan was eager to get the money in her account before he changed his mind, so she sat forward knowing it would give her client a blimp of her tits. 'Once the money is in my account we can arrange a day that we are both free to meet.'

Boom, a notification on her mobile phone from the bank; funds had just been transferred. She smiled at him; she was on fire now with some of the poses she was doing. Buzzing with what she'd earned, she agreed she would meet him at the weekend at eight o'clock in a place just on the edge of Manchester City centre. He'd already told her what to wear and how she should have her hair. Sabrina walked back into the bedroom and sat twiddling her hair as the punter gave Susan more instructions. Sabrina checked her wristwatch and shot a look over at Susan. It was time to say goodbye to her punters, time to have some fun with her best friend. The chat ended and Susan slammed the laptop shut.

'Right, let me get this back where it belongs. If Emma knows it's been moved, she will go sick.' Susan ran out of the bedroom with the laptop. Once she was back, she stripped out of her fancy undies, put her usual gear back on and used baby-wipes to take her make-up off. Suddenly she was back looking like the girl next door again.

Sabrina was intrigued by how much money her friend had earned and couldn't wait to ask her. 'Go on then, you've spent an hour online, how much have you got?' Susan pulled her faded jeans up and ragged her white t-shirt over her head before she sat on the edge of the bed, putting her trainers on. 'I'll just check now.' Susan grabbed her mobile phone from the bed. 'One hundred and twenty pounds.'

Sabrina whistled. 'What, you've just earned that now while I've been sat with you?'

'Yep, told you it was easy money, didn't I?' Susan was already working out what the cash would go on.

'Fucking hell, I thought you were just showing off.'

'Why would I lie to you. Honest, Sabrina, me and you could smash it. We keep it to ourselves and just do a few days a week to start with. Nobody will ever find out and, plus, it's not like we have our growlers out, is it? We are just flirting with these perverts, giving them a few shots of our boobs and that. We get ogled when we go out anyway, why not get some dough for it?'

Sabrina was thinking hard. Susan walked over and held her bank statement in front of her on her iPhone. 'There you go if you don't believe me. Like I said, easy money.'

Sabrina studied the screen, looking at another credit for two hundred pounds. 'What's that payment for? That's not from OnlyFans.'

Susan went bright red, fidgeting about. 'Oh, that's money a guy sent me to get some red lacy underwear so I can wear it for him next time I'm on live. I don't count that money with my takings because I will have to spend it on props.' Susan was impressed with her own lie.

Sabrina rubbed her hands together and Susan could see she'd already bought into this money-making idea. 'You will have to show me what to do. Oh my God, I will have to pad my bra out, I'm as flat as a pancake compared to you, bloody hell, I'll have to shave downstairs too, I'm not going to lie it's like a fucking Wildebeest.'

Susan burst out laughing as she stood up. 'Honestly, from what I've seen, there're guys out there into everything – whatever you look like, it's someone's turn-on. But this is our secret; we tell nobody nothing. Tell your family you have a job on the market or something because they'll want to know where your cash is coming from, won't they?'

Sabrina squirmed. 'My mam won't be arsed about me having extra money. She knows I sell bits of weed for our kid for extra cash and she isn't bothered about that, so I'll just say I'm selling weed if she clocks on.'

'Good, my mam thinks I've got more shifts in Sav's shop. I'll have to word him up about that too. He'll cover for me anyway, he's sorted.'

Sabrina and Susan were ready to go out now. Susan grabbed her jacket from the side and playfully punched her friend in the arm. 'I'll buy us Maccies. My treat. Imagine when we're both earning; we can piss off for the weekend and all that. I'm going to save as much as I can and by next year we should have enough to go to Ibiza for a couple of weeks.'

'As if your mam will let you go to Ibiza on your own. She still treats you like a baby.'

Susan stood looking at her refection in the full-length mirror and used the edge of her finger to fan her lashes out. 'They'll have to get used to the fact that I'm a woman now. I'll be eighteen soon enough. I'll be laying the law down to them both soon too and if they don't like it, they can piss off. I'm nearly seventeen and soon I can do whatever I want. I might even get my own apartment; I'll be able to pay for it at this rate, won't I?'

Sabrina was impressed. 'Good luck with that, your mam and dad are strict where my mam doesn't give a flying fuck. She's always telling me to find my own place anyway. On my life, that woman does my head in so I might be sharing that flat with you. We could work together and live together.'

Susan chuckled and rubbed her hands together. 'Come on, let's go and get some food. The world is our oyster now.'

Chapter Twenty

Bridie stood at the side of the bed and looked down at her husband as she plumped his pillows behind him. 'I'm going to nip down to the market and get some shopping. Don't try and do anything while I'm gone – get some rest, just like the doctor said.'

Bert yawned, sick to death of his wife treating him like an invalid. 'Bloody hell, Bridie, I'm not disabled. I had a bit of a funny turn, that's all. The doctor said if I take my tablets what he prescribed for me then I should be able to live a normal, healthy life.'

'Funny turn? It was a heart attack, Bert. I just want to make sure you're fighting fit and fully recovered. It scared the life out of me seeing you lay in that hospital bed.'

Bert held his hand up to her and she reached over and gripped his warm hand. 'I'm going nowhere anytime soon, love. And, like I've told you a hundred times before, the card game was just a one-off. I'd been having trouble sleeping, Dane had said I was welcome to have a gander, and I thought I would just have a go of it when you were in bed asleep. On my life, I don't have a gambling problem no more. I've been there and worn the t-shirt, you know the dance. You saved me from all that.'

Bridie looked deep into his eyes and let out a laboured breath. 'I hope so for your sake, Bert. When you got yourself into a mess the last time, I thought we would never come back from it. It was probably one of the worst times in my life ever. It wasn't just the money we lost – it was the trust. I went to church every day for months asking God to help us both get through it.'

Bert didn't like the direction this was going. 'Will you get me some nice pork pies from that stall on the market? The ones with egg in them. Honest, since I've had my heart attack you've been feeding me like a bloody rabbit.'

'And that's how I'm going to continue. The doctor said to eat healthy, so if you can tell me where, in that conversation, he said give you pies and pints, then please let me know.' Bridie pulled her shoulders back and bent down to peck him on the cheek. She'd proved her point and that was the end of it. 'Right, I'll be a couple of hours, you know what I'm like when I get gabbing. And mind you listen out for the postman. I've ordered you some new slippers and a dressing gown that should be delivered today.'

Bert rolled his eyes. 'Bleeding slippers and a dressing gown, I may as well climb into my grave already,' he whispered under his breath.

Bridie had been gone for over half an hour. Bert had already read the paper and boredom had set in. He sat up as he heard somebody knocking on the front door. If he missed his wife's parcel then she would have a face on her all day. He could hear her now, 'One bleeding job I gave you and you couldn't even do that.'

He rushed out of the bedroom and down the stairs, hair stuck up and bare-chested. He opened the front door and gasped to catch his breath. Isaac stood snarling at him, hand resting on the doorframe, foot rammed inside the front door, no escape for Bert.

'Hello, stranger, glad to see you're feeling better. It still doesn't mean that you don't pay what you owe though, does it? I don't give a shit if you've had a heart attack or not, you still cough up.'

Bert was in a panic, head sticking out from the front door, making sure his wife was nowhere to be seen. 'Give a man a break. I've been in hospital, I'm lucky to still be alive. It was touch and go you know, I've beaten the odds to be even stood here.'

Isaac stepped nearer, his face only inches from the old timer's face. 'Not arsed, like I said. If you can't pay then I'll take it away.' Isaac eyeballed Bert. 'So have you got the three weeks money you owe me or what? I'm here for a good time, not a long time, so cough up otherwise I'll be taking something from your house to remind you how this works.'

Bert was struggling to breathe, his palm held against his chest. 'You can't do this to me. I've been ill.'

Isaac's tone changed. 'I'm not running a fucking charity here, mate. You borrowed the money, so you fucking pay it back. I'll ask one more time before my boys come in and start taking stuff.' Isaac whistled over his shoulder and two men came into the garden. Huge fuckers they were; big shoulders, crew cuts. Proper meat-heads.

'I'll get the money to you, Isaac, just give me time to get back on my feet again. Have you no heart or what?'

Isaac gave his heavies the nod, in no mood to listen to this old fart and the excuses he was making. 'Take the TV for now, lads.'

Bert tried blocking the front door but they barged past him, nearly sending him west. He followed them, pleading with them. 'I said I will get the bloody money. Lads, listen to me, I'll have the money to you in a few days.' His words fell on deaf ears; the guys were unplugging his television, flinging aside anything that stood in their way. Bert picked up the photograph of him and his wife that they had chucked onto the sofa from the telly and held it close to his heart. All he could do was watch. Isaac walked into the front room and spoke to Bert. 'If the payments are not made next week, we'll be back again and then we'll start throwing our weight about.'

'Bastards, you are, the lot of you. Have you no heart?' But the men had left with the television. Isaac made his way to the front door. 'See you next week. Hopefully you can make a payment then and save us going through this again.'

'Piss off!' Bert shouted after him.

Bert sat on the sofa looking at the empty space where the television used to be. He dropped his head into his hands. 'She'll bloody go ballistic,' he muttered. There was no blagging this. Unless . . .

Bert grabbed the brick he'd taken from the back garden and, checking no one was watching, smashed it through the glass of the front door. Aware Bridie could be back at any moment, he rushed to put the brick outside and got straight onto the next part of his plan. He ran into the front room and started flinging stuff from drawers, smashing a few ornaments. Then he ran back up the stairs to bed and dragged the duvet over his shoulder. He'd tell her he'd taken one of his sleeping tablets the doctors had prescribed, fallen back asleep and not heard a peep. She would believe him, wouldn't she? She had to.

Bridie spotted the broken window as soon as she turned onto their road. She froze on the spot and felt a rush of adrenaline surge through her body. 'Bert!' she started shouting as she dashed down the path and through the front door. It was open – they always left it on the latch. 'Bert, Bert!' Bridie rushed into the front room. She clocked the opened drawers, the mess the burglars had left; cushions thrown across the room, ornaments broken on the floor. Bridie fell to the ground and picked up a broken statue her mother had given her. Her fingers picked up small pieces of debris from the floor and she held them in her hands, eyes flooding with tears. Bridie paused then, dropped the statue on the floor. Her husband, where the hell was he? Instantly she imagined the worst – the shock of being burgled could have triggered another heart attack. Was he upstairs now, dead as a dodo? She ran up the stairs, gasping for breath, and rushed into the bedroom. 'Bert, we've been robbed! They've taken the telly and God knows what else. Bert, are you awake? Did you hear me? We've been robbed.'

Bert pretended to wake up, yawning, scratching at his head, a performance any actor would have been proud of. 'Love, calm down, what's happened?'

Bridie perched on the end of the bed and sobbed. 'They've taken the telly, Bert, smashed the front room up.'

Bert was out of bed now. 'What?! I've not heard a bleeding thing. After you left, I took one of my new pills. Knocked me out. I can't believe we had burglars and I slept through it all. I'll strangle the bastards when I catch them up.' Bert was already making his way down the stairs. Bridie followed him and stood at the living room door as Bert walked around the room taking in the mess and shouting at the top of his voice. 'I'll cut their bleeding bollocks off when I find out who's been in here. I know people who will hurt them. On my life, I'll string the fuckers up. How dare they come into our home and take things that don't belong to them.'

Out of habit, Bridie started to clean up, but everything she did seemed to be in slow motion. Then she ground to a halt. 'What am I doing? I could be damaging evidence. I'll ring the police, Bert, the sooner we can report this, the more chance we have of getting our stuff back. I'll just have a look around and see what else has gone missing without touching anything else.'

Bert barely let her finish the sentence. 'No, no police, they don't lift a finger for burglary these days. We'll sort this out ourselves. I'll have a word with a couple of the lads from the pub and we'll deal with this the old-fashioned way.'

Bridie shook her head. 'Don't be silly, Bert, we need to report this and do things properly. I don't want any trouble landing on my front doorstep. Let the law sort out these thieving fuckers.'

Bert knew his wife was angry when she started swearing, and if he pushed the wrong buttons now there would be no changing her mind. He needed to keep her busy. 'Bridie, you're right, the best thing we can do is have a look around and see if we can see anything else missing.'

His wife snivelled. 'The thought of someone being in our home makes me feel sick inside. I can't wait to get everything tidied up, clean everything their thieving hands have touched.'

'Just go and see if they have taken anything else while I sort out the outside. I'll start by cleaning the glass up from the front door. I'll phone a lad I know who can fit another pane of glass. We need that sorting if we're going to be able to stay here tonight.'

Bridie was already on her way upstairs, her eyes red with tears. Bert started to clear up the shards of glass from the floor near the front door. He felt another sickening lurch of guilt as he heard his wife scream from upstairs. She stood up at the top of the stairs looking down at him. 'They've taken my jewellery from the box in the spare room: my bracelets, my rings, my necklaces, the bloody lot.'

Bert rushed up stairs to comfort his wife. Bridie was holding the empty jewellery box in her hand. 'Look, they have left nothing. That's all that I had left of my mother. Bert, you need to find these people and get my mother's stuff back. It's all I have left of her. Please get it back, please, I'll do whatever it takes. Your lads, police, whoever – just catch the bastards.'

Bert woke the next morning with no clue how he was going to keep the police from his door. But the answer came in the outrage of his neighbours. The news of the burglary seemed like the last straw for the Manor. Still reeling from the death of Matthew Murphy, an attack on the home of defenceless old-timers was adding insult to injury. The residents were up in arms, demanding that the police have more of a presence on their streets, and before he knew it, there was an emergency meeting called in The Griffin pub to show support for Bert and Bridie.

Dane was the spokesperson, and he addressed the local police community support officer who'd attended the meeting. 'We want answers, we want these animals off our street. This is a nice area; we all look out for each other and work hard for what we own. This robbery was in the middle of the day, on a busy street. This shows you that these thieves can and will strike at any time. We need police support, somebody walking our streets twenty-four hours a day. Bridie was too scared to leave her house today even for this meeting. We've already had a murderer living on our streets, we need to flush these scumbags out of our area and make sure they never return.'

'Hear, hear,' one of the residents said. Dane got a round of applause and the officer who had attended knew he would have to give these residents some peace of mind – but it meant biting back what he really wanted to say. The police were out on the streets every single day dealing with crime: armed robbers, drug dealers, murderers. Sure, a crime had been committed here but it was in no way a code red for the police force compared to what else was happening across the city every hour of the day and night. He tried the usual lines to calm the gathering, but nothing worked until he promised to get one of the nearby patrol cars to add the Manor to their beat.

Bert kept a low profile at the back of the pub, he just sat in the shadows listening to everything that had been said, relieved when the meeting was over. The PSCO had promised he'd leave 'no stone unturned' investigating the burglary, but Bert had seen how stressed and over-worked the kid was. He would ask a few questions, that would be it.

As the people left, Bert sat at the bar drinking a pint of bitter that one of the neighbours had got for him. After all, he was the one who'd been through the ordeal, hadn't he?

Dane stood across the bar from Bert. 'We need to stop these pricks once and for all. I've had a word with some of the residents and we're having a whip round for you and Bridie to get you a new TV and one of those Ring door-bells. You two should not have to worry about bleeding toerags robbing things from you that you have had to work hard for. Bridie has told the police exactly what her jewellery looks like, so hopefully – sooner or later – they might get a lead to get her mother's belongings back home where they should be.'

Bert rubbed at his arms as if a bag of ants had been sprinkled over him. 'Thanks, Dane, my Bridie is in pieces with all this. She's already saying that she wants to move. It's a crying shame that we don't feel safe in our bloody home anymore.'

'I'll have a new TV with you the first thing in the morning, mate, and I'll personally fit the doorbell. The police are all over this now and we'll flush these rats out for sure. I'm going to be extra vigilant now and anybody who looks dodgy in the neighbourhood will be getting their collars felt.'

Bert ran his finger around his pint glass. 'Thanks, Dane. Thank you to all the residents for supporting us too. It means a lot.'

Dane walked away to serve someone else, and Bert sat staring into space. He knew he was in deep and if anybody found out the truth, he would never be able to hold his head up in this area again.

Chapter Twenty-One

B rooke stepped off the plane and felt like a new woman. Dublin was an amazing place to have visited and she was already wondering when she could book another trip. The people had been so friendly, the food was great, and the music was on another level.

Lee was by her side now and they were holding hands. Brooke turned and smiled at him. 'Thank you so much for this weekend. It was just what I needed. I feel refreshed and ready to face the world again.'

He reached over and kissed her cheek. 'I'm glad. I can see the changes in you already. You actually slept last night instead of tossing and turning all night long.'

'That might have been the vodka, Lee. I've barely been sober all weekend. I feel like I need a detox now to cleanse my body.'

'Well, it was worth it. But if your body is a temple, we could look at a spa weekend for our next trip if you fancy it?'

Brooke nodded. She was going to be a yes person from now on. She'd realised just how much of a prisoner she'd been while she was with Vincent.

When they got back to Lee's, Brooke walked into the house and dropped her black cabin case down on the floor. 'I'll make us a coffee. You sit and put your feet up.'

'Cheers, babes. I'll just check my work emails while I've got a chance.' Brooke headed into the kitchen and flicked the kettle on. She was humming a tune as she opened the kitchen cupboard, then stood back in confusion. The cups in the cupboard were all in an identical position. She rushed into the front room in a panic. 'Lee, please tell me you put all the cups the same way in the cupboard?'

He lifted his head up from his mobile phone, no clue what she was going on about. 'Brooke, just calm down, take your time and tell me again.'

She paced around the living room. 'The cups are all lined up in military order.'

Lee stood up and took her back into the kitchen. 'Are you trying to tell me you're flipping out because the cupboard is tidy? Show me what you mean.'

Brooke pointed inside the cupboard and spoke in a distressed voice. 'Vincent always made sure the handles all faced the same way. Look, each of them is facing the same way, each exactly the same distance apart. He walloped me once because I put them in the wrong order.'

'Babes, I probably put them in like that so they all fit into the cupboard. Chill out!' He took her in his arms, kissing the top of her head. 'It's fine, babes. Think about it, how on earth could anyone get in here without us know-ing? I'll have a quick check around, but I'm sure I would know if anyone had been in here. Plus if Vince found you, I think he'd want to do a whole lot more than tidy up after you.' Lee let go of her and went to have a look around the house.

Brooke was properly spooked, the hairs on the back of her neck standing to attention. She lifted her eyes to the ceiling as she heard Lee walking about upstairs.

'Everything is fine, nothing has been touched,' he shouted back down.

Brooke was calming down. Maybe it was her mind playing tricks with her. She'd been through a lot lately, she told herself, perhaps it was no surprise she was finding it hard to let go of her past.

Lee was back at her side. 'Go back in the other room and I'll finish making the brew.' Brooke went back to the living room and curled up on the sofa, angry with herself for even thinking her ex-husband had been to this house. She had to stop letting him mess with her mind – they were separated now and she wanted to have him out of her head as well as out of her life.

Lee came back in the room holding two cups in his hand. He sat down and continued reading his emails. 'Oh for fuck's sake,' he moaned.

'What's up?'

'My boss has booked me to go away this weekend, London. Apparently there are a couple of potential clients he wants me to meet, could be a great opportunity for the company if I pull it off. He's always doing things like this to me. Why doesn't he speak to me first and see if I have any plans before he books in meetings and all that.' He carried on reading the email. When he'd finished he reached over and picked up his drink. 'Why don't you come with me? It's a double room and once I've had my meetings, we can go sightseeing in London.'

Brooke thought about her pledge to say yes to everything, but knew she couldn't walk out on her responsibilities. 'Thanks, Lee, but I'm going to get ready for being back at work on Monday. And I should start going to see some flats. Like I said, I can't stay here with you forever.'

'You can stay here with me as long as you want. If I'm being honest, I thought you would just move in with me anyway – especially after the great time we had in Dublin. What's the point in paying rent on another gaff when I've got a place here for you to stay. It's a no-brainer.' Brooke knew what he was saying was fair, but still she needed her own space, to answer to nobody. 'I know what you're saying, Lee, but we're quite new to each other. I know we have history, but this here is real life. You might hate me and my habits after a few months and can't stand the sight of me. I think we should take things slowly, don't rush.'

Lee nodded his head, scared of being too much too soon. 'Whatever makes you happy, love. Anyway, let's chill today and watch a few films on Netflix. I told you I would look after you and I will. Just a takeaway later, nothing to stress about. What do you think?'

Brooke smiled, tiredness setting in her body now. Lee started to get the fluffy throws ready for the sofa and flicked on the TV, looking for a decent film to watch.

Brooke tried to shut out the questions and anxiety in her mind, but something still didn't sit right with her; it was eating away at her. Vincent was a bomb waiting to go off and his silence was spooking her out. She needed to be ready for him.

Chapter Twenty-Two

Anthony trudged along the canal in the midnight hour. He could hear traffic in the distance and people shouting from the other side of the canal. There was no way he was staying with Vincent again, the man was ready to flip; pissed all the time, chatting pure nonsense that he didn't understand. His own mental health was bad enough without someone else's adding to it. Anthony kicked a stone and stood watching as it plopped into the murky water. His feet moved slowly towards the water's edge and he sat down on the edge of the canal, just staring at the black surface. Anthony kicked slowly against the wall at the edge of the canal. He turned his head as he heard voices behind him. He clocked the homeless crew all sat about behind him. Well, he was homeless now, wasn't he? Maybe there was safety in numbers. Anthony jumped to his feet and headed towards them, realising now how little it took to go from nice life, nice house to down and out.

Anthony was apprehensive as he spoke to the guys on the edge of the group. 'Alright, lads? I don't suppose I could chill here for a bit with you? The mrs has kicked me out and, well, I'm fucked if I'm being honest, got nowhere else to go.'

A man in what looked like his early sixties, but could have been twenty years either side of that, stepped forward in a long grey coat, with dirty white trainers that were at least three sizes too big for him. 'Have you got any money? If you buy some booze, we'll all be your friend, won't we, lads?' He gave a quick look behind him and chuckled loudly.

Anthony pulled a twenty-pound note from his jacket pocket and waved it about. 'I've got enough for a few drinks.' And that was all that was needed for him to be accepted into the group. Anthony found a wonky old chair and plonked himself down on it. He looked at the men and thought how normally he'd have crossed the street to avoid blokes like this; the stench of booze and unwashed clothes, none of them had a full set of teeth between them, rough as bears' arses the lot of them. And now he was grateful to be accepted, to be welcomed in by people who asked nothing of him but some beer money. Anthony blew his breath into his hands and rubbed them together. 'Bleeding hell, how do you lot survive in this cold weather? I've only been sat here a few minutes and I'm freezing my balls off.'

A guy who introduced himself as Jesse offered Anthony his hand, calloused and filthy as it was. He said he was the head of this group and had been homeless for many years.

He knew this place like the back of his hand, knew everyone who stepped onto the canal each night. 'You get used to the cold after a bit. Get a blanket from over there and throw it over you. It might stink a bit of cat-piss but, aye, it will keep you warm.'

Anthony reached over and gripped a tartan blanket. Bloody hell, Jesse was right; it did stink but, hey, beggars couldn't be choosers, could they? Anthony necked a mouthful of vodka and stared out into the night. 'I bet you see all kinds on here each night, don't you?'

Jesse rubbed at his cold nose and chugged hard on the dimp he'd just lit up. 'You can say that again; brasses, fights, affairs, we see it all, don't we, lads?'

A man to the left of him began to talk now, slurring his words, pissed. 'We get all sorts from the gay village doing everything down here too. Bobs gives them a good kicking if he gets the chance, batters them and takes what he can from them.'

Anthony turned to face the man, a terrible question taking shape in his mind, a question he couldn't even bear to think, let alone ask. He needed to find out more. 'Why would he batter someone just because they are gay?'

Jesse stepped in again. 'He's not what you'd called modern, is Bob. He's a bitter bastard to be honest – thinks everyone else is ruining his life, his country, his chances. Truth is, he's done a pretty good job of ruining his own life.'

The drunk guy couldn't resist chiming in again. 'Still, he's had some decent stuff from his little scheme; iPhones, watches, bracelets. He battered that one who was found in the canal dead last month. He never killed him though, just gave him a good hiding and took his phone. You should have heard him when he heard the man died; shocked he was because he only gave him a few digs, ragged him about a bit.'

Anthony felt as if his heart had stopped. 'So, the man who died and was found in the canal was one of Bobby's victims?'

The man looked like he realised he might have said too much and clammed up. Anthony passed him the vodka and turned his chair to face him, he had to get him talking again. After he'd necked a mouthful of vodka he started again, talking about the night Matthew died. 'I watched the whole thing, you know. The dibble came around asking questions here, but I told them fuck all. Bobby gave the man a few slaps and that was it. No way we were grassing him up. It was somebody else who flung him in the canal. I could hear them arguing, screaming at each other. I couldn't see who it was, but I know it was them who pushed him into the canal and got off. If I wasn't as pissed as I was, I would have got up closer to see what was going on, but I was steaming drunk. Pissed my pants and all that, didn't I, Jesse?'

Jesse was coughing as he rolled a cigarette. 'You're always pissed, pal, from morning until night you're steaming drunk. New guy, ignore anything he's saying to you because he's off his head more than he's straight.'

Anthony was still buzzing; a lead. 'When does Bobby come here? I'd like to shake his hand – he's just trying to keep our streets clean.'

Jesse stood at the side of him, having a piss, and turned his head back to answer him. 'Not sure, he just comes and goes whenever he feels like it. He's an addict so God knows where he lands. Every day is different for him but I'm sure he hangs out in Harpurhey, well, that's what he told me anyway.'

Anthony swigged a massive mouthful of vodka. He was staying put for now, in the hope this Bobby guy returned. The information was circling around his mind. So, if Bobby just gave Matthew an arse-kicking and robbed him, who on earth was the other person he was arguing with after this? It could only be the real murderer. Anthony stared out into the midnight sky. He was going to find out who the killer was and clear his name. He'd show them all that he was innocent all along. First thing in the morning he was going to see Bronwen, tell her the news, tell her there was a murderer still on the loose who'd killed her son. She might never forgive him, but she might just hate him less.

A big, fat rat ran past his feet and scrambled into the nearby bushes. Jesse started to laugh. 'We're all the same here, lad. Cats, rats and dogs, we all have the same home. Society think we're vermin, but the real rats – they're the ones who hide in plain sight.'

Chapter Twenty-Three

B ert looked like he'd lost some timber; his face was thin, cheekbones showing. Bridie came into the front room and looked at him. 'I'm thinking of getting a dog. At least we will have some protection at night if the dog barks, plus it will get us both out exercising when we take it for a walk. What do you think?'

Bert didn't look keen; a scruffy mutt in his house, pestering for food and walks, no thanks. 'I think you're potty, woman. There have been no burglaries in the area since we were robbed so hopefully it's the end of it. No need to get a bloody guard dog.'

'It's not just protection – it's affection, too. I can see you walking a dog about, Bert, they say they're man's best friend. You might even love it.' Bridie sat thinking, a warm smile on her face 'Maybe a little dog, a Yorkshire terrier or something like that.'

'Yapping bleeders, they are. If you're going to get one, what about them Frenchies? Dane has one and all it does all day is sleep, low maintenance.' He didn't see a Frenchie scaring off Isaac and his heavies – maybe he should convince Bridie she needed a Pit bull.

'Nah, I'm going to speak with Dane and see what he recommends. He's always had dogs and I think he's the right person to ask. I'll go and get a basket and blankets ready for it. Hopefully, by the end of the day, we should have a new family member.'

Bert was just glad Bridie was leaving him alone for a bit. Since the burglary she'd barely let him out of her sight. He checked his wife was gone and stood staring out of the front window. Vincent had just left his house and driven off in a hurry to wherever he was going. It was perfect timing. Bert was going to nip round and play the good neighbour – just checking out the window he'd seen Vince leave open.

Bert scurried round to Vincent's back garden and headed straight to the open window. He dragged over a nearby chair and clambered through the window. He was too old for this lark, but he'd committed now, Bert thought as he crashed down on the other side. He was nowhere near as fit and agile as he used to be. Bert got his breath back as he looked around his surroundings. No use giving himself another coronary. Slowly he made his way into the living room looking for anything of value. He opened drawers, searched every nook and cranny looking for some cash. Zilch. Bert made his way up the stairs next and crept to the first bedroom. His eyes were drawn to a whiteboard with photographs of Brooke on it, blue and yellow Post-it notes stuck all over the board, arrows pointing one way then another. Bert edged forward and studied the board. This was weird; addresses, times. It was a mission in progress. But all the arrows pointed towards Brooke.

Bert felt troubled, but this was no time for him to start playing Sherlock Holmes. He needed stuff he could flog. Bert started to search the bedroom for any cash or other valuables. Bingo. As he opened the bedside cabinet, he found what he was looking for; a wad of twenty-pound notes, a watch, a necklace. He rammed them into his pocket and knew he would have enough this week to keep Isaac from his back, maybe even to make sure he never came banging on his front door again if he got enough for this little lot. Bert scarpered down the stairs, knowing not to push his luck looking for more. He already had his work cut out to make this look like a robbery, make it look like thieves had been through this house just like they'd been through his own. He started to throw things about, launched cups at the walls, opened all the drawers in the kitchen. Bert stood looking at the mess he'd created and opened the back door with the gold key stuck inside the lock. Job done. Bert was outside now, head down, identity hidden.

Bert stashed the money he'd just got and rammed the other goods in his jacket pocket. As soon as his wife came home, he'd go to the pawn shop and sell his swag. By the time everyone on the road would be gossiping about the break-in, the goods would be long gone. Nobody ever suspected the little old guy, did they?

Chapter Twenty-Four

Vincent sat in his car. He'd been parked here for a few hours watching Lee's house. Of course he knew where his mrs had been staying; he was ex-military, he could find anyone if he put his mind to it. He screwed his eyes up as he spotted a man coming out of the house carrying a small suitcase. The vein at the side of his neck started pumping with rage and he whispered under his breath, 'Come on, dickhead, come to Daddy.' Vincent let out a menacing laugh as he reached over for the bottle of vodka and swigged a large mouthful of it. 'Showtime.'

Lee put his suitcase on the back seat of his car and sat in the driver's seat. Leaving Brooke for the weekend when she was clearly still so vulnerable was lying heavy on his heart, and he was in two minds to ring his boss and tell him to shove his job right up his arse. Lee reached inside his jacket pocket and gripped his mobile. A quick text before he set off on his long drive to London wouldn't hurt.

Missing you already XX

Right, time to go. He reached over and clipped his seat-belt in and was ready to start the engine when the world went dark. It all happened so fast. Pain in his head, pounding at his body, eyes closing, no strength to open them anymore, breathing shallow, the darkness pulling him down.

Vincent stood over Lee and spat at him. 'Did you think you could take my woman again and I wouldn't do anything about it, you prick?' He paced one way then the other. The room he'd brought him to was dark, and the only light was from a tiny window above. You could see the whites of Vincent's eyes as he sat down and stared over at Lee's seemingly lifeless body. He'd not killed him yet, no, this twat could suffer just like he had. Vincent hummed a tune and looked up and out at the silver moon. The first part of his mission was complete. The target had been detained, ready for interrogation. Vincent had so much to ask this geezer. He wanted answers, wanted to know the truth about his wife. He snarled as he heard the moaning from across the room and stood up slowly. When this runt opened his eyes, he wanted to be the first thing he saw; make sure he'd remember his face for the rest of his days, even though there was little of him showing apart from his eyes, burning with venom. Vincent was dressed in black with a black hat pulled down low over his head. He looked like he did when he was in the forces, dark and dangerous. The groans were getting louder, Lee's body twisting and turning.

'You see, mate, you should never touch another man's woman and think you can get away with it. Brooke is my wife, my life.'

Lee tried to focus; his vision blurred, there was ringing in his ears. 'Who are you? Where am I?'

Vincent let out a menacing laugh and bent his body down closer to his victim. 'You're in your worst nightmare, mate. Welcome to my world, prick.'

Lee cowered and tried to bring his arms over his head to protect himself, cover his face.

Vincent peeled his hands back; he wanted him to see him, see every inch of him. 'Brooke is my wife. We had something special, and you fucked all that up, made her hate me.'

Lee knew now who Vincent was and he felt his blood run cold as reality kicked in. A part of him had hoped Vince had just hired some thug to beat him up – but if this was Vince himself, every kick, every blow would be personal. 'Brooke told me your marriage was over. I would never have gone near her if she would have told the truth.'

'Lies, fucking lies.'

'It's the truth, mate, I'm sorry. It was just something that happened.'

Vincent roared at Lee. '*Just something that happened?* You messed it all up, ruined my marriage. My head is messed up with it all. Every time I close my eyes, I see you fucking my wife! Do you know how that feels? Do you fucking know?' he screamed at the top of his voice.

Lee knew he'd have to pull it out of the bag here and try and calm this guy down; he was raging, eyes popping out of their sockets. 'OK, mate. I'll level. She loved you, told me she would never leave you. I knew that from the start. Honest, I never stood a chance. It was you all along, only you. She only slept with me to hurt you – she used me to make you care.'

Vincent walked back a few paces. He sat down on a wooden box and pulled his cigarettes out of his pocket. The sound from the dripping pipe was all Lee could hear. They were in an old warehouse, damp, cold and derelict, he'd worked that out. But Greater Manchester was full of places like that.

Vincent had been planning this for weeks. He'd spotted Brooke one day when he was working in the area and followed her back to Lee's place. Of course he'd broken into the house, had to see what kind of life she was leading – it had taken all his self-control not to burn the gaff down. Instead, he knew if he just sent her a sign, Brooke would know he'd been in there. She was next on his list, the next to face the consequences of breaking his heart again. But first he had to deal with this waster. Vincent chugged hard on his fag, just watching Lee, listening to every pain that surged through his body. He wanted this man to suffer, to feel hurt like he had. Vincent stood up and squashed the fag out under his size twelve black boots. He inhaled fully, his chest expanding. 'I'll be back and then I'll decide what happens next. Just so you know, Brooke is mine. Until she takes her dying breath that woman is mine. Until death do us part.' Vincent walked out of the room and locked the door behind him. One down, one to go.

It was late by the time Vincent got back to his house. He was hyped for going to see Brooke, but this stopped him in his tracks. He dashed from room to room. Some bastard had been in here, robbed him. He walked out into the back garden and stepped back, looking at his house. This was his castle, his home, his safe place. Vincent nodded. He'd catch the robbing fuckers; he'd catch them red-handed. And when he did? They would pay, and he was going to enjoy it.

Chapter Twenty-Five

Anthony stood waiting outside Bronwen's house. He'd wait there all day if he needed to. He was desperate to speak with her, tell her he'd found out some information regarding her son's death. Although he realised he wasn't going to be popular – not just because Bron hated him, but because anyone wouldn't want him on their doorstep in this state. He looked rough and stank of something rotten, dark-brown mud was underneath his fingernails, a fug of alcohol around him.

The wind picked up and Anthony zipped his coat up fully, trying to keep warm. He clocked the front door opening. There she was, in full view. All he needed was ten minutes of her time, just to tell her what he knew. It was now or never. 'Bron, can I please just speak to you for a few minutes. It's about Matthew, about the night he died.'

Bronwen was shocked to see him, lost for words for long enough to give him chance to say his piece.

'Bronwen, I've got a witness from the night Matthew died. Well, not a witness like, but a confession of sorts. This man knew it all, said Matty was battered first by a man who robbed his phone, then someone else came along, he heard them arguing, shouting at each other, and then the man pushed him into the canal.'

Bronwen stood looking at Anthony, the fight from her had gone, no strength any more to deal with anything that was flung at her. 'I never thought I'd say this, but it makes no difference to me any more. He's gone and nothing will bring him back. Everything that I loved has gone. I'm just an empty shell now.'

Anthony had to fight his urge to reach out, all he wanted to do was put his arms around her and tell her he was there for her. His voice was softer, he rested his hand on the top of her shoulder. 'Please can we just sit down somewhere so I can tell you everything I know, please. I want to clear my name and get whoever is responsible for this locked up behind bars. Please, Bronwen, please. I owe Matthew that much.'

She looked deep into his eyes and the love they once shared flashed into her mind. 'You can have ten minutes and then you're gone.' Bronwen started to walk back down her garden path as Anthony followed closely behind.

Bronwen looked at Anthony in more detail. He didn't look like the man she once loved; he looked older, more hollow. He could feel her stare and fidgeted about in his seat, nervously. 'Every night I've been on the canal searching for the answer to Matthew's death. In your heart of hearts, you know I would never hurt a bone in your son's body. Yes, I hated the way you treated him like a baby sometimes, but I would never have hurt him. I know I need to talk to you about me being at Alison's house, but firstly let me get this from my chest before my head explodes. As soon as I'm done here, I'm going straight to the canal, then onto the police station and telling them exactly what I know.'

Bronwen was listening now as he relayed everything that he'd heard. 'I'm going looking for this Bobby guy – I want to get to him before the dibble, I'll fuck him up proper. Then I'll make sure he's arrested and questioned about that night because he was there, Bronwen, he was the one who assaulted and robbed Matthew first. And I don't want to rub salt in the wound, but I heard he had it for anyone he thought had come from the gay village. So I'm going to teach the cunt that Matthew was more of a real man than a thieving, prejudiced little shit will ever be.'

Bronwen dropped her head low and snivelled. 'If what you are saying is true then I'll rest when that bastard is charged and locked up. I want justice for my boy, make sure whoever did this to him rots in hell.' There was an awkward silence. Anthony coughed to clear his throat and looked over at her.

'I know you hate me at this moment in time and I hate myself for ever putting you through this. I was pissed, sick to death of us arguing, and when Allison came on to me I realised I just wanted to be wanted. It's no excuse, I know.'

Bronwen rubbed her face. 'You broke us, Anthony. You're right about one thing though – I can never forgive what you did. You put it all on the line for a quick shag with the estate bike. How could we ever come back from that? I'm not only a grieving mother, I'm a laughing stock.'

'No, Bronwen, you're not. The people around here love you and are supporting you. I'm the one they all hate, and I need to fix that. I swear to you now, I won't rest until I find this Bobby guy and bring him to justice. As for losing you, I'll never get over that. I'm sorry from the bottom of my heart and if I could fix it I would.'

Bronwen dabbed a tissue into the corner of her eyes. 'Just find whoever murdered my son and then I will rest.' Anthony sobbed as he listened to her pour her heart out. 'Every day is grey without him. I watch the clock tick away knowing he'll never be coming home through that front door again. He's taken my heart with him, Anthony, I just feel numb every day. There's no life in me, no nothing. I'll die from a broken heart, I know it. I can't eat, can't sleep, nothing makes sense anymore, nothing.'

'I can't even imagine how you feel, Bronwen. Matthew meant a lot to me too. We had our laughs, our man chats when you weren't there. I'm suffering too. On my life, I feel broken inside.' He walked over to where she was sitting and fell to his knees, reaching out and holding her cold hands in his. 'We'll find the truth out, Bronwen. As God is my witness, I'll find out the truth.' He kissed the ends of her fingers and looked up into her eyes. 'I love you with all my heart, Bronwen, with every inch of my heart.'

Bronwen stared at him, as if she was looking through him rather than at him. 'I can't do this right now, Anthony.

You've said what you came here to say. Now go and find this Bobby. Please just give me some peace. Find him. And as for me and you, I could never love you again – not just because of what you did, but because I'm broken now – how could I ever love again with a heart that will never heal?'

Chapter Twenty-Six

Susan looked over at Sabrina and flicked her hair back over her shoulder. 'Come on, you, hurry up. We are supposed to be there by eight bells. I want to be gone from the house before my mam and dad come in from shopping. That's all I need, them two pecking my head asking a thousand and one questions.'

Sabrina fastened her silver strappy shoes and stood up, unsteady on her feet. 'Oh, for crying out loud, how am I supposed to walk in these heels? I feel like I'm walking on stilts.'

Susan chuckled. 'Just practice walking up and down the bedroom, you'll get used to them, I did.'

Sabrina stood still now. 'I'm not sure if I want to come with you, Susan. You know me, I'm up for anything normally, but this all seems dodgy as anything. We don't know these guys, and what do they want us there for, anyway? They're weirdos if you ask me.'

'Stop being a muppet, Sabrina. We're going for a few drinks with these guys. The man said it's a party and he just wanted some pretty girls there with him to look at.'

'And that's all? To look at? Come on, Sue, you're not that daft?'

Susan hunched her shoulders, blushing slightly as she applied her candy-pink lip-gloss. 'Well, it's up to you if you're coming or not. He's paying us good money to go so if you want to turn the cash down, then fine. *I'm* not walking away from that kind of money.'

Sabrina was rattled. 'I just want to feel safe, that's all. How many times have you seen it on the news about these guys grooming girls and doing God knows what to them?'

Susan looked at her friend. 'There are plenty of times I don't feel safe – pervy guys on the bus, blokes who put a roofie in your drink if you turn your back, dudes who follow you back when you're walking home. There are bad men everywhere if you let your guard down. At least here I'm going in with my eyes open. If you want to, bring a blade. You carry one when we're out on the estate so bring it with you now too. You're always telling me that if anyone started with you that you would stab them up, so bring your knife if that will make you feel any safer.'

The bedroom door swung open and Emma was standing there looking them both up and down. 'Where the hell do you think you're going dressed like that?'

Susan panicked. 'We're going to a party, aren't we, Sabrina. I've told my mam that I'm staying at Sabrina's house tonight anyway, so it's sorted.'

Emma looked puzzled. 'So, whose party is it and why are you lying to my mam about where you're staying?'

Sabrina could see Susan was flapping and jumped into the conversation. 'Because Duffy is going to be there tonight and your sister is all over him like a rash.'

Emma looked doubtful. 'Well, I'll ring you later to check in with you.'

Susan flipped. 'Oh piss off, Emma! Like I'm going to be answering my phone to you when I'm out in the mix with all the crew. Tell me you would answer to Mam or Dad if you were out having a drink with your mates. You act like you're my mam – don't forget you're only a year and a half older than me so you can drop the high and mighty bit.'

Emma raised her eyebrows high. Her kid sister was right, but still, she still wanted to make sure she was safe. Susan sprayed her new Victoria Secret body spray across her body and smiled at Emma.

'Lighten up, will you? I'll be fine.'

Sabrina hooked her silver shoulder bag over her shoulder and glanced back at herself one last time in the mirror. 'Ready when you are,' she said.

Susan walked to the door and pecked her sister on the side of her cheek. 'See you tomorrow. Remember, if Mam and Dad start asking questions, have my back, like I would have yours.'

Emma watched them both walk down the stairs and smiled. Sabrina could not walk in her heels, she was wobbling and unsteady on her feet. Emma walked back into her bedroom. Now was her time to earn some money. She switched on her laptop, and her night began.

Susan stood rubbing her arms as they waited to meet a guy her client had sent to pick them up. He'd said his name was Hassan, and he'd be in a silver car. Susan spotted one pulling up in the distance, music thumping from it.

Sabrina huddled closer to her friend. 'Is that him? I'm not sure about this, Susan. Honest, my heart is beating like nobody's business.'

'Just breathe, will you? Sort your head out and let's pull this off. Just think about the money. I'll do the talking when he pulls up, but don't just be sat there like some nerd. These guys think we are confident girls, party girls, so let's give them what they are paying for.'

The silver car flashed its headlights at them. Susan gripped Sabrina by the arm, virtually dragging her with her. 'Right, confident girls we are, just keep telling yourself that.' Susan opened the passenger door and Sabrina got into the back of the car.

'Hi, Hassan. Nice to meet you. You're our driver for tonight, aren't you? The one who will drop us off later.'

Hassan looked to be in his late thirties, and he smiled at Susan. 'The lads can't wait to meet you both. There's plenty of beer and sniff there, so don't worry.'

Susan swallowed hard. Come on, she didn't mind a drink or two, but drugs, no way was she shoving that shit up her nose.

Sabrina leaned on the back of her seat and joined the conversation, wanting to know more. 'So where is this party, is it local or what?'

Hassan lit a spliff and chugged hard on it before he passed it over to Susan. 'It's not far, stop worrying, will you. You'll have a good time.'

Susan looked at the joint in her hand and wasn't sure if she was going to have a drag of it or not. She'd had weed before, but it wasn't something she made a habit of. She placed it in her mouth and looked over at the driver as she sucked hard on it, she passed it over to her friend. 'Here you go, Sabrina. Get a few blows of that and loosen up.'

Sabrina declined the offer; she wanted to keep a straight head and see what these creepy blokes were all about. She listened to every word Hassan said; the more he spoke, the more she didn't like what he was saying. The car stopped at some traffic lights and Sabrina whispered to her friend. 'Susan, get out of the car. Come on, let's go home. This doesn't feel right. Think about it. He's giving you drugs already and we're not even there yet.'

Susan just shook her head but Sabrina was done. She flung open the car door.

Hassan was in a panic now. 'Get back in the car, you fucking idiot. You're going to get knocked down.'

Susan was fuming too, not with Hassan, but at her friend for embarrassing her. 'Sabrina, what the hell are you doing? He's sorted, you're making a fuss about nothing. Half your family sell gear so why are you freaking out about a joint? Please, just get back in the car.'

Sabrina stood with the car door open and a car behind them started honking its horn.

Hassan was furious. 'Hurry up and get back inside otherwise I'm driving off.' Sabrina swallowed hard and you could see she was in two minds. 'I swear down if you lay one finger on any of us, I'll report you. I've got brothers, you know. Big names in the area who will chop you up if anything happens to us.'

Hassan started laughing and watched her get back into the car. He sped off and turned the music up, bass pumping and blocking any chance of more conversation.

When they pulled up a few minutes later Susan straightened her dress as she got out of the car. She waited for Sabrina to join her before she dragged her closer and whispered in her ear. 'Get a grip, you, and sort your head out. Don't mess this up for us.'

Sabrina still had that feeling deep in the pit of her stomach that told her something wasn't right. Hassan led the girls down the garden path of the house they'd parked up at. It was a big, posh house set in its own grounds. These guys had dosh for sure, Sabrina could tell that much.

Hassan walked inside through the double oak doors and led the girls to the back of the house. He opened the back door and pointed at a building set inside the grounds of the house. 'There you go, ladies, that's where the party's at. Follow me.'

Susan was eager to get inside and get a drink down her neck to calm her down. Sabrina was doing her head in. If she ever got work like this again, she was going it alone for sure. Susan followed Hassan inside. The lighting was dim and she smiled as she heard music playing and spotted some other girls sat about the room; young girls, just like they were.

'See, cushty, just like I knew it would be.' Susan smiled at her friend.

Hassan pulled Susan to one side and whispered into her ear. 'You have someone who wants special time with you.'

Susan knew the guy she was here to see was her best client, but she didn't like the sound of meeting him privately – she'd rather stay here in the party. 'Special like what?'

He smirked. 'Like a bit of a lap dance. A bit of slap and tickle, you know the score.' Susan gulped. When she was onscreen, she was the one calling all the shots. Now she was here and meeting this guy in person, she wasn't sure if she was up to it. She reminded herself who she was and repeated it in her head several times. 'Confident girl, party girl, rich girl.' She followed Hassan towards a door in the back wall.

Sabrina was about to follow her friend when Hassan grabbed her back by the arm. 'It's her he wants, just her.'

Sabrina frowned. 'So why can't I go with her? I'm her best friend, you know. We do everything together, don't we, Sue?'

Susan panicked when she heard her friend use her real name, but she distracted herself by thinking of the money, the pound signs flashing in her mind's eye. 'I won't be long, just chill over there and have a few drinks.' Susan carried on walking and followed Hassan into the side room. The lighting was much darker here, she could barely see. He opened the door and stood back so she could walk inside. The door closed behind her. A cold chill passed through her body and, all of a sudden, her mouth became dry. Susan walked further into the room, slowly, a strong smell of Oud filling her senses. A man sat in an armchair facing her. His identity was hidden by a mask, but not the normal one he'd worn on camera. This time, through the gloom, she could see he was wearing a 3D mask of a dog's face. It made her shudder slightly, but then he spoke and the familiar voice brought her courage back. She started to move over towards him; get the job done and get out, she told herself. 'Hassan said that you wanted a lap dance.'

The man looked over at her, she could see his big brown eyes through his mask. 'Come and sit here first, we can talk for a bit.'

Susan made her way to the chair facing him. She sat down and crossed her long tanned legs. She always wore false tan now, always made sure her body had a golden tan. There was an eerie silence, she could only hear his breathing and through the wall the beat of the music in the other room. Susan hated the quietness and stroked a single finger up her leg, just like she did when he was behind the screen. 'So put some music on that I can dance to then.'

The man chuckled and reached over to the speaker. The music played and Susan stood up. She was no lap dancer, but if this guy was paying for her to dance then she was dancing. Susan remembered all the poses her sister had taught her and reminded herself it was all about the tease. She flicked her head over her shoulder and slowly her body bent one way then another. She straddled him and bent her body back. She even started to relax into it – she was doing it, teasing him, making him hungry for more. She rubbed up and down his body with hers and she could feel his erection through his jeans. Just as she was wondering when the song would end, the man reached over and turned the music off. He passed her one hundred pounds. 'That's on top of what I paid you for coming to the party – a little treat just for you for that dance.'

'Cheers for that,' she said as she shoved the money down the front of her bra.

The man sat forward in his seat and his voice was low. 'You can earn some more money if you want?' She watched as the guy snorted what she guessed was cocaine from the small table at the side of him. He jerked his head over to her. 'Come and get a line, it will make your night so much better.'

Susan checked her money was safe in her bra and looked over at the line of white powder on the table. 'I don't do drugs.'

'That surprises me, I thought you young uns all dabbled in a bit of sniff. Anyway, there is always a first time. I'll give you another fifty pounds to get a bit.'

Susan stood looking over at the white line of cocaine. Her mind was doing overtime: another fifty quid, another fifty quid to spend on clothes. She couldn't get hooked on the stuff after one sniff, could she? Plus if he'd just had some, it must be OK stuff, rather than cut with rat poison and all the other stuff she'd heard about. She walked up to the table and snorted the line of powder. How bad could it be? She knew loads of people who had done it. Susan closed her eyes as the rush filled her body, a wave of adrenaline pumping from her toes to her head. Susan smiled over at the man. She was on top of the world, confident, ready to party. Now she needed to get Sabrina to have some of this stuff, that would sort her nerves.

The man stood up and turned the music back on. He passed her a drink and watched as she necked it in one mouthful with a cunning look in his eyes. 'Dance with me,' he whispered in a low voice.

Susan felt his large hands around her waist. He looked deep into her eyes and she tried to pull his mask off. He gripped her hand tightly and growled at her. 'The mask stays on, it never comes off. Ever.'

As she tried to focus on his words, Susan felt strange; the room was spinning, his voice fading with every second. All of a sudden her legs felt weak and she could feel him carrying her over to the double bed at the side of the room. It was like she was having an out-of-body experience.

A few moments later, the door swung open and Sabrina rushed into the room, sick to death of waiting about for her friend. The men she'd met in the other room were perverts here and she was fed up with fighting them off and telling them no. All they wanted to do was get her drunk. Sabrina stood with her hands held over her mouth as she saw her friend on the bed and the man in the mask on top of her.

'Susan, what the fuck?' Sabrina ran over to the bed, she could tell straight away that her friend was out for the count. 'What the fuck have you done to her, get your dirty fucking hands off her now before I ring the police.'

Sabrina dug her hand deep into her pocket and pulled her knife out, waving it in his face, ready to cut him up. 'Get off her now, you have like two seconds before I plunge this deep inside you. Susan!' she screamed. 'Susan, wake up, come on, we need to get out of here.'

The man rolled off her and Sabrina dragged her friend up from the bed, always watching the man, waving the blade over at him. Susan was like a dead weight, she didn't know where she was or what day it was. With all her might Sabrina gripped her and dragged her out of the bedroom. Susan was coming around and her eyes were opening slowly. Sabrina was sweating, desperate to be out of here as soon as possible.

The cold air hit Susan and she stood spewing her guts up as they hid away in the shadow of a bus shelter not far from where they'd been. Sabrina was crying. 'Susan, that guy was doing stuff to you, touching you. What were you thinking? I knew it was a bad idea coming here. We need to ring the police, tell them what this lot are doing.'

Susan sat back on the seat in the bus shelter and dropped her head between her legs. 'One minute I was fine and the next, the next...' Tears started flooding from her eyes. 'I don't remember anything.'

'The dirty git must have drugged you. Come on, let's ring the police and have the lot of them charged – we know where they live.'

Susan wiped the tears from her eyes and looked up at her bestie. 'No, nobody must know about this. Please, don't tell a soul. I've been an idiot. Please, Sabrina, promise me that you'll tell nobody about this. Swear down that this stays between us.'

Sabrina bit down hard on her bottom lip. 'It all stops now then; you stop going online and you never speak to that pervert again. And even if we're not telling the dibble, you need to get down the clinic tomorrow and get yourself seen.'

Susan nodded feebly.

Sabrina hugged her friend tightly in her arms. 'He was having sex with you, Susan, I saw it with my own two eyes. I was going to stab him up and he knew it.'

Susan covered her ears with her hands and pressed them firmly. 'No, please don't tell me anymore. Just forget about it.'

Sabrina used her mobile phone to ring her brother, Scully. He was always picking her up when it was late. He wouldn't ask any questions, he never did. Sabrina stepped out of the shadow of the bus shelter, found out what street they were on and made the call to get them home. Tonight they'd walked a dangerous line and learned a lesson they'd never forget – dance with the Devil and you're going to get burnt.

Chapter Twenty-Seven

'Vincent was as drunk as a skunk in the pub last night and he was declaring he'd been robbed too. All the residents are meeting up later on today for another meeting. Dane said even if he has to walk the streets every minute of every day, he'll find out who these robbing bleeders are. A few of the others were up for around the clock surveillance too,' Bridie told her husband. As terrible as it was to know the burglars had hit the street again, she felt better knowing it hadn't just been their house targeted.

Bert carried on brushing his hair. 'Pointless, if you ask me. A bunch of civilians squaring up against a set of burglars who clearly know what they're doing. I mean, there could be a gang of them. What if they attack the patrol, what then? I for one won't be putting my name forward. Let the police do their job. I thought you always said that.'

Bridie shoved her polka-dot yellow dress over her head and sat down next to her husband. 'Well, that was before they came back and hit Vincent's. If we take this lying down, the Manor will be crime central before we know it. Plus I've had a bit of a breakthrough with my missing jewellery too. Madge from the pawn shop is going to let me look at the CCTV. I mean, I swear it was my necklace I saw in there. The managers are just being crafty saying nobody has been in selling knocked off stuff because they would get into deep trouble if they're seen to be buying stolen goods, won't they? But Madge is sympathetic, said she'd find a time when her boss isn't in so I can go look and see if I recognise anyone – and she left a message last night saying the coast was clear this morning.'

Bert bolted up from the bed. 'Tell you what, I'll go and have a look. You stay put, I don't want you getting involved in any of this. Like I said, we don't know who we are dealing with.'

'Piss off, Bert, I'm going to look at some CCTV footage, not challenging anyone. It's my jewellery, it meant a lot to me, and I won't give up until I find it.'

Bert followed his wife into the bathroom and watched her brushing her teeth. 'Bridie, I don't want you going anywhere – they aren't reasonable people, the folk who fence stuff to the pawn shop. Let the coppers do their job and stop bloody meddling in dangerous business.'

She looked at him through the bathroom mirror and spat the toothpaste into the sink. 'Save your breath, Bert, I'm going. I don't see what the harm is. I might see who the thief is so you should be happy that I might solve this without you having to go out on one of Dane's vigilante patrols.'

Bert stood on the landing, a look of blind panic on his face. Bridie walked past him and, almost without thinking, he moved. His hand pushed into the small of her back in one quick shove. Bridie tumbled down every stair, crashing into the wall. Bert stood watching as the silence burnt into him. Then the screams started and shook him out of his trance.

'I'll ring an ambulance, love, just stay put, don't move, I'll ring an ambulance.' Bert scuttled down the stairs, stepping over his wife's collapsed form.

Bridie was moaning and groaning, bright-red blood pouring from her knee. Bert was on the phone to the emergency services. He ended the call and ran back to his wife's side. He held her hand. 'Bridie, you're going to be alright. The ambulance is on its way. You gave me a shock there, I thought you were a gonner.'

Bridie's eyes were open wide and with every pain that surged through her body she gripped her husband's hand tighter. 'What happened?' she moaned.

'I think you lost your footing or something. I tried to grab you, but it was too late. Have you taken your blood pressure tablets, you might have had a dizzy spell or something?'

Bridie just lay still now, looking up at her husband's face. 'I'm feeling faint, Bert. If this is it, and my number's up, remember I love you and I always will.'

Bert choked up, crying. He turned towards the door, not to hide his tears but his guilt. Sirens rung out in the distance. 'You're going to be just fine, love. Just stay put, petal, let me open the front door and go outside to see where they are.'

Bridie didn't want to let go of his hand and he had to peel her fingers back one by one. 'I'll be straight back, love, just give me a few minutes to see where they are.' Bert struggled to stand up. He looked down at Bridie's injuries and cringed. What kind of monster had he become? 'Just stay there,' he said as he opened the front door. Bert stood looking down the road, pacing one way then the other. It felt like forever but as the minutes ticked by he was too scared to go back in. He'd heard stories of people dying waiting for an ambulance. At last he could see the ambulance and he waved his hand frantically. 'Here, she's in here,' he shouted at the top of his voice.

The paramedic got out of the ambulance and rushed straight into the house with his kit. Bert rushed behind him, trying fill him in. 'She was at the top of the stairs and I think she had a funny turn or something. She just fell down the stairs smashing into the walls. I tried to grab her, but it all happened so fast. Please tell me she's going to be alright, because if anything happened to my Bridie, I don't know what I would do. She's my world, always has been.' Bert had never fancied himself much of an actor but in that moment, he believed his own story. The other medic comforted him and started to take some more information, asking what medication his wife was taking and how long she'd been on them. Bridie was given some pain relief and she was out of it now, talking but not making any sense. Once they'd put her onto a stretcher, they were ready to leave. Bert asked to go with her, but they told him to pack his wife a bag and make his own way up to the hospital. As the ambulance drove off, he felt a wave of nausea hit him. He'd almost killed his own wife just to hide his own sins. What if she babbled to the medics? What would she say? He was in deep now, too deep.

The sound of the ambulance had brought all the neighbours out and straight to his side, comforting him. Joanne and Frank Dury tried to calm him down. Frank spoke to him. 'Come on, Bert. Bridie is a fighter, it will take more than a fall down the stairs to stop her. Come in ours for a bit. Joanne will make you a nice hot cup of tea for the shock.'

Joanne nodded. 'Bert, just come inside for a bit and try and calm down. Frank will whizz you up to the hospital, don't worry.'

Bert was escorted into the Drury household. What good neighbours he had, always looking out for him.

Chapter Twenty-Eight

Anthony sat in the shadows on Tavistock Square in Harpurhey. This was the place to be if you were ever looking for someone. It was like a watering hole in the desert and, at some point, anyone who was anyone on the dodgy side of town would pass through here every day. Anthony had done some homework on Bobby Owen and since he hadn't showed up at the canal yet, his mate had told him he got his drugs from here.

Anthony perched on a step, positioned so he could see all the square. He'd already clocked a few smackheads getting served up and knew it was only a matter of time before Bobby came to score. Anthony sat chewing on the side of his fingernail, gnawing at the skin. He wondered where the police presence was on this square. He'd seen so much crime here already and he'd only been sitting here for a few hours. Dodgy guys in the corner of the square selling bent goods; TVs, watches. Old ladies cashing in prescriptions to the dealers who sold them on. Shoplifters handing out bags of clobber they'd nicked to order. You name it, you could get it here. Still, today he was glad the police were absent – it made his next steps a hell of a lot easier.

Anthony was alert as he spotted a man entering the square from his right. He pulled his shoulders back. Was this his man? He wasn't sure – you couldn't exactly look addicts up on Facebook – he was going to have to try the old-fashioned way. Anthony stood up and walked a few paces nearer.

'Yo, Bobby!' he shouted.

The man looked over at him and Anthony could see the guy didn't know whether to get on his toes or not. Anthony had to be quick. 'Bobby, our kid said you're the one to come to if I needed a new phone.'

Bobby nodded, proud he could get his customers anything they wanted for a price. 'Yeah, what you after?' He bounced on the spot.

Anthony hesitated, trying not to visibly wince at the smell of this guy, and quickly looked around him. 'I've got a few things I need.'

Bobby loved a business proposition and rubbed his grubby hands together. 'Give me a second to score and I'll come and see you. I'm roasting my tits off and need to sort myself out first.'

Anthony nodded his head. 'I'll wait here for you.'

'Sorted. Like I said, I'll be back soon to see you.' Bobby slouched off to one of the other guys lurking in the shade of closed shops.

Anthony walked back to the step and once he was there, he never took his eyes from Bobby. He was as thin as a rake; if he gave him any shit, he'd knock the fucker out for sure, put him on his arse. He'd shit bigger than him. He couldn't believe this scrawny waster had beaten Matty up – he was going to enjoy taking his revenge.

Anthony's fists curled into two tight balls at the side of his legs, knuckles turning white. Bobby was on his way over to him. Christ, his eyes were barely open and his words were slurred. The fix had hit home clearly and the guy was on another level.

'Yes, pal, what can I do for you? And if you want something special, it's cash up front?'

Anthony made sure nobody could see them and patted the spot next to him for Bobby to sit down. He pressed Record on his mobile phone, nestled in his pocket. 'Right, Bobby, it's like this. I'm going to ask you something and if you start chatting shit then I'm going to kick ten tons of shit out of you, so it's up to you. I've been talking to your pals down by the canal and they told me you battered Matthew on the night he died, took his phone.'

Bobby was trying to stand up now, but Anthony had gripped him and came nose to nose with him. 'I was accused of killing him that night and you're the only one who can help clear my name. You said someone else was with Matthew after you, heard arguing.'

Bobby was shaking like a leaf, stuttering. 'I seen fuck all, seen nothing.' Anthony swung his head back and headbutted the addict, a reminder to let him know this wasn't going to end well for him if he didn't start talking. Bobby was dazed, crying but no tears coming from his eyes. Anthony's voice was fierce now, meant business.

'Start talking because if you don't, I'll take you somewhere and I'll do you in. Like I said, you can help clear my name, nobody else. So, unless you start talking, I've got fuck all to lose and I'll end you.'

Bobby had no other choice and, through the haze of his high, started talking. Alright, he admitted, he'd robbed somebody and nicked his phone, surely that was a robbery charge and an assault, nothing more, he told Anthony. He could handle a few months in prison, Bobby said, it might even help him sort his head out anyway and get off the smack – it cost more on the inside that it did round here. Bobby rubbed at the sores on his head and licked at his scabby lips. 'Mate, I'm sorry if you knew the kid. I was desperate, needed to score. I only kicked him a few times, all I wanted was his phone. Look, do I look like the sort of fella who could KO someone? He was singing and pissed out of his head. I just gave him a few slaps, had his phone away and got off. After a few minutes I turned back around and thought I would go and make sure the kid was alright because I'm not a bad twat, you know. I've got no time for those fairies from the gay village but I'm not a killer.'

Anthony clenched his teeth – fighting the urge to knock the prejudiced fucker out there and then, but he knew he had to let him continue.

'I was standing back in the darkness as another guy was pulling him from the floor. They started shouting at each other and the other guy was going sick at him, ragging him about. It was none of my business then, so I got off.'

'What did they look like, this other bloke? Was he big, small? What colour hair?'

Bobby shook his head and pulled his scruffy cap from his head, scratching at it like he had nits. 'I don't know, I didn't take much notice. Like I said, I was going back to just make sure the lad was alright, that's all.'

Anthony sat thinking. He looked at Bobby. 'Will you tell the police what you've just told me?'

Bobby squirmed, the thought of being arrested getting the better of him. 'Nah, mate, I could handle a stretch for robbery, but if they can't find this other bloke they'll pin it on me.'

Anthony's eyes widened. 'Where is the phone you nicked from him, tell me that then.'

'Sold it.'

'Who to?' Anthony's patience was fraying.

Bobby knew he was in danger of getting a belt if he didn't tell this guy everything he wanted to know. He'd grassed people up before to save his own neck and today was no different. 'It's a ginger guy who works in Cash Generator up the road. We have a thing going where he buys all the phones from me. He meets me around the corner and he bungs me the money. Doesn't go through their books or anything, like.'

Anthony had more to go on now but still this rat held the information to clear his name. Anthony gripped Bobby by the arm and pulled his mobile phone from his pocket. 'Hello, police please.'

Bobby was in a panic and tried wriggling free, but he was going nowhere any time soon. He was a prime witness; the only living soul that could help clear Anthony's name. He was staying put.

It didn't take long for the police to show up, scattering anyone else lurking in the square. The police arrested Bobby and gave Anthony an address to email his recording to. But he kept back the part about Matthew's mobile phone being sold. No, that was his next stop, getting more evidence to help clear his name and avenge his stepson.

Anthony walked into Cash Generator and pretended to browse the goods. Although he knew it was there, he'd never even stepped inside before. Anthony did a double-take as he recognised a familiar face.

Ben walked over to him. 'I've not seen you in here before, what are you looking for?'

Anthony was stuck for words. This kid had more front than Blackpool. The last time he'd spoken with him he was just like the rest of the community, calling him a murderer, scum of the earth. 'Have you got a minute, Ben?'

Ben checked the time on his phone. 'Erm, I'm due on my break in twenty minutes if you want to wait. What's up?'

Anthony stuttered; his voice low. 'The police have just arrested a man who saw what happened the night Matthew died.'

'No way, who have they arrested?' Ben gulped.

Anthony was aware that people could hear him now and clammed up. 'I'll stick around outside until you're free.'

Not long after, Ben walked out and over towards where Anthony had been sat waiting. He was white as a sheet – unsure if he was going to speak to a killer or a hero. Ben licked at his lips and sat down next to him. Ben lit a fag up and passed one to Anthony. 'I only get fifteen minutes break, so I need to make sure I get a few ciggies in before my break is over. Anyway, I'll shut up while you fill me in.'

Anthony sucked hard on the cigarette and blew a thick cloud of grey smoke from his mouth. 'It's a guy called Bobby Owen, who the police have arrested.' Anthony shared the whole sorry story – all apart from who he sold the phone to.

Ben looked like he was going to faint, but pulled himself together. 'So, Skanky Bobby robbed Matthew and gave him a few slaps?'

'Yep, scum-bag he is, rancid. But, ay, he sung like a budgie when I twatted him. I knew there was more to this story. Like I've told everyone, I'm innocent. I'm a cheat, yes, but I'm not a fucking murderer.'

'Does Matthew's mam know about this new stuff?'

'Yes, I called her on the way over here. I know she will never forgive me for what I did that night, but I'll sleep better knowing my name has been cleared.'

Ben shook his head, reached over and patted Anthony's arm. 'Sorry, mate. Me and Malc were good friends with Matthew and when it all came out, we had you down for doing him in. Come on, you were always having a pop at him for being a mummy's boy.'

Anthony growled over at Ben. 'I'm not denying that, but it was the truth and he even said himself that his mother needed to stop treating him like a baby. I loved Matthew like I would have my own son. I would never have harmed him.'

'So the police are charging Bobby then?'

'Yes, but probably only for assault and robbery. They have to find out now who else was on that canal and who Matthew was arguing with because Bobby seen them, heard them.'

Ben checked his phone. 'I better get back into work. Moaning bastards they are if you're late back from lunch.'

Anthony reached up, grabbed his arm and looked him directly in the eye. 'There's something else I've not told the police yet, and I think you'll want to hear this. Bobby told me the phone he took from Matthew he sold to you. I need that phone back, there might be things on there that could help find the killer.'

Ben was sweating now, had to sit back down on the step. He looked over at Anthony and knew there was no getting out of this. My, how the tide had turned. 'Listen, Bobby always sells me stuff. I just make a few quid here and there. I'm fuck all to do with the murder.'

Anthony smirked over at Ben. 'Now you know how I feel, mate. Welcome to my world. I want that phone back. Once I've looked in it then I'll take it to the police so they can use it as evidence.'

Ben was up in arms. 'So, you're going to grass me up then. Fucking hell, like I said, I just make a few quid. Don't have me down as part of this investigation. I'll lose my job, get a criminal record.'

Anthony was in the driving seat now and you could see he didn't know how he was going to play this. He sat cracking his knuckles and licking at his lips. 'I'll come with you now to pick the phone up, or have you sold it already.'

Ben was in a panic. 'No, it's still at my gaff. I've not even switched the stupid thing on – I can't believe it's Matty's. All this time I've had it sitting in a drawer and it might have the answer on it. I've not had time to clear anything off it yet because before I sell them on, I usually reset it all. Anthony, can't you just say Bobby sold the phone to someone else. It'll have my fingerprints all over it. Please don't do this to me, I'm begging you.'

Anthony stood up and straightened his coat. 'Move your arse. Let's get the phone and, after that, we can sort out what we're going to do about you.'

Ben was near tears. 'I just need to run back in work and tell them I'm leaving. I'll have to say I've got a family emergency or something.'

'Tell them what you want, mate, just get me that phone.'

Chapter Twenty-Nine

D ane stood at the front of the small crowd in the pub, his voice loud, smashing his clenched fist against the table below him. 'I say we man the streets and catch these bastards red-handed, there are enough of us. These are our homes we're talking about. The police have done fuck all, so I say let's take this into our own hands and do this the old-fashioned way.'

The door opened slowly with a slight creak, and you could have heard a pin drop as Bronwen walked in. She'd not stepped foot in here since the death of her son and although she'd been forced herself to go out occasionally, to pop to the shop or visit Matthew's grave, still fresh, she was nowhere near ready to go back to normal life. What was a normal life for her now, she wondered. Losing a child was every parent's nightmare. The books she'd read told her to take everything day by day and remember the good times she'd shared with her son. But nothing made sense anymore. As soon as she closed her eyes every night, her son's face was there looking at her, his murder never leaving her mind. Maybe one day she would be able to think of his face with joy rather than anguish, but now she looked like she had the weight of the world on her shoulders. Bronwen scraped a chair back, all eyes on her. Dane nodded his head over at her and spoke in a low voice. 'Good to see you here, Bronwen.'

Alison was working behind the bar and as she spotted Bronwen it looked as though the ground had fallen out from under her. Bronwen had made it clear that while she directed most of her rage at Anthony, she wasn't letting Alison off the hook. Most of the locals had heard Bronwen calling Alison a dirty slut, calling her out for sleeping with a man whom she knew was in a relationship.

'Come and sit down, Bronwen. Help us all come up with a solution to these robberies,' Gaynor said before any trouble kicked off between her friend and her barmaid. The landlady stood next to her husband and listened as he addressed the group again.

'Frank, I need you by my side on this. You can hold your own. What have you got to say about this, are you in? You've got two beautiful daughters – I bet every parent is worried sick that their innocent kids could run into these scum criminals targeting our estate.'

Frank Drury nodded his head and looked around the pub for other men who could have a go and not be scared of a bit of a fight. Frank ran his eyes over Vincent, who was necking his pint at the bar, and shook his head at Dane. Maybe a couple of months ago this man would have been asked to stand with them all but recently, with the amount he was drinking and the nonsense he was spouting, he was as much use as a chocolate fireguard. But Dane knew which of the other neighbours he could count on, which of them could look after themselves if the situation called for it, and by the end of the night there was a rota put together to man the streets until the crime in this area had stopped.

Bronwen stood up and coughed to clear her throat. 'Can I just have a few words before you all go home? I know you all had my back while the police searched for Matthew's killer and I'd rather tell you all direct than have folk whispering behind my back. Anthony has uncovered that on the night my son was murdered, he was beaten up and robbed by a man called Bobby Owen. Ant has informed the police of what he knows, and I'm pleased to say the scum-bag has been arrested and is with the police as we speak.'

'They should string the waster up!' one of the regulars shouted out.

Bronwen carried on speaking, her desperate urge to get justice making her voice louder and clearer than ever. 'This Bobby fella claims that on the night that Matthew was murdered another person was with him after he'd robbed him and left him, and that he heard them arguing and shouting at each other. So, while I'm glad to say there's progress, you need to know that I won't rest until we know if there is still a murderer on the loose. We're the Manor – and I know you all want to see whoever did this caught too. I hear you're setting up patrols; it's a brilliant thing you're doing for our community – but you need to know the kind of people you'll be up against. The kind of

people who wouldn't think twice about killing an innocent boy on his eighteenth birthday.'

Dane looked at his wife, Gaynor, and raised his eyebrows.
He was all up for catching some burglars, but a murderer,
this was serious stuff. But they couldn't back down now.
'We're all behind you, Bronwen, and we'll keep our ears to
the ground to see if we hear anything on the grapevine.'

The men who'd signed up to man the estate all gath-
ered around Dane and the rest of the community started
to go their own ways. Bronwen stared over at the bar and
finally clocked Alison. She gritted her teeth and was about
to stand up, but Gaynor dragged her back by her arm.
'Don't do it, love. Between me and you, we're just waiting
for the chance to sack her. Honest, if she puts one foot
wrong, she's out of the bleeding door. You've got bigger
battles to fight than your beef with her.'

Bronwen sat back down. Maybe now was not the right
time and this could go on the back burner for now. She sat
nursing her drink and staring not at but through everyone
else there. The pub to her would always be full of ghosts
now – the memories of Matthew's last night playing over
and over.

The doors opened and Malcolm and Ben came in. Ben
looked sheepish as he walked over to his friend's mum. He
pulled the chair back and shot a look over at Bronwen. 'I
swear to you now, I didn't have a clue it was Matthew's
phone. You know me, I always do a bit of wheeling and dealing to earn a few quid. I've aways bought stuff from Bobby
and never had anything like this before. It was just in my
drawer waiting for me to reset it. It was flat too – no photo

on his lock screen, and you know Matty said phone cases were naff, so how was I to know it was his? I'm sorry though, Bronwen, I really am. If I'd known, we could have charged it up or even taken it to the pigs. I feel awful. I know that's nothing compared to what you're going through, Mrs M.'

Bronwen touched Ben's arm. 'Thanks, Ben, love. It took guts for you to confess to Ant about the phone when he asked you and not lie and say you'd already sold it on. I'm not mad at you – who am I to judge what you do to earn a bit of extra dough? I'm just glad we are starting to get some answers. I think I knew deep down that Anthony was not the one who killed Matthew. He has his faults, but he's not a killer. I know that now. I think I was just lashing out – I wanted answers. I still do.'

Malcolm nodded at Ben. 'Go and get the beers in, mate. Bron, what are you drinking?'

'No, I've just got one. I'm going to drink this and head off home. Anthony is coming round and hopefully we can sit in a room with each other without me wanting to strangle him.'

Ben headed towards the bar and Bronwen looked over at Malc. 'How have you been doing? I've been meaning to give you a ring, but I don't seem to have the energy to do anything anymore. It's like all my strength has been sucked out of me. I just about function every day.'

'I know what you mean. I'm the same. I went to his grave the other day and just sat there talking to him, telling him how much I miss him.'

Bronwen's eyes clouded over, and she choked up. 'He'll be with you, Malc, he will be with us both. Sometimes I feel his presence at the side of me.'

234

Malcolm shivered. 'So, what do the dibble know about this other suspect they're meant to be looking for?'

'I don't know, this is the missing part of the jigsaw. Bobby told Anthony he didn't get much of a look at him, so who knows what they'll do – but it's a lead, at least.' Bronwen could see Malc was getting upset and tried to change the subject. 'You'll have to call around to mine one night with Ben and we can have a proper catch-up. The house seems so empty without you two there every night. I feel I've not just lost Matthew – I've lost all of you lot too. All the mucking about, the jokes and laughter in the house.'

'I know. Yeah, I'll defo still come around. I feel like I need to, I'm lost without coming to your house. You know with him at home and all that.' Malc looked down at his feet while he spoke.

Bronwen knew he was talking about his stepdad and shook her head. 'Is he still having a go at you? How many times have I told you to just get your stuff and come and stay at mine anytime you need. The man is a bully.'

'He's not as bad as he used to be. I just keep out of his way. It's my mam I feel sorry for. Since she came back, I can't just leave her to deal with him, she wouldn't last two minutes.'

'I don't understand why women put up with an abusive partner. I swear if Anthony would have ever laid a finger on me, I would have scratched his eyes out.'

'I know. I've told her time and time again to leave his sorry arse but she tells me it's complicated, tells me it's going to change, that he's sorry. All the same old crap that

235

wifebeaters always say. It makes me realise you never know who else is taking a swing at their partners in private. I bet some of these old boys here have done it – and look at us, neighbours and not knowing.'

Ben was back, and he passed Malc a bottle of Peroni. 'Bloody hell, Dane is really going to town over there on his vigilante squads. I'd hate to be in their shoes when it all kicks off. Frank is game as fuck too; I just heard him saying he's got a baseball bat and an iron bar to take out on his patrol with him. He's asked if I will go too.'

Bronwen shook her head. 'No, lads, just leave it to the police now. Let them do what they do best. I don't want you two putting your lives on the line when the killer's still out there.'

Bronwen looked at her son's two friends and a warmth filled her body. 'He was so lucky to have you two. It means such a lot to me to know that you cared for him like the way you did. Malc, you always protected him, even when them bullies from school were giving him a hard time you sorted it out and made sure they never went near him again and you, Ben, you never judged him. He was proud to call you both friends.'

Ben gulped as a wave of emotion gripped him, he bit his bottom lip. 'Always my friend, no matter where he is now.'

Chapter Thirty

Brooke walked about the salon, edgy and anxious. Her friend Amy went to her side and pulled her into the back office. 'He's out of your life now. Stop thinking about him. You know as well as me that if Vincent wanted you, he would have been in here kicking off.'

Brooke flicked the kettle on and stood with her back to the wall. 'I'm just spooked, that's all. Lee is working away and I just feel vulnerable.'

'That Lee seems to have come in your life at the right time, if you ask me. I'm a great believer in fate, Brooke. I know he hurt you in the past and left you high and dry, but he's here now and standing by you. And he's a bit of alright too. I wouldn't kick him out of bed.'

Brooke went bright red and slurped a mouthful of her drink. 'I just feel like I should be building my life back on my own, not depending on another bloke to make me feel whole. He never stops telling me how sorry he is for not speaking out for me and telling his wife that he loved me and not her. He said it was circumstances at that time; his kids, the finances. But it's all happened so fast.'

Amy rolled her eyes. 'It is what it is, Brooke. I always say only look back to see how far you have come and now is your time to be happy. Vincent has dragged you down for years and if you're being honest with yourself, you should have ended the relationship years ago.'

'I know, I know, but I just felt guilty. I was the reason Vincent was drinking, I broke him in two and I wanted to fix him, make him be alright.'

'Stop it, Brooke. I'm sick of hearing it. Vincent had problems before you and Lee got together. You told me yourself he hadn't touched you in months. That's not normal, is it?'

'I blame the days he was in the army. He's seen some bad shit you know, the worst.'

Amy looked doubtful. 'If he was struggling with his mental health then he should have got help, not searching for all the answers he needs at the bottom of a beer glass or taking it out on you.'

'I think he has that post-traumatic stress. I told him that too and he nearly bit my head off telling me it was me who wasn't right in the head, not him.'

'It's called gas-lighting you know. I researched it and it's when someone makes you think you are going crazy, blaming you for everything. You should Google it. I bet you can see yourself and Vincent.' She paused. This was a ciggie moment and if she was going to tell the truth here then she needed a fag in her hand. She passed one over to Brooke and held the lighter underneath it. She took a few drags and crossed her legs before she carried on. 'I never told you before because you always made excuses for Vincent, always had a reason why you put up with his shit. Even when he came to our Christmas party when he wasn't invited demanding that you got your arse home. I've seen the bruises too, don't think that I haven't. You lied for him, Brooke, told me you'd fallen or banged yourself. Come on, love, you need to get up early if you want to get one over on me. I knew exactly what was happening, but you covered up for him, not ready to see the real truth. All the girls here saw it, but you just plodded on in complete denial.'

The tears streamed down Brooke's cheeks. 'I'll never get myself like that again, Amy, never.'

Amy smiled and reached over to hug her friend. 'I'm glad to hear it. I'm always here for you if you're struggling, but for now put a smile on your face and let's glam our clients up.' They both necked their coffees and stubbed their fags out. Just before they went back into the salon Brooke reached over and grabbed Amy by the arm. 'Thank you, Amy. I needed to hear what you had to say. The clouds are shifting, and I think I can see the rainbow at last.'

Vincent looked down at Lee and loved that he had control over him; he could see the fear in his eyes, see that he didn't know what was going to happen next. He should have done this as soon as he heard Brooke was back with him. He plonked down on the wooden crate, sparked a cigarette up and growled over at his captive. 'You're a prick, do you know that? We could have worked things out, Brooke and me, sat down and solved all our problems but you coming back has changed all that. If you're out of the picture again, we still could.'

Lee sat up straight, pulled his knees up to his chest, felt the dried blood on his head and his cheeks. He'd had enough. If he was going to die then he just wanted it over with – there was no reasoning with a man like Vincent, he may as well as just give him the honest truth. 'It's your own fault. If you'd have treated her well then she wouldn't have gone elsewhere, looking for comfort. I'm not arsed what you do with me anymore, but I'll speak my truth and let you know you're a loser. Brooke was right – you're tapped in the head, pal.'

Vincent roared at the top of his voice, 'I'll fucking end you! Shut up, before I do it now. Honest, I'll send you to meet your maker.'

Lee swallowed hard and looked over at Vincent. What was the point in dragging this out? Although a small voice in his head was screaming that if this man wanted him gone then he would have done it by now. Should he fight? His body was filled with pain and his left leg was useless, maybe it was broken, he wasn't sure. 'Brooke deserves happiness. You've had your chance with her and fucked it up. If I make her happy then let her go. Come on, admit it. You've abused her for years, pal, made her cry, beaten her, so what the fuck do you still want her for?'

Vincent swigged a mouthful from the bottle that he'd stuffed in his pocket before he'd ambushed Lee. 'Because she's my wife, pal, my property. How many times do I have to tell you?'

'Bullshit,' Lee whispered under his breath. 'You can never own a woman like Brooke. And me, what do you want with me? If Brooke wants you then so be it, but let the fucking woman choose herself, don't force her.'

Vincent sat thinking. He'd not slept properly for weeks, and Lee could see he was practically dead on his feet. 'I'll be going to see *my* wife and asking her myself, don't you worry about that. She probably thinks I've walked away from her, but she should know me better than that. Until death do us part. I'll never walk away.'

Lee shot a look around the room; no way out but through the door. He licked at his lips frantically and knew in a few minutes Vincent would be gone and he'd be his prisoner again. 'So you're just going to leave me here while you go and hope Brooke takes you back?'

Vincent let out a menacing laugh and stood up with his head held high. 'I've not decided what I'm doing with you yet. You're here and nobody but me knows it, so if you never returned home then anyone would just assume you did a bunk – a work trip that you never came back from.'

Vincent didn't give him chance to say anything else, he left the room. Lee listened as the door was locked behind him and he punched his clenched fist into the wall at the side of him. He'd been to martial arts classes for years and he had decent moves to take any man down when he was fighting fit. But like this? Limping and dizzy from the beating Vince had given him when he grabbed him? He wasn't so sure. But it looked like he had no other choice. The next time Vincent came here again, he would be ready for him, would take him down by any means. But for now, all he could do was sit waiting, worrying about Brooke and what her psychopath of a husband had planned for her.

Chapter Thirty-One

Emma closed her laptop. It had been hard graft tonight and the punters were not parting with the cash like she'd hoped. A poxy hundred quid she'd made tonight, nothing compared to what she was expecting to earn. She needed to distract herself so quickly got changed and headed down the hall to her sister's bedroom. Susan had been quiet lately and she wasn't as loud and as bubbly as usual, but speaking to her had to be better than chatting shit with skinflint blokes on OnlyFans.

Susan was laid on her bed watching the television. Emma edged inside the room pretending that she was looking for something. Not a peep from her sister.

'I've done shite tonight. I don't know what's up with them, tight bastards they are, not willing to spend any money.' Emma walked over to the bed and plonked down next to her sister. 'How come you've got a face like a smacked arse too? Is it boy trouble because you've not smiled for weeks.'

Susan rolled onto her side, dragging the duvet over her shoulders, blocking the world out. Emma gripped the duvet and yanked it back. 'Aw, is my little sister having boyfriend trouble? Come on, tell me what's happened, I might be able to give you some advice.'

Susan was wrestling with the corner of the quilt that she had hold of and was pulling at it with all her might, face bright red. 'Piss off, will you? I'm not in the mood. I'm due on and I've got bad cramps.'

Emma chuckled out loud, but still kept hold of the duvet so she could see her sister's face. 'I thought you had work tonight. It's nearly six o'clock so you better start getting ready. You know my mam and dad will kick off if you're skipping shifts.'

'I can't be arsed with work tonight. I'll just phone in sick. Sav's sweet, he won't mind.'

Emma was stern. 'Listen, the deal was that you tell my mam and dad that you are picking up more shifts at the shop and that's where the extra money comes from. Don't balls this up for us both.'

Susan took a breath. 'I'm not sure if I want to do the OnlyFans page anymore. It's grubby and I hate not knowing who's looking at me.'

Emma frowned. 'You've been earning good money so what's changed your tune all of a sudden?'

'Nothing, it just freaks me out. I thought I'd put it out of my mind when I shut the laptop but it stays with me – like something's crawling on me.'

'Bloody hell, Mrs Prim and Proper. Since when have you been arsed who's looking at you? I thought you loved the attention. You've been telling me it's bloody easy money up to now and how you are saving up. I don't buy this. What's changed – and I mean really?'

'Nothing,' Susan snapped back. 'I just don't like it anymore. It was fun at first – something new, but now it feels like I have to fake a smile, even when I'm off camera.'

Emma plonked down on the bed and fanned her long nails out in front of her. 'I get what you mean. After all, it's work – no one loves their job really, do they? It's up to you though, be skint or have money, the choice is yours. I was thinking that we could even join up together, give these punters a double bubble and get some seriously decent money coming in that means we don't have to do this forever. I reckon that two of us can rake it in if we team up and really tease them.'

'God. That's fucking hanging, Emma. I tell you I'm quitting and you try to get me to go all girl-on-girl. Well, no way. I'm not doing it anymore I've decided. I'll work for Sav and earn my money the boring way. I'm sorry I even got involved in it all if I'm being honest.'

Emma was livid. 'Don't start all that now. It was the best thing since sliced bread the other month and now you're turning into some kind of nun.'

'Yeah well, things change, I wish I could turn the clock back. You should watch out for yourself too – it's not a nice place on there.'

Emma was sick of hearing her sister's lecture and marched to the bedroom door. 'Don't be begging me to set you up again in a few weeks because the answer will be no.

You go and work for pennies at Sav's and let me be the one who earns the big money for doing virtually nothing.'

Emma was gone and Susan jumped up from her bed and shot a look at the clock. It was time to get ready for work. She was looking forward to getting some fresh air on her walk to the shop – her room felt stale and lying on her bed just made her thoughts race more. Even when she tried to get to sleep she kept thinking of the man in the mask. At least at the shop she was busy, distracted.

It was Halloween and Susan knew the neighbourhood kids would Trick or Treat the shop as well as all the local houses. Angela was a right misery and already she'd had a chat with Sav asking if she could just cart any more kids who'd come into the shop in hope of some free sweets, but Susan thought it was cute. She stood looking at the boxes of washing powder she had to stack the shelves with. Sabrina said she would call in tonight, but up to now she'd not seen sight nor sound of her. Angela was watching Susan's every move anyway. 'Do you have a problem, Angela, or what?' she hissed over at her.

Angela came out from behind the counter and stood over Susan, who was now bent down stacking the shelves. 'Yes, in fact I do. You've been doing the same shelf now for over twenty minutes. You should have finished that box and be onto stacking the washing-up liquid by now. I'm going to have a word with Sav about you. He thinks the sun shines out of your arse, but he doesn't see you staring into space wasting time, does he?'

Susan stood up tall and went nose to nose with Angela. She was getting told. 'Why on earth are you always on my back, are you jealous of me or something? What difference does it make to you if I'm stacking washing-up liquid, bin bags or bleeding magic beans?'

'You're lazy, that's why. I work my arse off and Sav never tells me that he appreciates me, yet with you he licks your arse always praising you.'

'That's not my fault, is it? Deal with it and get over it. Why don't you piss off back behind the counter and get the job done you get paid for instead of worrying about me?'

Angela looked like she'd sucked a lemon. 'I'll be telling Sav, don't you worry about that. I never thought he should have given you a job anyway. God knows why he did when he knows as well as everyone around here what kind of girl you are.'

Susan was fuming. 'Do whatever you want, Angela. And what do you mean, everyone knows what kind of girl I am?'

Angela started to walk away. 'You know what I mean. Don't think I've not heard you and Sabrina talking. I know exactly what you two have been up to with the boys from the estate, with that Duffy lad.'

Susan looked relieved, glad that Angela hadn't heard anything about what she was really up to. But all the same, she wasn't she going to let her talk to her like that, no way. Susan made sure nobody was in the shop and kept her voice low. 'Just because you can't get a leg-over with someone like Duffy, don't be jealous of me and the action I'm getting. Remember, we all hear everything in this shop and Mr Perkins from down the street isn't shy at coming forward, is he? I know all about the secret little meetings you have with him. The walks in the park and the times he comes back here when you're locking up on your own, so put that in your pipe and smoke it, yo-yo knickers.'

Angela was beetroot, with none of her usual sniping responses. Two youngsters came into the shop just at the right moment and stopped the argument dead in its tracks. Susan raised her eyes over at Angela and smirked. Game set and match in her eyes. The kids ran to the counter and screamed at Angela, 'Trick or treat.'

Angela had lost her appetite for her usual yelling at the kids and instead just leaned over to grab a packet of sweets each for them to get rid of them. But Sav came running from the back wearing a mask and making barking noises. The two kids screamed at the top of their lungs and ran to their mother who was waiting outside the shop door. He quickly whipped the mask off, laughing his head off. 'Oh I'm so sorry, Mrs Cross. I just couldn't help myself. I'm a big kid at heart and wanted to see if I could scare them. Halloween is my favourite time of year.'

Mrs Cross could see the funny side of things and held her two screaming kids close to her legs. 'Stop crying, you pair, it's only Sav. Come on, look at him, it's Uncle Sav.'

As they walked off, Dane sauntered in. 'Alright, Sav, just letting you know that our surveillance starts tonight. We need to catch these fuckers red-handed. Frank is doing his rounds tonight and we've got you and your brother down for Friday night if that's alright with you. I know you missed the meeting we all had, and I just took it for granted that you would want to be involved, especially with you having a business in the community.' Dane knew exactly what he was saying, and he phrased his remarks carefully, so Sav had no choice but to join the night watch.

Susan stood listening to the conversation. 'Does my dad know about this, Sav, because I know he'd be up for it.'

'He's already signed up,' Dane answered. 'One of the first he was. God help the scrotes if he gets his hands on them. He's got you and your sister to think of.'

Susan went into the back office. She needed a cig break and Sav was cool like that; he let her smoke in his office rather than having to go outside when the weather was bad. She flopped down on the black leather chair and lit up. Her phone vibrated with a message and she pulled it from her pocket and stared at the screen. She'd set up the OnlyFans app on her iPhone and hadn't deleted it yet. Illuminating the screen was a message from the man who'd raped her. 'Jay' he called himself on screen. She felt sick. She thought quitting going on camera was the fastest way to forget about what happened but seeing his name, his message, brought everything back. What did that prick want after what he'd done to her? He clearly thought he'd done nothing wrong if he was still messaging her. She checked nobody was about and opened the alert with her cig held firmly in her hand. She took a deep drag before she read the words.

'I miss you. Please speak to me. I've sent you a present, hope you like it.' Susan's colour drained from her face. Where had he sent a present to? Did he know where she lived? She stubbed her cigarette out and sat staring into space until the strident sound of Sabrina's voice cut through from the shop floor. She'd know what to do for sure. Susan stood up and walked back into the shop. Sav was still talking to Dane, giving it large about what they would do to the robber when they collared him. Susan shook her head. It was all bullshit – playing Billy Big Bollocks to each other. She knew Sav was as soft as shit and to hear him talking like this made her stomach churn. If this community wanted some real harm to come to somebody, then they should have asked Sabrina's brothers. Forget this 'all talk, no action' banter, Sabrina's siblings had all been to jail and the stories she'd heard about them would make anyone's toes curl. Sabrina had hidden a gun for her brothers once; Susan remembered her bringing it into school in her school bag. They'd both held the gun, taken selfies holding it. Stupid really, but it had felt wild and grown up at the time.

Angela growled over at Susan, making sure Sav heard her. 'Susan you've just been on a break, and I need the washing-up liquid out on the shelves as soon as possible, so tell Sabrina you can talk when you finish work, not now.'

Sabrina rammed her two fingers up at Angela and eyeballed her, unblinking. She'd had many a run-in with Angela and the last time she'd had proper words with her she'd launched a can of beans at her head. She'd been barred for a month, or until Sav had forgotten. So Angela was aware of Sabrina's temper and made sure she wasn't a sitting target, shielded behind the till.

'Wind your neck in, Angela, and get your own work done,' she replied. Susan grabbed Sabrina, they both were laughing their heads off.

'How long before you finish here?'

Susan shot a look over at the clock on the wall and replied. 'Half an hour I've got left, so go and wait for me on the park. Who's out tonight, is Duffy out?'

'Yeah, the full crew are out. They're all heading down to Tavistock Square.' Susan cringed and hesitated to reply. 'Sack that, my dad will go sick if he knows I've been chilling on there. You know what he's like.'

'How's he going to find out? I just thought you could nick a bottle of vodka from here and we could get steaming drunk.'

Susan was aware that Angela may be listening and led Sabrina back out of the shop. 'I'll see what I can do.'

'Get some cigs too. I'm skint and we don't want to be bumming fags from the guys, do we? Last time I had to do something hanging with one of them to get a fresh pack.'

'Just get gone and I'll see what I can do. But I need to see you – I got a message from Jay just now, he said he's sent me a present. I'll let you read it when I see you, but for now piss off before I end up losing my job.'

Sabrina couldn't hide her disgust. 'That guy needs locking up. On my life, I can't unsee what I saw, dirty git he is.'

'Shut up, will you? Angela will hear. I'll see you soon.'

Sav watched her wave her friend off and walked over to where she was. 'Angela has been in moaning about you again. Do me a favour and please try not to wind her up. You know what she's like. Just do what she asks you and save us both the earache.'

'It's her starting it, Sav, she's always on my case, bothering me when I'm working.'

'I know, but just bear it in mind that she's your line manager.' Sav went back into his office and Susan could see him on his laptop. He was so hard-working and she was so grateful he'd seen some potential in her, given her a chance. She felt terrible nicking from the shop, but she figured everyone must do it to make up for the crap wages. She'd get her head down and work solidly for the rest of her shift.

———

Half an hour later, Susan patted the bottle down in her pocket and made sure the cigarettes she'd stashed down the front of her bra weren't on show. 'See you tomorrow, Sav, have a nice evening!' she shouted behind her as she left the shop.

'See you tomorrow,' he replied.

Susan walked down the busy road to meet Sabrina in the park. She was edgy tonight and forever checking over her shoulder. The OnlyFans message had freaked her out, put the fear of God in her. She should have deleted her account, but a part of her wanted to know who was messaging her, still stalking her profile even though it was inactive. This freak was persistent, she knew that much now, and what if he knew where she lived? Maybe she should tell Emma, come clean about going solo, she would know what to do for sure. If Sabrina didn't have an answer, she'd have to tell her sister – it would drive her mad with worry keeping this to herself. She'd never be able to walk down the street without thinking he was there, watching.

Sabrina was drunk already and as soon as she spotted her bestie heading her way, she ran towards her with open arms. 'Our kid is chilling with us tonight and he said he will get us some scran later. Did you bring more booze?'

Susan could see Scully sat smoking a spliff. He was such a dude; he oozed confidence and was a true bad boy. He was nearly twenty-one and he'd been in and out of prison for short spells ever since he turned eighteen. He had status around these parts, and nobody messed with this kid if they knew what was good for them. Scully was always tooled up, always ready to stab someone up if they ever crossed him. Sabrina was proud of her brother's reputation and if anyone ever gave her any shit she always threw his name into the mix to protect herself.

Duffy clocked Susan walking over and nudged his mate. 'I'm going to shag her again tonight. She's been blowing hot and cold for weeks, but I know she wants me.'

His pal chuckled and high-fived him. 'Yeah, nice one. I might try my luck with Sabrina. Look at her, she's twisted already, she'll be game for anything. I got a suck from her the other week, but keep that to yourself. Scully's over there and if he hears anything about me and his sister, he'll have something to say.'

'Lips sealed, mate.'

Susan came to join the group. Scully looked her up and down and smiled at her. 'Yo, Suze, come and sit here with me, it's been ages since we've chilled together.'

'I know, you're always banged up jail, that's why.' Scully laughed out loud and patted the space on the brick wall next to him. 'Well I've been out now for three months this time, so fingers crossed I stay out.'

Duffy nudged his mate, his voice low. 'What the fuck is his game? He'll be getting told if he thinks he can just walk on in here and mess with my girl.'

His mate raised his eyebrows high, still checking nobody could hear him. 'She's not really your girl, is she? You've not put a label on it, so she's fair game.'

'Nah, I'm going straight over there.'

'Good luck with that because, by the looks of things, she's all over him.' Duffy glanced over to where Susan was sitting. His mate was right; she was flirting with Scully. Sabrina was between the two groups, singing, dancing, ready to party all night long.

Scully kept his voice low and whispered into Susan's ear. 'I'm getting off now, but I'll be in Tavistock Square later on if you want to hook up?'

Susan flicked her hair back over her shoulder and smiled at him, trying to play it cool. 'Okay, but don't leave it too late because I have to be in by twelve.'

'Aw, still a little baby, aren't you?'

She was right back at him. 'No, I just respect my parents, that's all.'

Scully jerked his head at her as he jumped down from the wall. 'Laters.'

It wasn't long before Susan was as drunk as Sabrina and although she told her about the message from Jay, the alcohol had numbed her anxiety and she decided she would force it to the back of her mind, enjoy her night. But this guy had raped and drugged her, she knew that however much she drank now, however loud she laughed with her mates, the nightmares she'd been having would return. She knew now she should have reported him, had the police track him and his mates and charge the lot of them for grooming young girls. But the shame she would bring on her family – her dad would have never forgiven her, would have disowned her. Plus a part of her knew what certain coppers would say – she heard what they said when they cleared her and her mates off the corners and benches where they hung out. She knew they called them scum, knew she'd get blamed for setting up the OnlyFans account. Yes, she would have to do things her way for a bit longer and now Scully was on the scene she had all the protection she needed.

Chapter Thirty-Two

Bronwen walked along the canal. It was past midnight and another night she couldn't sleep. The wind was howling and she had her big black coat on with a grey scarf tucked down tightly inside it, but she still felt cold to her bones. It was like she hadn't been able to get warm since she found out about Matthew. Bronwen stopped dead in her tracks, looking at the bright lights in the distance. Manchester was still alive; she could hear music coming from the bars and clubs in the distance. What was one lost soul in a city of thousands? Bronwen carried on walking until she got to the place where her son's body was found. She made her way to the bench set back behind her and sat down, holding her head in her hands. She sobbed. Slowly, she pulled the candle and the lighter she'd brought out from her pocket. It was going to be hard to light it tonight, the icy wind was sharp and unforgiving. She flicked the lighter near the candle and cupped her hands around it.

'I'm lighting this for you, Son, because you were always the shining light in my life. Wherever you are, I hope you are at peace. I'm not the same without you, Son, I never will be. I've not touched your room yet because it's so hard to say goodbye. I feel like a piece of my heart has gone since you were taken, and I don't even know if I can carry on without you. I've looked at the tablets you know, lined them up ready to end things. But I can't do it, not until I get you justice.' She inhaled deeply and shook her head looking into the flame. 'Ben and Malc miss you too, we all do. You had so much to live for, so many things that you wanted to do, why would anyone ever take that away from you? Why? I don't understand son. What am I missing?'

Bronwen jumped as she heard rustling behind her. She twisted her head back and screwed her eyes up trying to see in the dark, nothing. She stood up and looked all around the area. It was a scary place by anyone's standards and not somewhere where she would normally have felt safe – but since she'd faced the worst, nothing scared her. What more pain could anyone cause her than what she'd already suffered? Two men came walking towards her now, holding hands, kissing each other, full of life.

'Night, love. Get yourself home, it's bloody perishing tonight. You should be at home tucked up in bed.'

Bronwen nodded at them both. 'I am going home now. Enjoy the rest of your evening.' As they danced past her, she smiled to herself. Her son had loved Canal Street. But he'd never told her he was gay – was he still working it out? He'd spoken to her about girls when he was younger, but he'd never brought anyone home – man or woman. And now he never would.

Another man was walking with speed towards her. 'Bloody hell, Bronwen, I knew you would be here. I've been ringing you for ages. What are you doing down here on your own?'

'I just needed to come, Anthony, see with my own eyes where my son met his end. I couldn't sleep so I thought I'd try to come down and talk to him. I even brought a candle, but the pissing wind kept blowing it out. Look at my finger, it's burnt from trying to re-light it.'

Anthony hugged Bronwen and looked deep into her eyes. 'I will stay with you if you want? You're freezing, you can't sit out here alone.'

'No, just take me home. I've said what I needed to say to my boy. I just want to go home now. Anthony, will you come back with me?'

'Of course I will. Bronwen, I know I keep saying it, but I love you with all my heart and I promise you now that as long as I live that I will never hurt you again. If you take me back, I'll spend the rest of my life making things up to you.'

She squeezed his hand. 'One day at a time, Anthony, I can only take one day at a time.'

Chapter Thirty-Three

Bridie was back home after a short stay in hospital. She'd broken her arm and her body was still covered in bruises, but the doctors had said it was a miracle she'd not broken her neck. Bert sat on the edge of the bed and looked over at his wife. 'If you give me the money, I'll do the shopping. I can nip down the market and get us a nice piece of steak each. Just write a list down and I'll start to get ready.'

'If you wait for a bit, I'll get ready and come with you. We can get a taxi there and back. I should be alright.'

'No, you looked after me after my ticker played up, and now it's my turn to look after you. On my life, Bridie, watching you fall down those stairs scared the life out of me, and it's given me a wake-up call. I mean, you do everything for me, cook, clean, wash all my clothes. I've been the luckiest man alive, and I want to pay you back.'

Bridie smiled over at her husband and nodded her head. 'Pass me a pen and piece of paper and I'll do a list of the things that we need. I don't think we need a lot anyway, just a few bits to tide us over.'

Bert watched as she scribbled down the shopping list.

'If you can, get us a couple of vanilla slices from Greggs. I just fancy one with a nice cup of tea.' Bridie finished the list and reached inside her purse and pulled out four ten-pound notes. 'It won't be more than that, but take forty pounds just in case you see something else that you think that we might need. In fact, get four cakes because I think Beryl might be calling in later. She rang me last night and said she was up this way today.'

Bert pulled a face and started to put his jacket on. Beryl was a right gossip and when they were all younger, he'd had a few run-ins with her when she shoved her nose in his business. He swore it was Beryl who'd told Bridie she'd seen him down the bookies after he'd meant to have quit. Bert bent down slightly and kissed the side of his wife's cheek. 'Put a film on and rest. I'll be back soon.'

Bert stepped out of the house and started to walk down the street. A dark car was parked up in the distance. He knew without needing to see through the tinted windows that it was the loan man he'd been swerving all week. The passenger door opened, and Isaac shouted over at Bert, 'Get in, pal, you know what I want so don't piss me about.'

Bert didn't know what to do, it wasn't like he could outrun the younger man; even if he nipped down one of the snickets the car wouldn't fit down.

Isaac's voice got louder. 'I *said* get in, Bert.'

Bert slid slowly into the car, but kept the door open slightly. 'Isaac, the mrs has been in hospital, surely you must have heard that she fell down the stairs?'

'Not arsed, like I said last time, just pay me what you owe me. Two weeks in debt, pay up. What we got for your crap telly only covered the interest.'

Bert patted his jacket pocket and pulled out the cash his wife had just given him. 'I've only got the shopping money. I should have the rest of your money sometime this week, just bear with me until I get the money together.'

Isaac let out a menacing laugh. 'Mate, do I need to send the heavies in again or what?'

Bert swallowed hard. 'No, please. I'll get the extra money together, I will, just give me until the end of the week.'

Isaac snatched the forty pounds out of his hand and shoved it in his shirt pocket. 'I'll have that for now and I'll be expecting another payment before the week is out. My advice is to keep out of the bookies, mate. I have eyes and ears everywhere and they keep telling me you're always in there betting on some fucking donkey. End of the week. Now, piss off out of my car.'

Bert was trying to get out, but Isaac pushed him and he stumbled out of the car. 'End of the week!' Isaac shouted from his car window as he drove past him, 'End of the week.'

Bert dusted himself down and stood looking up at the sky. What the hell was he going to do now? He dug his cold hands in his pocket and trudged towards The Griffin. Somebody would buy him a pint in there, they always did.

Bert stood at the bar and listened as Frank Drury spoke about his plans for his night shift walk around the estate. They clocked Bert and shouted him over. 'Are you having a pint or what, Bert?' He nodded his head and Frank waved his hand over at Alison the barmaid. 'Get Bert a pint, love, and put it on my tab.'

Bert went to join the men. Frank was speaking about the route the men were taking tonight and the times they would be starting. Bert stayed quiet and slowly sipped at his pint. Dane joined in. 'I had a word with Vincent last night and he refused to lift a finger. So, Frankie my boy, when you're out tonight don't bother looking out for his gaff. If he can't be arsed joining us, then we can't be arsed checking on his house. It's only right, isn't it?'

Frank nodded his head and so did Bert. 'He's on another level lately, him. Alison was telling me some of the stuff he was saying to her about his wife, said he freaked her out. Has anyone seen anything of his mrs or what, because as far as I know she was only supposed to be going to see her friend for a few weeks?'

Bert nodded his head. 'That's what Bridie told me – she doesn't think he's right in the head.'

Frank nodded. 'Vincent has some serious shit going on and he's not the same man he was, if you ask me. I'll try and have a chat with him when I see him and give him a shoulder to cry on. It's obvious something's wrong and he might just need someone to talk to. I mean, you never know what people are dealing with under the surface, do you?'

Bert took a large mouthful of his pint. He'd have to go back home now, make up some excuse to his wife where the money had gone. Bert was in a dark, deep hole, and he was going nowhere fast. The truth was creeping up on him every single day and it wouldn't be long before his secret was out.

———

'What do you mean, you fell over and lost the money, Bert?' Bridie was furious when Bert told her his tale.

'I just tripped and landed on my arse. Look at the state of my pants, full of mud they are. I got up to sort myself out and by the time I realised I'd lost the cash, it was nowhere to be seen. I mean, I went back and looked everywhere, but you know what this place is like. Kids will have pocketed that the moment they found it. Anyway, you should be asking me if I'm alright, not about the bloody money I've lost.'

Bridie sat up in bed and looked down at her husband's muddy shoes and pants – he had specks of dark-brown mud on the side of his face too. She wriggled about in the bed and started to get up.

'What the hell are you doing, get back in bed. I'm fine, just a bit shaken that's all.' Bert felt anxious at the thought of Bridie being up and about again – it would only take one little chat with Isaac and it would all be out in the open.

'No, I'm sick of lying in bed. I'm fine and need to get back to normal as soon as possible.' Bridie was a strong woman and, once her mind was made up, there was no telling her. She started to get ready. 'I'm still alive and a broken arm won't stop me living my life. I'm going to go down to the market myself, the fresh air will do me good. And you know me – a bit of local gossip will cure me faster than anything. Give me half an hour down the shops and I'll know everything that's going on.'

Chapter Thirty-Four

Brooke tried Lee's phone again, still no answer. She'd been worried that things were moving too fast, but now she'd not heard from him since he went off on his work trip, the silence seemed strange. She sent him another text message.

```
Give me a ring when you're free. Missing
You. Love Brooke xx
```

She sent the message and sat scrolling through her photographs. A picture of her and Vincent came up and the sadness filled her face and her eyes clouded over. She'd loved her husband with all her heart at one time and no matter how much she tried she could never make him happy, herself happy. That guilt she always felt crept back into her thoughts. It had made her put up with the abuse for years and even now it meant she couldn't put the past behind her.

Brooke stood up and ran her fingers through her hair. It definitely needed a wash, was greasy. She walked out of the room and headed upstairs. She decided she was having a pamper night; would wash her hair, put a face mask on, paint her nails. She flicked the radio on and walked upstairs to run the bath. As she entered the bathroom, she froze. Her heart started beating like a speeding train as she looked at the towels on the handrail. Each of them was folded more neatly than her and Lee ever left them – with military precision. She sprinted out of the bathroom and started to search every room for her husband. Nothing. Brooke eventually sat down on the bed with her phone and rang Amy from the salon. 'He's been in here, Amy. The towels in the bathroom are straight just like he used to put them.' Brooke was almost hysterical.

Amy tried her best to calm her down. 'You need to call the cops, Brooke. Tell them your abusive ex has been in your house. Well, Lee's house.'

Brooke cried down the phone at her. 'Phone the police and say what, the bloody towels are in a straight line, they'll think I'm a bleeding nutter.'

Amy stayed on the phone for a few more minutes to calm her friend down and tell her she was coming over. The call ended and Brooke sat on the bed shaking like a leaf.

Only a few minutes later, Amy walked into the house and hugged Brooke. 'Calm down, will you, calm down. You can't let him get in your head like this.'

'I'm not going loopy, Amy, please tell me I'm not losing the plot. Come upstairs and have a look at the towels. I was fine and I was going to have a pamper night, but this has just freaked me out.'

Amy took her coat off and dropped her black handbag on the floor in the hallway. 'Come on, let's have a look then.'

Brooke went up the stairs first and opened the bathroom door fully. 'Have a look for yourself and then tell me I'm losing it.'

Amy stepped inside the bathroom and looked at the bath towels. 'I'm not being funny, but I don't know what you're going on about.'

Brooke stepped inside the bathroom and she blinked as she looked over at the towel rail. 'It wasn't like that before, they were straight, the same distance at each side of them.'

Amy looked at the towels again – they looked like they'd been slung on the silver rail, no neat folds. She used her soft voice. 'Babes, you have been under a lot of stress lately and maybe it's just your mind playing tricks with you. You need a good night's sleep.'

Brooke was having a panic attack. 'I know what I seen, Amy, please believe me. Maybe I messed them up when I was in shock at seeing them.'

Amy looked around the bathroom and in the mist on the mirror was a smiley face. 'Look at this, you will be telling me Vincent did this too in a minute.'

'He's been in here, Amy. He changed the towels, and he has drawn that smiley face. I'm not fucking potty. He's – what did you call it? – gas-lighting me.'

Amy gripped her by the arm and looked directly in her eyes. 'Breathe, bloody breathe, woman. Come on, let's go back downstairs and sit down for a bit. I've brought a nice bottle of red wine over and we can have a few glasses. It will chill you out and help you sleep.'

Brooke seemed in a daze now, her mind doing overtime; was she imagining all this or what, she started to question herself.

Amy poured two large glasses of wine and passed one to Brooke. 'Here, get that down your neck. I brought you some of my calming pills over too. Just take two of them and they'll take the edge off your anxiety.'

'I need more than pills, Amy. What the hell is happening to me? I'm questioning myself now about what I saw.'

'You're just tired, love. I've been like that when I'm stressed out, I don't know if I'm coming or going.'

'Do you really think that's what it is, Amy? I've scared myself half to death tonight. Maybe I need some counselling or something. I've been through some bad shit lately and I probably need some help coping with it all.'

The tears streamed down Brooke's cheeks and Amy passed her a white tissue. 'Come on, love, dry them eyes up. This is the new you. Remember what you said the other day about getting back to being you, the happy you.'

'And I was until tonight. It was like my life was flashing before my eyes and I couldn't breathe.'

'That's stress for you. When is Lee back home, anyway? No wonder you're feeling scared when you're living here on your own.'

Brooke ran her index finger around her glass and spoke. 'I've texted him a few times, but he's blanked me. I know he said he was in lots of meetings, but a quick text back wouldn't have killed him, would it?'

'I know, give him a ring, see what the score is with him. You don't need gameplaying from a guy when you're just starting out. This should be the honeymoon period.'

Amy's words hit Brooke hard. 'Thanks for coming over here so fast, Amy. If Lee can't be arsed contacting me then it will be his loss. I'm going to start house-hunting tomorrow and get my own place.'

Amy smiled. 'There you go. Panic over, get that drunk and get another glass down your neck. Fuck men, who needs them anyway? Girl power!'

They both raised their glasses in the air and celebrated the choice Brooke was making. As the ruby wine sloshed as they clinked their drinks, neither one of them noticed the figure reflected briefly in the dark glass.

Chapter Thirty-Five

Susan answered the doorbell and took the parcel from the postman. Once the door was closed, she ran upstairs as her mother shouted after her. 'Who was that?'

Susan shouted back to her. 'Oh, it was only the postman with my parcel from Pretty Little Thing.'

'Bloody hell, girls. Stop ordering stuff like there's no tomorrow. Save your money like I keep telling you.'

Susan ignored her mother's comment, motored into her bedroom and locked the door behind her. She threw the box on the bed as if it carried some kind of disease. She walked one way then the other, chewing on her finger-nails. Finally, she sat next to the brown parcel and stared at it. She didn't know what was in it but she knew already where it came from. There was every chance *he'd* touched this box, the same hands that had touched her body without consent. She ripped the box open. A Pandora box fell out onto her knees, and she wasted no time in seeing what was inside. Layer on layer of wrapping – like some twisted game of pass the parcel where you never really wanted the music to stop. Under the final layer of tissue paper there was a silver necklace with a charm. 'I miss you', it read. Susan flung the box and the chain to the end of the bed and sat looking at it with her knees pulled up to her chest. A message on her phone broke the spell and she snatched it up, half-fearing it was Jay, that he was watching her somehow, knowing that she'd got his creepy gift. She reached over and read the text.

Fancy hooking up?

She wasted no time replying.

Yeah, what time and where?

The message was sent, and she sat desperate for a reply. Scully had already told her not to tell Sabrina. This was their secret and he wanted to keep it that way. But word could get out easily if someone saw just the two of them together. Even when she had sat with him in Tavistock Square, all eyes were on her. She could tell the other girls who chilled there were all envious of her. Duffy had changed his tune too. He'd only ever texted her at weekends before – and only when he wanted a quick hook-up – but now he was messaging her every day trying to get a date. But Susan only had eyes for Scully now; they had connected, spoken all night long on the square and even shared a kiss. Scully made her feel safe, protected. She felt like she could tell him anything and he wouldn't judge her. After all, he'd been to jail, committed crimes since he was a teenager, so how could he condemn her. Maybe she would tell him about what happened to her. He would fix it, sort out all the bad men who were there that night.

She smiled as his reply came through – a time and place to meet. Now she had to get an outfit together and make sure she looked her best. Scully was a prize catch for sure and now she had him interested in her, she wasn't letting him go for love nor money. Her phone started ringing – Sabrina's name was flashing on the screen. She panicked, said she'd go and watch a film with her tonight. What would she tell Sabrina about going to the cinema; she hated letting anyone down. Sometimes it was best to say nothing, she figured, and ignored the call.

Another message pinged. Scully. He was keen. Knowing he had her back made adrenaline race through her. She looked at the necklace she'd thrown down on the bed. Maybe she could turn this to her advantage. She opened her bedside cabinet and placed the new necklace into her drawer. She slammed it shut and started to send a message through the app to Jay.

Thanks for the gift, but it will take more than that to keep my mouth shut about what happened that night. I want a pair of train- ers: size five Nike Air Jordans.

She sent the message before she lost her nerve.

Susan sat in Scully's black GTI Golf later that night and listened to the tunes playing; the bass was pumping and anyone who walked past the car looked at them both. Scully looked mint tonight in his black tracksuit. She could smell his Savage aftershave and she couldn't stop telling him how good he smelt. He passed her the bottle of brandy. Susan had been drinking for hours now and felt the heat in her veins. She looked over at him and smiled. 'If someone had hurt me, would you help me?'

He didn't even look at her, just kept his eyes in front of him. 'Goes without saying.'

Susan took a breath. 'I need someone taking down. I'm not proud of what happened, but I need you to help me get those men off the streets and make sure they never put anyone else through what I've been through.'

Scully was alert, facing her now as she started to tell him all about what she'd been doing, the words flooding out. After she finished, she dropped her head. 'I'm not proud of what I've done, I was just after making some extra money. Sabrina told me it didn't feel right, but I just ignored her and carried on.'

Scully smashed his clenched fist onto the steering wheel and growled over at her. 'What? My fucking sister was there too? I'll do every one of them in. I'll cut their balls off, the dirty twats.'

Susan realised she'd just dropped her best friend in it too and tried to backpedal. 'They never touched Sabrina, she was only there looking out for me. And she did – she pulled a knife out and she was going to stab them up. If it wasn't for her coming in it could have been a lot worse.'

Scully was fuming. 'So how does this Jay guy contact you?' Susan came clean about the rest of the story; the text messages, the gift.

Scully scoffed. 'Nice one. I think you've got the nonce running scared. But he owes you more than a fucking pair of trainers. Tell him you want a couple of grand to keep your mouth shut otherwise you will go to the police. It's easy money for us both, isn't it?'

Susan wasn't sure if she heard him right, but nodded her head. She'd had enough of making money this way – she just wanted him scared off, wanted him to feel as frightened as she had. 'I was thinking I could set up a meeting and you could show up and tell him what's what – threaten to give him a good arse-kicking if he comes anywhere near me again.'

'An arse-kicking. For shagging young girls? I would do more than that, I'd stab the fucker up. But...' He paused. 'Set it up. I'll get a few of the lads involved and we'll sling him in the boot of the car and take him for a ride somewhere.'

Susan gulped. She wasn't sure what she'd started. But Scully had her back, and that felt good enough to shut down the voices in her head saying she'd just pulled a pin on a grenade.

Susan kissed Scully passionately just before he dropped her off at the end of the street. He gripped her face and looked deep into her eyes. 'You don't worry about a thing anymore. You just sort out that meeting and I'll take care of the rest. Remember, tell him you want money to buy your silence. He'll shit himself and pay up. This could be a good little earner for us, Susie my girl. Remember, tell nobody nothing.'

Susan got out of the car and started to make her way down the street towards her house. She was nearly home when she looked at the wasteland at the back of the estate. There was a shadow of someone pacing back and forth.

Her heart was pounding as she started to run towards her house. After all, there was still a murderer on the loose.

Susan stepped inside the house and kicked her shoes off. Her mother stood facing her. She examined every inch of her. 'Have you been drinking?'

Susan wobbled slightly. 'Wow, Mam, just leave me alone, will you? I've just walked in through the door and you're pecking my head.'

'Don't you bleeding talk to me like that, you cheeky cow. Whilst you are living under my roof then you do as I say and drinking and rat-arsed is not what I want for my daughters.'

Susan held the rail to go upstairs and turned back to reply. 'Moan, moan, moan, that's all you do, woman. Give it a break, will you? I'm going to bed.' Before her mother could get another word in, Susan was up the stairs.

Susan lay in bed and looked out at the silver moonlight shining into her room. She pulled the duvet up and tucked it tightly under her chin. The room was spinning now and she felt sick. Her phone beeped and she had to struggle to focus on the words. Jay.

He'd agreed to send her the trainers, but now she had to up her game and get some money out of this guy if she wanted to keep Scully on side. But she wasn't ready to ask for money yet, no, she'd wait for the trainers to arrive and then she would drop the bombshell on this pervert. She replied to the message to keep him sweet. 'Thank you.' If he was ever going to agree to meeting her, she had to be nice, let him think he had her back in his grip, then Scully could swoop in.

Chapter Thirty-Six

Bert scurried along the back of the houses in the pitch black, listening to animals darting into the muddy marshland. If he was spotted by anyone, he'd tell them he'd heard a noise and he was checking it out. He was everyone's idea of a law-abiding citizen after all, and he wanted to show he was doing his part to help the community. In truth he was struggling to walk tonight, his arthritis playing up, his body still sore from where Isaac had shoved him out of his car. He was dressed in black with a dark-navy bobble hat that Bridie had bought him for when he went fishing. Before he'd pawned all his fishing gear for money to spend at the bookies. His black leather gloves looked too big for his hands, but they'd have to do. Bridie had been snoring her head off when he'd left her and had been for the last few hours. He'd watched and waited; he was a night owl at the best of times, always up until the early hours watching his boxsets, history channels. And tonight, with a mission to complete, he wouldn't have slept a wink anyway.

Bert looked back at his house and up at his bedroom window. How the hell had he ended up like this? He never, ever thought that he would have to rob houses again in his life. When he was a teenager, he'd often turn a house over with his mates. They were all skint back then and he had had to try and help his mother put food on the table somehow. He was agile in those days, quick, in and out like a rat up a drainpipe. Plus, he had his mates by his side to back him up, not working alone like he was doing now. But he had to stop the loan shark coming to his front door again. He had no other options. His feet crunched over the branches as he walked, the sound of scuttling making him flinch. Bloody rats, they were all over the place.

Bert looked at a house at the end of the fields. It was a new family who had moved onto the Manor estate and up to now nobody knew a lot about them except they travelled a lot. Bert's head hung down low as he picked up speed towards the back garden. The adrenaline was pumping around his body, head in the game.

Bert found the back gate was already open and he quickly clocked a kitchen window that was left slightly ajar. Thank God for that, he'd only just healed from breaking the last window. And less damage meant less noise. It made him feel slightly better – he was teaching these folk a lesson they wouldn't forget. What did these idiots expect, not securing their property when they were away from home? Probably had more money than sense. Their loss would be his gain. In he went. For an old man he could still move quickly when he wanted to.

Once Bert was inside, he pulled his slim torch from his inside pocket and shone it around the kitchen. Nothing of any value here. He checked through the front window and spotted there were no cars outside. His thinking was right, this family must have been on holiday. He hated confrontation so he was relieved he could do this without a fight. Bert knew most likely that anything valuable in this house would be kept upstairs – hidden away under the mattress or deep inside some drawers. He'd been in the game before and knew all the secret hiding places people would stash anything of value. Bridie was the same, always hiding money in her bedding box, in the airing cupboard.

He crept up the stairs, hoping there would be no alarms or cameras to disturb. His breathing had quickened, beads of sweat on his forehead. Bert proceeded with caution. Slowly, he edged into the bedroom – empty as he'd hoped. This was going to be a doddle and he started to relax. He pulled drawers open, dragged the mattress from the bed. Where the hell was the cash? The jewellery? He walked over to an ottoman full of bed linen and yanked the lid open. Bingo, beneath the sheets were wads of cash. He knew most of the people who lived on the Manor either didn't trust banks – or couldn't put their dirty money in those kind of accounts. With haste he picked up the bundles of money and stashed it straight inside his coat pocket. This was enough to keep Isaac off his back. Bert started to walk towards the bedroom door but stopped dead in his track. Maybe there were more goods to take? He turned back around and pulled more drawers open. Get himself a little nest egg. Shining the yellow light down in front of him, he found what he was looking for. This was a good graft; a few rings, earrings, and a bracelet. It was time to go.

Bert opened the back door and headed back out into the night with his hat pulled down firmly. He turned to close the door behind him when he was rugby tackled to the ground.

'Take the thieving bastard down, Frank, hold him while I get a grip of him.' Bert was like a sack of spuds. He tried wriggling free, but he was going nowhere fast. Dane dug his knee into his chest as he rolled him on his front and stared down at him. 'You're going nowhere, pal. We've been onto you for weeks. You think you can rob decent working people and get away with it, do you?'

Bert was struggling for breath as Frank rummaged through his pocket. He pulled the cash out and held it up in front of him. 'Thieving bastard,' he hissed as he carried on searching him.

Dane pulled his torch from his pocket and shone it down on the thief's face. His jaw hung low, eyes wide open. 'Bert, what the fuck?'

Frank stood up. He looked at the money and the jewellery on the floor and then back at Dane. 'Bert's the bloody thief?'

There was a silence for a few seconds before the truth of the matter hit Dane full on. He moved away from the old man like he was diseased. Bert rolled on his side to sit up straight, coughing and spluttering. 'Lads, I was desperate, the loan man was hammering at my door, they threatened to take everything that I own, anything of value. I was at my wits' end, had nowhere else to turn.'

Frank walked around in a circle. 'So it's been you all along?'

Bert swallowed hard and his eyes clouded over, crocodile tears but he was giving a good show. He snivelled. 'I'm sorry, I feel so ashamed. I'm a good man. You both know me and know I must have been desperate to do what I've done.'

Dane bit down hard on his lip. Bert was a mate, a regular in his pub. Frank could see he was torn, and he held nothing back. 'So, you robbed your own house, took Bridie's jewellery, let us all buy you a new television and Ring doorbell and said fuck all?'

Bert hung his head low like a brick was tied around his neck and shook his head slowly.

Dane urged him to answer. 'Bert, is that true?'

The old man nodded his head, eyes still looking at the ground. 'Frank's right.'

Dane's voice was raised. 'You silly old bastard. What the hell were you thinking? That's your bleeding wife. How could you do that to her? That poor woman has been out of her mind with worry thinking some louts have been in her house when all along it was you. Out of fucking order, Bert, bang out of order.'

Frank stood back with both hands on his hips. There was no way he was covering this up. Friend or no friend, the man was a thief. Preying on all his friends, hard-working people. His chest expanded and his nostrils flared. 'He's getting dragged to the police station. I know he says he's one of us, but don't fucking rob from your own. We all piss in the same pot, Bert, we all struggle to make ends meet.'

Dane pulled Frank aside to have a quiet word. 'We can't shop him in, he's an old man. He would never survive in the nick, he'd probably have another bloody heart attack or something. Can't we think of something else, it doesn't sit right with me grassing him up.'

Frank was sticking to his guns. 'No, Dane. I've not slept properly for weeks, neither has the mrs. This scum-bag has been prowling the streets looking to earn money – and for what? Gambling debts. He could have come to any of us and asked for help, but he chose to rob from us instead. I have no pity for him, pal, my mind is made up. You ring the police, or I will?'

Dane was put on the spot, looking over his shoulder at Bert. The man looked like butter wouldn't melt in his mouth, but the damage had already been done. This had been a crime-free community a few months ago and they were all at risk if they let it carry on the way it had been. Frank pulled out his mobile and held it to his ear. 'Police please.'

Bert broke down in tears when the dibble pulled up. It took two officers to pull him up from the floor. Bert looked over at Dane and Frank and shook his head. 'I thought you were my friends; friends don't blow you up.'

Frank was right back at him. 'And friends don't bleeding rob from each other, do they, Bert?'

The arresting officers couldn't hide their surprise. 'Bloody hell, and here was us thinking it was something to do with the kids on Tavistock Square and instead we should have been checking out old folks' homes. We'll need you two both in for formal statements in the morning.'

Dane grimaced. He wasn't usually one to call in the coppers unless he had to and he was feeling bad. Although he knew he'd done the right thing it still didn't sit right with him. 'I'd better go and break the news to Bridie, hadn't I? She'll be bloody heartbroken when she knows her old man is the one who's been robbing everyone, robbing her.'

Frank rolled his eyes and then his expression changed. 'I bet he had something to do with that fall that she had. I wonder if he was trying to do her in for the insurance money or something, because, let's face it, you hear about stuff like this on the news every day. Think about it, it would have been the answer to all his problems.'

'No way, Frank. He loves the bones of Bridie, been with her since he was a teenager.'

'Just saying, pal, you never know the day, do you?' The two men watched the police car drive off with Bert in the back of it, blue flashing lights but no siren. 'Do you want me to come to Bridie's with you or what, Dane? It's not fair that you should have to go on your Jacks.'

'Do you mind? It only feels like yesterday I had to wake her when Bert collapsed. She'll think he's carked it when she sees my face. Though what we've got to tell her is almost as bad. It will break my heart watching her face when she knows. Bridie is as straight as they come and even when the shoplifters are in the boozer selling all the knock-off stuff, she never buys it. I think she's a church-goer too, every Sunday she goes to Mass.'

'Well, she better start praying for her husband then and hope he mends his ways. We'll have to stress to her that we don't think any different of her. It was her husband who was the thief, not her.'

'Come on then, before I lose my bottle. Let's get this over and done with.' Bridie's house was in complete darkness as Frank and Dane walked down the garden path. Frank rapped the letterbox and stood back from the front door looking up at the top window, watching for any movement. Dane agreed that if she didn't answer on the next knock, then they would leave her until the morning. He knew how hard it had been to wake her after Bert's heart attack. But the curtains were moving at the top window, a face appearing.

'Bleeding hell, do you know what time it is? People are sleeping you know,' Bridie called down.

'It's only us, Bridie, Dane and Frank. We need a word with you.'

Her voice faltered. 'Is it Bert? Is he OK? He's not in the 'ozzy again, is he? Hold on, I'm coming down.'

Dane sighed and looked over at Frank. 'I'm not looking forward to this. Are you doing the talking or me?'

Frank shrugged and Dane knew it was down to him.

Bridie looked like she'd been dragged through a hedge as she opened the door. Her hair was wild, her face pale, her quilted powder-blue dressing gown on and matching slippers edged in cream fur couldn't hide the panic that was coming off her in waves. Dane swallowed hard and looked at her for a few seconds without speaking.

Bridie was never one to hold anything back and she growled at them both. 'Bleeding hell, has the cat got your tongue or what, spit it out – what's happened to my Bert? He was getting better – he's been taking his pills. Tell me what's happened?'

'It's not his heart, Bridie. Can we come in for a minute though? I think you might need to sit down for this.'

She studied his face. 'If he's been gambling again, you can both piss off and you can tell him the same from me. He was on his last legs and if he's been daft enough to play bloody poker again then it's his problem not mine.'

Dane edged in through the front door and followed her into the living room. She flicked the small lamp on and stood looking at them both with her arms folded tightly. 'Spit it out then.'

Dane took the main stage. 'Bridie, there is no easy way to say this, so I'm just going to say it. We've caught the thief. Me and Frank were on guard tonight and we caught him red-handed.'

Bridie perched in the armchair. 'Well, that's a bloody relief. I'll tell you something for nothing. I've not been able to rest properly knowing that someone is lurking in the neighbourhood while we sleep. I hope the police have been informed? I know you were all up for this vigilante stuff but the police have a job to do. Have you phoned them?'

'They have, Bridie, we're doing this by the book,' added Frank.

'Was Bert on one of your patrols then? Daft bugger should know better in his condition. But he's been on edge since the robbery. It's a good job he was with you boys because he said he was going to throttle them.'

Here it was, the bombshell. Dane cringed as the words fired out from his mouth, no more pussyfooting around. 'It was, Bert, we caught him red-handed and he admitted everything.'

There was silence. Bridie looked like he'd spoken in Latin for all the sense it had made. 'Can you say that again?' she said as she stuck her index finger down her lughole.

'It was Bert, Bridie. He's the thief. We caught him down the road, coming out of the new couple's house who've just moved in. He had money and jewellery stashed in his pockets.'

Bridie looked at Dane and then Frank and then Dane again. 'Stop pissing about, is this a wind-up?' Bridie stared at them and, as the silence told her all she need to know, her eyes flooded with tears.

Frank went over to her and hugged her. 'We were shocked too. He's the last person we expected to find tonight. I don't know what to say, only I'm sorry.'

Dane seconded that and hugged her too. She lifted her head up and held a stiff upper lip. 'Please go. I want to be by myself.'

Frank didn't need telling twice; he was already making his way towards the front door. Dane followed. 'Bert needs to tell you everything, Bridie. It's not our place to tell you what's been going on. He's down the station, but I'm sure he'll call when he can.'

'Just leave,' she repeated with a heavy heart.

Bridie locked the front door behind them both and trudged back into the living room to turn the lamp off. As she closed the door behind her she looked like the world was on her shoulders. The shame of it all. She was already imagining what people would say. Everyone whispering behind her back when she walked past them in the street. People judging her, calling her names, and all because her husband couldn't say no to a wager. Bridie went back to bed and pulled the duvet back over her body. She knew sleep wouldn't come so she gave in and sobbed her heart out. Then the penny dropped – it was him who stole her jewellery, him who took her television and now she was thinking about it, was it him who pushed her down the stairs when she was close to finding out the truth? All the sadness left body, and she sat up as if boiling hot water had been flung at her. Anger poured in; he'd promised her that his crime days were over, told her he would turn over a new leaf when they bought this house on the Manor estate, a fresh start, respectable. But it was clear. He'd lied to her, betrayed her and her trust. He could rot in jail for all she cared. She was washing her hands of him once and for all. 'Fool me once, shame on you,' she muttered. 'Fool me twice, shame on me.'

Chapter Thirty-Seven

Scully looked down at Susan's trainers. 'So, have you told him you want some money from him as well?'

She twisted her trainers one way then another, admiring her new sneaks. 'Yeah. I said that I would need more than a pair of trainers to keep my mouth shut, but I'm willing to keep quiet for a grand. I told him I would meet him and once he handed the money over then it would be forgotten about.'

'Dandy, you did well.'

Susan felt a glow at gaining his approval. This was the hardest bloke around and he was pleased with her. 'It's because of you, you know. You make me feel safe, Scully. I can't explain it, it took a lot for me to confide in you about what happened to me. Some other guys would have kicked me to the kerb for going on that website.'

He bent his head slightly and kissed the top of her head without meeting her gaze. 'Just keep that sexy mouth of yours shut and we'll both be on a good little earner. Say nish to our kid too. Sabrina will go sick if she knows I'm boning her best mate.'

'Boning?' she repeated. This was hardly the big romance she'd been playing out in her head.

'Well, you know what I mean. I just say it how it is sometimes and don't think about stuff before I put my mouth in gear.'

She pulled away from him. This guy was hot as hell, but if he was just using her for sex then he could do one. 'If I'm just a casual thing, then say it how it is. I want us to be exclusive.'

He could see she was upset and backpedalled. 'Wow, touchy. You might as well know I'm not into all that soppy shit. You'll get used to it after a bit – but if you don't like it you can do one now. We've slept together right, so in my eyes we're boyfriend and girlfriend, but that stays between us. I don't want every fucker round here knowing my business. I'm not going to be getting his and hers tattoos after one shag. Like I've said to you before, I'm a lone wolf and tell nobody nothing about what I get up to. Mates, women, even me mam – I tell people what I choose and nothing more. Being in prison does that to you; you learn to trust nobody and always keep your cards close to your chest. I've had birds in the past who've done the dirty on me, and I have to make sure you're the one before I start shouting it from the rooftops.'

Susan weighed his words. Was he sincere or just giving her a line? Scully lit a spliff up and took a long, hard drag of it before he passed it over to Susan.

'So, let me get the facts right. Emma, your big sister, is on OnlyFans too and she's raking it in?'

'Yeah, she's smashing it. I bet she's earning four or five hundred quid a night now. All she does is tease them and they are gagging for it; paying daft money to get a blimp of her tits and all that.'

Scully sat and tickled the end of his chin. 'So, you was earning good money too?'

'Yes, I didn't have as many followers as my sister, but I was still getting around three hundred quid a night on a good day.' She was relieved that he sounded impressed rather than appalled by what she'd done.

Scully leaned over and kissed her, stroking her cheeks softly as he spoke. 'I could look after you if you wanted to carry on doing it. I mean, make sure you never got yourself in a situation again. Think about it, we could both earn some decent money. I'm not that kind of guy either, who gets jealous. It's a bit of a turn-on for me that men are paying to get a blimp of you, if I'm being honest. They get to look, but I get to touch.'

Susan passed the spliff back over to him. This guy really cared about her, didn't he? He was like a modern-day knight in shining armour – respecting her, protecting her, so what if he'd done some bad stuff in the past – he was a man of action. 'I'm not sure. What happened freaked me out and I swore to myself I would never do it again.'

'That was then, this is now, and you have me by your side now making sure everything is kosher. If one of them pricks steps out of line, I'll fucking rip their head off and shit down their neck.'

She winced. He might not sound like a fairytale, but she believed him that he would protect her. 'Just let's get the money from Jay first and then we can talk about it again. Thanks, Scully, you really do care, don't you?'

'You bet,' he whispered into her ear.

Scully dropped Susan off at the end of the road and kissed her goodnight. He squeezed her arse as she started to get out of the car. 'Make sure this Jay guy doesn't back out. Keep him sweet and make sure he turns up.'

'I will, have faith in me and my powers,' she pouted as she walked up her garden path.

Scully sat watching Susan walk away and smirked to himself as he pulled his phone out of his pocket to make a call.

'Hiya, babes. I'll be there in twenty minutes, I just had some stuff to sort out with the lads. Do me a favour and run the bath for me? I've been working my balls off tonight and need to chill. I'll tell you about it soon enough. All I can say for now is get your bikini ready, we will be going on holiday soon if this job pays off. Love ya, see you soon.'

The call ended and Scully flicked the ignition. The tunes were pumping and 'Overseas' by D block Europe played at full pelt. He nodded his head as he sang along to the tune. This was going to be like taking candy from a baby. Easy money.

Susan said goodnight to her parents and went upstairs. She was humming a song and floating on air. She'd never felt like this before – like she was wearing armour or had superpowers. This must be love. She'd heard her friends talking about this feeling and the more she thought about it, the more she was convinced she was head over heels for Scully. Because all the signs were there, weren't they? He was on her mind every second of every day since they'd met. He was her last thought at night and her first thought when she woke up in the morning. And he was already protecting her, making sure she was safe, thinking about the future. She would marry him tomorrow if he asked her, spend the rest of her life with him, have his children. So what, he'd been to jail; her mam and dad would understand when she told them that was all in his past. And how open-minded was it that he would look after her when she was online talking to other guys? He was one in a million for sure. The only problem was that he was her best friend's brother. She never kept any secrets from Sabrina ever, but this was something she had to keep her mouth shut about. There was no way she was messing this up. Susan dragged the duvet over her shoulders and snuggled down for the night. She looked at her mobile and sent a message.

Thanks for being there for me. Love ya. Sue xxx

She looked at the message and read it a few times. She was debating writing more, opening up and telling him how she saw their future. No, she'd save something for their next date. She pressed the send button and held her phone close to her heart. Life was good again. She was back on track.

Chapter Thirty-Eight

Lee could hear noises outside the door. He jumped up and banged his fist on it. 'Can anybody hear me? Help.' He listened carefully, voices getting louder outside.

A reply, a kid's voice. 'Who are you?'

Lee nearly collapsed, he was weak, tired, dead on his feet. 'Listen, whoever you are go and get help, ring the police and tell them some nutter kidnapped me and banged me up in here. I'm hurt too. Please, if you do this, I'll make sure you get a reward.' No reply. He repeated himself and this time he got a response.

'My dad will go sick if he knows I've been chilling in the warehouse. I'll be grounded for months.'

Lee's voice was desperate, clutching at any reason he could think of. 'Kid, just ring the police and tell them there is a man trapped here. You've got a phone, right? You don't have to give your name or anything.'

'But what about the reward, how will I get that?' *For crying out loud.* 'Tell me how to find you and I'll make sure you and your mate get a hundred pound each, but be quick. The man who put me in here is very dangerous and he could come back at any time. I'm protecting you as much as me by telling you this.'

A reply. 'Right, we'll ring the dibble but as soon as you get out, we want the money. We will shove the address under the door to send the money to.'

'Yeah cool, just hurry up.' Lee couldn't imagine what Vince would do if he came back and found these kids.

A few minutes passed and a scruffy piece of damp paper, an old receipt, was rammed under the door with a name and address scribbled on it. He clutched at it like it was a golden ticket. 'I've got it now and I promise you I'll pay the money, but please go now, straight away, and ring the police. Tell them exactly where I am and tell them I'm hurt, say you think I maybe dying, that should get them here faster.'

'Right, we're going now!' the youth shouted back. Lee's legs buckled from underneath him. The clock was ticking now and he said a quick prayer that this ordeal would be over soon.

Bert dropped his head onto the table of the shabby police interview room and his voice trembled as he admitted what he'd done. The shame of it all was too much for him and he had to keep taking breaks from questioning to steady his voice. The duty solicitor shook his head as he heard the story unfold. Bert lifted his head up. 'I need to tell you something too. It's been playing on my mind, but I've not been able to tell anyone until now. The other house that I robbed was my neighbours', Vincent and Brooke's. She's been gone for ages now. My wife always said there was something fishy going on behind closed doors with the two of them. Anyway, when I broke into their house, I saw something that didn't seem right – a board with Post-it notes spread across it. It was sort of like a mission; Brooke's name and someone called Lee too. It looked like the kind of messed-up stuff you see on those true crime documentaries. If I was taking a guess at it, it looks like Vincent was planning on doing his other half in. Can you check it out, just make sure Brooke is alright. If I'm clearing my conscience then you may as well know that too.'

The officer scribbled something down and took the address of the couple. Once he'd finished, he passed it to his workmate and whispered something to him before he left. 'Thanks for that, Mr Hammond, but let's get back to you. I know you've admitted more than three burglaries. Is there anything else you would like to tell me?'

Bert sat looking at his hands. Then he glanced over at his legal representative and shook his head. 'No, that's the lot. Does my wife know where I am and what I've done?'

The detective nodded his head. 'Yes, I'm afraid she does. We had a warrant to search the house in the early hours of this morning so I'm sure she will know where you are.'

Bert closed his eyes and shook his head. 'She'll never forgive me for this. I've let her down again, let myself down. She's always been by my side through thick and thin and she told me time and time again that if I ever got on the wrong side of the law again, she would wash her hands of me.'

The police officer knew what he was going to say next would hit home with Bert. 'I can inform you that we asked your wife whether if you were granted bail you could go back to your home but she refused point blank.'

'So what does that mean, I can't bloody go home?'

His solicitor coughed to clear his throat, he had to explain this further. 'Without a bail address you are snookered. Unless you can give us the details of someone who would be willing to let you live there for a while.'

In his outrage, Bert had forgotten about his crime and was up in arms. 'It's my bleeding house too. She can't tell me I can't go back there. Where does she expect me to go? I'll have a word with her and make her see some bloody sense. I'm entitled to a phone call, aren't I?'

The police officer spun his black Biro around in his fingers. 'Your wife has also lodged a request for a restraining order too. I can't tell you more, but I can state that she felt her safety was at risk in your company.'

Bert smashed his fist down on the table causing his glass of water to spill. 'Don't be silly. Look at me – I'm a bleeding pensioner. She's just saying that because she's angry at me. Just let me speak to her and I'll put her straight.'

The officer spoke in a stern tone. 'Sir, these are serious allegations and if the CPS decide to give you bail then you will have to go into a bail hostel if you have nowhere else to go. I must remind you that the crimes of breaking and entering and burglary are very serious, and you'll be lucky to escape a jail sentence. Even if your cooperation is taken into account. If, that is, you've told us everything.'

Bert gulped and sat cracking his knuckles. 'I'm an old man, I have a dicky heart and I have high blood pressure too. I can't go to jail. I wouldn't last a minute.'

Time moved differently when you were stuck in a cell, and it felt like forever until Bert's initial hearing. But he'd been looked on favourably for pleading guilty, and his bail application was granted – Bert had stood at the charge desk and the duty officer read out everything that he'd been charged with, including his bail conditions. He wasn't allowed anywhere near the Manor estate or his wife, and he had to be at the bail hostel by 8pm every night. Bert signed the document and slid the pen back over to the officer. 'I'm not a bad man, I just got myself into debts and couldn't see a way out, pal.'

'If I had a pound for every person who's stood there and told me that, I would be a rich man and could retire from this job. All I can say is that crime never pays, ever, and we always end up catching you.'

Bert folded his charge sheet neatly and placed it in his jacket pocket. 'How am I going to get to this hostel place, I've not got a carrot to pay for the bus or a taxi?'

'Afraid I can't help you there, sir.'

Bert took his property bag, pulled his shoelaces out and started to thread them back into his shoes. It looked like he was getting there on foot. A big, fat salty tear fell from his eye and landed on the floor near his feet. He'd messed up big time and he knew it. He'd always been able to pull things out of the bag before. But he'd come to the end of the road. That day with Bridie when he'd pushed her – he'd known then that you don't come back from something like that. Even if no one could prove anything, how could he ever look himself in the eye again? He'd lost it all. Bert trudged out from the police station and looked up at the night sky. Looking up at the silver stars he whispered under his breath. 'I'm sorry, Bridie, sorry to everyone who I have hurt.' He zipped his coat up and looked down at the address on the piece of paper held tightly in his hand. It would take him over an hour to get to this place. He had nobody to ring to help him, nobody who would come rushing to his side. Bert had never felt more alone than this moment in all his life. Alone and scared.

Chapter Thirty-Nine

Anthony plugged the iPhone in to charge it up. He'd not given it to the police yet after Bronwen persuading him not to. Ben wasn't a bad kid, she knew that. He'd been a good friend to her son and she didn't want him to ruin his life by landing him with a caution or a record. She'd told him she felt she was looking out for Matthew by looking out for his mates. And Anthony just wanted his own name cleared – and if the phone helped that, then he had no beef with Ben. Bronwen had been upstairs in bed for at least an hour, but he wouldn't be able to rest until he'd got into this phone. The start-up screen flashed up on the phone, but it kept getting stuck at this stage and never starting up. He'd bought a new charger today and hoped this time was the charm. Anthony lifted his head as he heard the dog whining. He whistled. 'Come on, lad, I'll take you out for a wee while this bleeding phone starts up.'

His four-legged friend dashed to his side. Anthony grabbed his fags and stood with the back door open as

Scooby ran about sniffing and looking for his ball. It was cold tonight, winter had truly kicked in; icy wind, rain that felt more like hail and trees blowing in the distance. Anthony shivered and whistled for Scooby. 'Come on, lad, it's bloody freezing out here, I'm freezing my balls off.' The dog ran straight in and circled near his legs, rubbing its cold fur up and down his legs. Anthony chuckled and moved the dog away. 'Go and get in your basket.'

Scooby knew the word basket and headed straight to it. Anthony flicked his cig dimp into the drain at the back door. He'd clean the drain tomorrow, first thing when he got up. Bronwen hated that he never picked up his cigarette dimps and he wanted to keep her sweet, nothing else stressing her out.

Anthony returned to the sofa and reached for the iPhone. Finally, it had sprung to life. Bron had told him Matthew's code and the anonymous black screen changed into a riot of colour. Sadness filled his eyes as he scrolled through the photographs stored there. There were great memories on this phone, alongside plenty of photos that he'd never seen before. Bronwen would love these. Great memories captured of times when they were all happy and looking forward to life. As he stared at a snap of Matthew, he couldn't hold the tears back. 'Mate, what the hell happened to you? I know we had our ups and downs, but you were a good lad and I loved you like my own.'

Scooby could sense something was wrong and came to Anthony's side, rubbing his head against his hand. He jumped up on the sofa and snuggled down next to Anthony. Bronwen would have had kittens if she knew the dog was on the sofa, but this was their little secret when she went to bed. Anthony tickled Scooby and showed the photograph to him. 'I bet you miss him too, don't you, lad.' The dog licked the screen. Anthony carried on flicking through the snaps but stopped dead in his tracks when he came to a certain photograph. He sat up straight and moved the dog from his lap. He dragged his finger over the picture to enlarge it. He gulped and quickly went through every other picture stored on the phone, getting increasingly flustered. To confirm his suspicions, next, he went through every message.

'Fucking no way,' he whispered under his breath. 'Surely not.'

Chapter Forty

Brooke lay in bed reading. It calmed her down, helped her relax. She was sure tonight was the evening Lee had said he'd be back – before he'd started ghosting her. But he had to come home at some point – even if it was just to give her marching orders. Until then, she needed to keep her mind busy, stop herself imagining Vincent was around every corner or in the house rearranging stuff. The book was a welcome escape and she forgot about her own fear for a while as she read about a woman who had the odds against her and pulled through. She only had a few chapters left to read and already she had decided she couldn't go to sleep not knowing what happened next. That was a sign of a good book, wasn't it? Brooke had only just got the habit and after reading a novel Amy had given her, she was hooked. Every time she was in Asda she always grabbed a new release to add to her shopping list. Being lost in a story was the only time she wasn't looking over her shoulder. Brooke reached over now and picked up her glass of wine. There was only a mouthful left and there was no point leaving it. She had to admit that helped numb her fears as well. Brooke was engrossed in the plot and even the wind howling outside didn't bother her.

Brooke finished her novel now and closed the book, leaving it on her chest. The main character had found her Mr Right after years of toxic relationships. The woman from the story had given Brooke hope – perhaps there was a happy ending waiting for her somewhere. But tonight her eyes were heavy. She remembered a quote she'd read from the book and whispered it under her breath before she fell asleep. 'If you do what you've always done, then you'll get what you've always got.' Change, she had to believe in change.

It was nearly three o'clock in the morning and the rain was still hammering against the windowpanes when Vincent crept into the bedroom. For a big guy, he could move quietly, and the sound of the storm outside gave him the cover he needed.

He stood at the bedside with a can of petrol held in his hand. Carefully he upended the can, the open spout pushed into the blankets so it silently seeped all over the sheets, soaking into the mattress and only as the can emptied, still pressed into the sheets, did the heavy smell of the fumes start to escape. He covered his mouth with his scarf as he shook every last drop onto the bed. He placed the petrol can silently on the floor before he sat on the edge of the bed. Gently, more gently than he had touched her for years, he reached out and touched the top of Brooke's shoulder.

'Wakey, wakey, wifey.' He never took his eyes from her, waiting for the moment she realised it was him and not her lover who was in bed with her. 'Brooke. Come on, sweetie-pie, open those eyes.'

Brooke stirred slightly, still half asleep, mumbling. 'Lee, I wasn't sure if you were coming home tonight. Get in next to me I'm freezing, snuggle up.'

A switch flicked in Vincent's head and he gripped her by the throat and dragged her up, so he was nose to nose with her. 'You slag, did you think you could walk away from me and that was it? No, no, no. It doesn't work like that.'

Brooke was wide awake now, filled with fear as his chilling words sank into her ears. She swallowed hard, the tang of the petrol attacking her senses, every inch of her body shaking with fear.

Brooke remembered the book she'd just read and how the woman found her inner strength. 'Just go, Vincent, I've got nothing to say to you. We're done. We have been for a long time.'

She pulled away from him, but he held firm.

'I've been thinking about this moment for a while now and I've planned each and every manoeuvre. I bet you're wondering where lover boy is, aren't you?'

She screamed at the top of her voice, wriggling, trying to get his dirty, mucky hands from her body while looking around to see where the smell of fuel was coming from.

She saw the fuel can, thinking he'd come to torch the place. Brooke had a look of terror in her eyes as he continued. 'No phone calls from him, no text messages. Strange, isn't it?'

'What have you done with him? I swear if you've so much as hurt one hair on his body I will stick a knife in you myself. You're washed up, Vince. A failed soldier, a failed husband.'

'Sssh, baby girl. Your words can't hurt me now. Stop worrying about him. I've been here for weeks, watching you. The towels, the cups, you know that was me, don't you? I like to send you little signals, play with your mind like you've played with mine.'

Brooke knew she couldn't break free, she had to try something else. Her voice was softer now, the one she used when she wanted him to calm down. 'Please just go, Vince. You can go and find happiness somewhere else with someone who has not hurt you like I have.'

He looked like a broken man. 'It's gone too far, Brooke. My mission ends here today. No more pain for any of us. No pill can cure my broken heart, Brooke. I've tried to repair myself and rebuild me, but nothing works when you're not by my side. You have Lee now and the thought of him with his hands on you torments me every minute of every day. We had a fight and you ran straight back into his arms. The affair never ended, not in your heart. I'm a dickhead for ever believing a single word that came out of your mouth, woman. The pair of you must have been pissing yourselves laughing at me behind my back.'

Brooke knew now wasn't the time to remind Vince they hadn't just 'had a fight' but that he had beaten her black and blue. She had to keep him talking. 'Don't be silly, Vincent. The night we fought was the first time I had seen Lee in a long time. He just helped me out, that's all.'

His voice roared. 'Helped himself to my woman don't you mean?' He flicked the lighter in his hand, smiling at her. 'It's time for you to go now, end my misery, you won't be able to torment me any more. I always said if you weren't going to be mine, you couldn't be anyone's.'

'Go on then, Vincent. If I'm to die tonight, then so be it. I would rather be dead than spend another second in your arms pretending I'm happy. Go on, do what you're doing and get it over with.' She could barely believe the words coming out of her mouth. She sounded like she had a death wish. But she realised she couldn't placate him any more. 'But before I go, let me say my piece. I don't love you anymore. My life has been worthless for so long now that I don't remember what happiness even is. You stole that from me. Do you know how it's been for me living with you lately, never knowing what I'm coming home to, wondering if I will get a belt from you, a kicking.' Her eyes were as bright as the flame dancing on the lighter as she carried on talking. 'I've served a longer sentence as your prisoner than my sin deserved and I'm not doing it anymore. Let's get this over with because I don't fear you anymore. Look at me, Vincent, look into my eyes. Go on, you'll see nothing but strength and courage. Just like you told me you had when you were a soldier. You will never break me again, ever.'

These were strong words, and Vince didn't know what to say. He didn't have power over her anymore if she didn't fear him. He tried again, determined to break her will. 'I'm going to burn you alive, make you suffer.'

'Do it!' she growled back at him. 'And you can die with me.' She clenched her fists and jumped on him. She might not be able to escape him, but she could take him down with her. She sank her fingernails into his eyes and she was punching and kicking, anything to try to floor him.

Vincent scrambled up from the bed and gripped her by the hair, dragging her one way then the other. His hand went back and he swung his flat palm right into the side of her face, sending her head sideways. 'Get over there, you daft bitch!' he screamed.

Brooke was still screaming like a banshee – she'd had years of hiding the beatings from her neighbours, but she wasn't staying silent any longer. She wailed and roared as the punches landed, until the last blow landed on her chin and she fell flat on the bed, out cold.

In the silence, Vincent pushed her legs onto the bed, reached down and gripped the lighter. Before he could spark the wheel he heard noises coming from outside, then the smash of glass and splintering of wood as the front door was smashed down. He shot a look outside the window and could see blue flashing lights. There was no time for last words. He flicked the Zippo and threw it on the bed. 'Mission complete,' he spat as he scrambled out from the bedroom.

It was only moments later that the bedroom door flew open, but the bed was already in full blaze; a wall of fire between the end of the bed and Brooke's unconscious body as police stormed the room. They darted to the far end of the bed and dragged at Brooke's arms. Thick black smoke was filling the room now, clawing at everyone's eyes and throats.

'I've got her,' the officer shouted back to the other officers. 'Get an ambulance here as soon as possible and phone the fire brigade.'

Brooke was carried to safety and out of the house as sirens filled the street. She was coming round, coughing and whimpering.

'Brooke, can you hear me? I'm here with you now, you're safe.' Lee was by her side, his face as bruised and battered as her own.

The police spread the net wide to look for Vincent, and soon there were flashing lights and door to doors at the Manor. Dane spoke to one of the officers and he filled him in on what had happened. The residents were in complete shock when they heard Brooke was in hospital with her injuries.

Bridie stood watching the street from behind her curtains. Normally she'd be the first one accidentally out in the garden if there was a police car parked up. But she couldn't go out and speak to her neighbours after her husband had been arrested, could she? He'd ruined everything she'd ever worked for. Her lovely home, the close friends she had, even the lovely garden she spent hours tending to felt tainted. Bridie turned back and looked over at the suitcase placed at the end of her bed.

Tomorrow she was leaving the Manor, never to return. The For Sale boards would go up as she left, and she'd already arranged to go and live with her sister in Blackpool. The way she felt right now, she wouldn't see Bert again until her dying day if she could help it. Bridie straightened the covers. The house was as neat as a pin – she'd do anything for a quick sale, the removal men could handle the rest. She had a taxi ordered for early the next morning and could already feel her time left in this house was nearly done. Bridie looked around the room and sadness filled her heart; the memories, the laughter, all flooding her mind. Everything she'd seen from this window – and never realised worse things were happening inside.

———

Vincent sat on the train keeping his eyes down and his face pointed away from any CCTV. He had a bottle of whisky stashed in his pocket he was taking frequent swigs from. His ticket was one-way and wherever he was going, he wasn't planning on coming back. He'd always told Brooke he had friends all around the world and if he wanted to, he'd vanish without a trace. He just had to get out of this city, reach some of his old squaddie pals in Spain, and then he could put all this behind him.

———

The train had only just pulled out from Manchester Piccadilly when it slowed again. Bloody railways. Vincent shut his eyes with his head resting against the cold window – he was done with Manchester. Then it all happened so fast. Armed response officers stormed the carriage with their guns pointed at him. They twisted him up in seconds. He was used to being able to overpower anyone, but their training was sharper and fresher than his – even without the whisky he'd drunk. He was marched back down the train to where the final carriage was still at the platform. They scrambled him through the station and threw him in the back of a police van. There was only one place he was going now.

Chapter Forty-One

Anthony jogged along the towpath with his coat zipped up tightly; he was running and stopping, running and stopping, out of breath. Wheezing, he stopped and dropped his hands onto his knees as he spotted someone familiar on the bench facing the canal. Malcolm looked shocked to see Anthony and had a puzzled look in his eyes. 'What are you doing here, it's late?'

Anthony stood weighing Matthew's best friend up and down, not sure what he was going to say next. His voice was shaky and he knew once the words were out there was no taking them back. 'It was you, wasn't it? You who flung him in the canal?'

Malc looked stunned. 'Are you drunk or something, Anthony? I haven't got a clue what you're going on about. I come here most nights like I told you and Bronwen. I miss my friend and being here helps me deal with his loss. I talk to him every time I'm here and find peace.'

Anthony walked one way then the other, never taking his eyes from the young lad. 'There's no point denying it. I've read the texts message you sent to each other, seen all the photographs of you two together, the selfies, the shots of you two loved up, kissing.'

Malc held his head back, nostrils flaring. 'Bullshit, I'm not gay.'

Anthony walked around him and started to speak. 'The night Matthew died, you left with girls, and he messaged you asking you to come back and meet him on the canal. I've seen the texts. He told you it was his birthday and you'd both agreed to tell everybody you were together.'

Malcolm stuttered, still in denial. 'Nah, mate. I don't know who Matthew was texting, but it wasn't me.'

'Look, kid.' Anthony waved the phone in front of him. 'You can either tell me the truth now or I'm taking the phone to the police, and they can deal with you.'

Malcolm knew his number was up. He bit down hard on his bottom lip. 'You don't get it. Matthew was in love with me. I told him we could never be together, but he wouldn't listen. He was threatening to tell everyone about a few nights we shared – kisses when we were both high. He said he'd tell my stepdad. Do you know what he would have done to me if he would have heard that about me? He hates queers. He wouldn't have understood.'

Anthony was listening, but aware this lad could run at any second.

'I told Matthew that night I'd come back to the canal to talk it out. But when I arrived, he'd already been battered.

311

I was trying to help him, but he kept saying he was going to announce to the world that we were together. He was stumbling all over the place – I don't know if it was from the booze or from the beating Bobby gave him. But he kept on at me and when he grabbed me, I pushed him and he fell into the canal. He hit his head on the way in. I tried my best to help him, but he was a dead weight. The water just pulled him down.' Malcolm broke down crying now, tears spraying from his eyes. 'It was an accident. A daft fucking accident.' Malc dried his eyes with the cuff from his jacket and shot a look over at Anthony. 'Now you know. And now I need that phone from you. Nobody can ever know. The police have got Bobby for beating him up, robbing him. So what if Bobby claims he saw him talking to someone else after? He's a junkie – the police won't keep looking too hard for anyone else. Grassing on me won't bring Matthew back, will it?'

'No, but Bronwen needs to know what happened with her son and you have to man up and tell her how her son really died.'

Malc launched himself at Anthony, then tried to scarper, but Anthony grabbed him by the ankle. He pinned him down and held him in a death grip. 'Do the right thing, Malc. There is no getting away with what you have done.'

But even though Malc was small, he was strong. He flipped Anthony over onto his back and with one roll, he spun into the canal over his head. Without a backward glance, he sprinted into the night.

The homeless man had seen everything and jumped into the canal. He gripped Anthony by his coat and pulled him to the side. The cold water was like an iron fist around them, but Anthony hauled himself back up onto the path, dragging his rescuer behind him.

Anthony was shivering, chest heaving to get air back into his lungs after swallowing so much of the murky canal water. Once Anthony found his breath he spoke to the man. 'You didn't have to do that, I'm forever thankful.'

The man just nodded his head, still struggling to get his own breathing under control. Anthony dug his hand in his pocket and emptied his wallet of a wad of sodden notes. 'Here. Go and get some warm clothes and a hot drink. As soon as I'm sorted out, I'll come back here and find you and thank you properly.'

Anthony was already making his way back down the path towards home. He knew anyone who passed him would think he was mad – a huge guy, soaking wet, tearing through the Manchester night. They'd think he was high or on the run. But he didn't care. He was cleared. He'd solved a murder and justice would be done.

Chapter Forty-Two

Susan stood waiting for Jay. Scully had drummed into her exactly what was going to happen. Once the car pulled up, she needed to get the guy out of the car and near the bushes where she was. She was shivering, and not just from the cold. It was nearly time.

The car pulled up and her phone buzzed with a text. She sent one back asking Jay to get out of the car and come to where she was standing, but he insisted she should get into his car. Susan panicked and tried ringing Scully, but there was no answer. Slowly, she made her way to the dark alley. She could see the outline of a man sitting in the car with his headlights dipped. With caution she edged forward, trying to get her eyes to focus – was that Jay or his mate? She was spooked; all she had to do was sit in the car and speak to this man. He would pass her the money and it would all be over. Scully wouldn't let him drive her off anywhere this time. She inhaled deeply and told herself she could do this. After all, last time she was selling her body, this time she was selling her silence. So she could handle that. Susan opened the car door and leaned in. 'So, did you bring the money or what?'

Jay. He was wearing the familiar mask. He held a brown envelope up and waved it in front of his face. 'It's here, so just sit in here for a few minutes, then I'll give you the money and you can be gone.'

Susan hesitated, still not sure if she was safe or not. But the money was there looking at her, within reach. She lowered herself into the seat, but kept the car door open fully.

'Go on then, say what you have to while I count this and I can get going.'

'I've missed you. Missed our chats online. I'm sorry what happened that night and I can promise you nothing like that will ever happen again. I just needed more of you, wanted to be inside you.'

Susan felt sick. But she thought about the money, about Sully's protection. 'I might be back online soon, but it will cost you more than it did before. I will never meet you again, but we can go back to the old arrangement if you want?'

Before he could answer, Scully opened the driver's door and snatched the envelope from the man's hand. He dragged Jay from the car and she could hear him screaming, pleading with his attacker not to hurt him anymore. Susan got out of the car and ran to where the attack was taking place. She was horrified and looked away. 'Stop it now, he's had enough.'

Her words fell on deaf ears, Scully was still kicking the crumpled shape of the man. Then there was a flash of dull silver and a pool of blood seeping into the floor. Jay's body shook a few times and then he lay motionless. Scully stood over him and kicked at his body one last time. 'Dirty cunt!' Susan screamed at the top of her voice and ran as fast as she could from the scene.

Scully ran after her and once they were away from the body, he dragged her into a dark alleyway and shook her by the arms. 'Calm the fuck down, will you. That creep got what was coming to him. Look, we got the money too.'

Susan was gagging, sweating, in complete shock. 'Don't touch me, leave me alone. You told me you would just give him a slap if he didn't hand over the money. You stabbed him. You killed him, Scully, he's dead.'

Scully gritted his teeth together and pinned her up against the cold brick wall, nose to nose with her. 'Listen, you daft cow. That's what he deserved. You keep that mouth shut and we'll all be happy. We had a good earner from him, just like I told you we would.' He counted three hundred pound from the envelope and held it out towards her. 'Here, your cut.'

Susan shook her head. It's blood money, Scully. I don't want any part of it. You keep it.'

Scully chuckled and stashed the money back in his pocket. 'Fair enough. After all, I did all the work, you just shook your money-maker.'

'Just leave me alone, Scully. I never want to see you again, ever.'

He sniffed hard and kicked his foot at the floor. 'So you saw a bit of blood, that's what you have to deal with in my line of work. Keep your mouth shut and we'll be sweet. If you start talking, then expect a call from me or one of my boys at your gaff. You do know what happens to grasses, don't you?'

Susan cowered away from him, scared. She didn't breathe out until he turned on his heel and walked out of the alleyway. She was alone now, scared, petrified of what lay ahead. She was as guilty as Scully was and she knew it. Her rapist was dead, but she as good as had blood on her hands. Stains like that never left. And what could she do? Even if the police believed her – an underage kid who'd been messing in online porn – what would they do? If they so much as knocked on Scully's door he'd hurt her, stab her up just like he'd done with Jay. Susan looked up at the night sky and howled like an injured animal.

Chapter Forty-Three

Angela Towen stood outside the shop and placed some flowers at the front door alongside the others that were there at the base of the closed shutters. She started to read some of the cards and the tears pooled in her eyes. She'd worked here for as long as she could remember and always thought that one day Sav would make her manager. Even had dreams of buying the place one day. So his tragic death had hit her hard. He was such a nice man and for anybody to stab him and leave him lying dead outside his car was too much for her to get her head around. Why would anybody do that to another human being? He'd always been the kind of man folks could rely on – he gave some of the residents here tick until they could pay him, and he was always sending food parcels out to people in the community who needed it. 'Heart of gold' she'd written on her card. Angela watched as other residents came to join her. Frank and Dane and their wives placed flowers

outside the doorway, weeping. Gaynor looked over at
Angela. 'They will catch whoever did this. What kind of
low-life could do that to a man like Sav? They were probably trying to do over the shop or carjack him – but they
walked away with nothing but blood on their hands. Filth.
But if the coppers don't get him, our Dane will. He's
already stopped the burglar. We're not going to take this
crimewave lying down.'

Angela sobbed, tears falling onto her lips as she pulled
her black coat tighter around her waist. 'I don't know
what I'm going to do now. I've worked here for so long.'

'You will get sorted out, Angela. If you want, you can
always come and do a few shifts at The Griffin.' She looked
to the side of her and raised her eyes at her husband.
'Can't she, Dane? We are looking for some good staff,
aren't we? We've had to fire Alison – caught her out the
back with one of the delivery guys.'

Dane agreed. 'Yes of course, Angela, you're always
welcome to come and work with me.'

Joanne Drury snuggled into her husband and squeezed
at his hand. 'You don't know how precious life is until something like this happens, do you? I'm having second thoughts
about living around here anymore. Look what's happened
over these last few months. I thought we were safe here.'

Frank cradled his wife and kissed the top of her head.
'I know. I was saying to Dane how lucky we are with our
girls and how we want to keep them safe and away from
this kind of shit. I mean, look how badly our Suze has
taken this. She'd only worked here a couple of months but

she cried and cried since I told her the news. She's a mess if I'm being honest with you. Won't leave her room.'

———————

Back at number 6, Susan cried as she packed her bags. She didn't know how long she had before her parents got home. She couldn't stay here a moment longer. The guilt was choking her. Emma came into her bedroom and clocked the sports bag rammed with clothes.

'And where do you think you're going?'

'Just leave me alone, Emma. I don't want to speak to you. It's all your fault this happened anyway. It was you who told me to do it, you.'

Emma came further into the room. 'What the hell are you talking about?' Emma grabbed the packed bag and put it behind her on the bed. 'You're not going bloody nowhere until you sit down and tell me what has gone on.'

'Fuck off, just leave me alone. I'm going and that's the end of it. The sooner I'm away from here, the better.'

Emma could see this was serious. She stood up and gripped her sister's wrist. 'Just calm down and tell me what's wrong. Bleeding hell, Suze, it can't be that bad.'

'It is, it's bad, Emma. I could go to prison. I was there, I watched him do it.'

Emma led her sister back over to the bed and helped her sit down. Her voice was softer now. Emma looked her sister directly in the eyes. 'You can tell me anything, you know that.'

Susan snivelled and played with her fingers nervously. 'It was Sav. Sav who wore the dog mask, Sav who talked to me online, Sav who I met. Sav raped me. And now it's Sav who's dead because I told Scully. I never told you anything about it because I knew you would go mental because I had been going online without you. Because I did everything you told me not to do.'

Emma stood up and walked to the window in shock. Her eyes clouded with tears as the story her baby sister had just told her hit home. 'I should have known better. You're right, it was me who got you into selling photographs of yourself. And of course I knew you'd try to do it solo, I just turned a blind eye to protect my own hustle. You've been going through everything that happened to you on your own and you never told me a thing. I introduced you to this world and it's my fault that it happened. Susan, I'm so sorry. You're seventeen – still a kid and I've let this happen.'

'It's not your fault, Em, I'm just as much at fault as you are. We both just got caught up in something that seemed so easy. It was fine on camera. I should never have agreed to meeting anyone though. And I should have gone to the police – not told Scully. He's said if I breathe a word that he was the one who stabbed Sav up then he will come looking for me, send his boys to deal with me. I thought he loved me, Emma, when all along he was just the same as all the others. Just out for himself.'

'He's a prick and the sooner you tell the police what happened, the sooner he will be locked up.'

'No!' Susan shrieked. 'I was part of it. We were getting money from Sav to keep my mouth shut. I never knew it was him. I swear down on my mam's life I never knew it was him behind the mask. It's all so twisted.'

Emma sighed. It had all seemed so simple. A few clicks, a few poses, a few quid. Now people were dead and more blood would be spilt if they told anyone. This was the ugly truth.

The bedroom door opened slowly and Joanne was stood there crying, the colour drained from her face. She walked into the room slowly and fell to her knees. 'I heard everything, bloody everything.'

Emma ran to her side and pleaded with her mother. 'Mam, I was only doing it to earn some decent money. I hated that job I was in, just couldn't stand going to work every day for shit money.'

'My sweet girls, showing your bodies to anyone who would pay for it. I don't get it – is that what the world has come to?'

Frank was shouting his wife's name from downstairs and when she didn't answer he came looking for her. As soon as he looked into the bedroom, he knew something was wrong. He stood with both his hands on his hips as he looked at the scattered clothes all over the bedroom floor. 'Susan, if your mother has told you to clean the bloody room then do it. How many times does she have to tell you?'

Joanne lifted her eyes up to her husband and shook her head. 'I wish this was just about the bloody state of the bedroom, you better sit down.'

Frank looked at Emma and then Susan and then his wife. 'So, is someone going to tell me what is going on or what?'

Joanne closed her eyes, the pain in her heart clear as she told her husband everything that had gone on.

Frank never said a word, just stood up and walked out of the bedroom. Joanne followed. 'I'm going to do what's right,' she snivelled.

Susan heard somebody knocking on the front door and she ran to her bedroom window to see who it was. Two police cars outside and a van. She ran to Emma. 'Please, Em, please don't let them take me.'

Susan was arrested and brought down the stairs in handcuffs. Emma wasn't far behind her, crying her eyes out. 'She's just a kid, she was vulnerable. Please don't take her. It's my fault.'

Frank and Joanne sat in the front room as the officers took their daughter out from the house. A female officer came into the living room. 'I know how hard this must be for you both. You've done the right thing in phoning us.'

Frank stood up and walked into the hallway with the officer asking questions about what would happen next. Once the police had left, he walked back into the living room and looked out the window. There was a For Sale board outside Bridie's house.

Joanne followed his gaze. 'Bridie had the right idea. We're selling the house. I want us gone from around here as soon as possible. I can't stay here after all this.'

Frank held her hand tightly. 'I know, love, I know.'

Chapter Forty-Four

Malcolm sat on the cold ground at Matthew's grave. He'd been here most of the night and he was sitting next to the little wooden cross that marked the spot until the headstone was ready. A laminated photo of his best mate was pinned to it, fluttering slightly in the dawn breeze. He took a long, hard drag from his cigarette and inhaled the morning air. A blackbird was bobbing about near the graveside and it caught Malc's attention. 'Is that you, Matthew? Come on, squawk if it is?'

The bird flew off. 'I wish I was free like you, blackbird.' Malc's hand closed around a handful of dank soil, lifting it up then dropping it slowly. 'I did love you, Matthew, but it wasn't our time. My family are hard men, fighters as you know, and if they knew I was gay I would have been dead in an alley before the news even got out. You had a good family, mate, a mother who would have loved you no matter what you did or who you loved. I told you so many times that wasn't my case. It won't be long until the dibble catches up with me and arrests me. Everyone will know our story then anyway, won't they. So, you kind of got what you wished for. Bit late though, 'ey?' He picked up another handful of soil and sprinkled it down through his fingers. 'I've missed you every single day since you've been gone and, given the chance again, I would have shouted out from the rooftops just how much I loved you and what we could have had. I'm sorry, Matty, sorry for not believing in us. I lied to save my life and it cost yours.' Malcolm shot a look behind him as he heard the cars pulling up at the cemetery gates. 'Love you, Matthew, always will. I have to go now, but no matter where I am in life you will always have my heart. God bless.'

Malc walked to the end of the row of graves where an officer met him. As he was read his rights and the handcuffs were placed on his wrists he looked down at the uneven rows of headstones and memorials. This was what life came to in the end – a few words on a stone. The only thing that really mattered was the love you left. He hoped Matty knew he was sorry, that the truth was all he could give to Bronwen. He was silent as they led him back to the gates. He turned back one more time and nodded his head at the grave before he got into the back of the police van.

Chapter Forty-Five

Susan cried her heart out as she was escorted out of her sentencing. She would be serving a five-year sentence for her part in Sav's murder. The judge had been lenient with her because of the rape she had endured, but there was no escaping her part in his death. Sav's wife had refused to attend. Sabrina and her whole family had left town as soon as Scully's name was in the news as a suspect. It was only Angela and her parents who'd turned up for the hearing.

Frank and Joanne Dury sat in court and supported their daughter the best way they could. This was every parent's worst nightmare. Even Emma hadn't come to court. She'd had a panic attack the first time she tried to leave the house after Susan's revelation, and now spent her time scanning the street for Scully's boys coming to make a call.

But they never came. Instead, Emma watched as a stream of new people arrived on the Manor. First the estate agents, with their shiny cars and For Sale signs. There were boards stuck in three gardens now. The McQueens' house was up for sale, although fire damage still marred the front bedroom window, making the house look like it had a black eye. Over the road, Bridie and Bert's looked like a doll's house in comparison – the front garden still as immaculate as Bridie had kept it. It sold quickly but no one had met the new owners yet. The Drury house was the largest of the three – 'perfect for growing families' the estate agents said as they showed couples round the place. 'A real community feeling' said the details on the property pages. Frank had scoffed when he'd read that – his family would never be the same again.

Even the local shop was up for sale. It was the end of an era and the residents that remained still crossed the street to avoid the place where Sav had died.

But for Bronwen leaving was never an option. Staying on Manor Road meant staying close to memories of Matthew. Every day she walked to the canal to sit on the bench that now bore a small gold plaque with her son's name placed on it. Love is Love was written underneath, and she hung on to those words. Malcolm had written endless letters to her and once she'd sorted out the visitor's pass, Bronwen was going to see him in prison. When the truth emerged, she found she could let go of all the hatred and rage. She'd forgiven her son's murderer. After all, Malc and Bronwen both loved Matthew, didn't they?

Bronwen had thought she'd never feel happiness again after Matthew's murder, but the day she found a postcard on the mat from Brooke McQueen she raised a smile. Brooke had recovered from the fire and sold her share in the salon to Amy. With the money she'd booked a flight to Australia, alone. She'd told Lee she had to do this solo – and in the note to Bron she wrote that when the house sold, she'd use the money to stay in Oz. Who could blame her, thought Bronwen. That woman had lived in Vince's shadow for too long – she deserved some sunshine.

Over in The Griffin, Dane smiled over at his wife and kept his voice low. 'I see the houses on the street have sold, we will have a full deck again soon enough, just in time to enjoy the refit. Angela told me someone has bought the shop too and they have offered her her old job back, how good is that? Maybe things are on the up again?'

Gaynor smiled at her husband and looked around the remodelled pub. The cheque that had come in the post from Bridie had surprised them both. She'd written to tell them Bert was in a care home now – he'd had a stroke before his trial date and would likely never regain consciousness. She figured Dane and Gaynor could do more good with Bert's share of the house money than she could. She'd planned a Caribbean cruise with her sister – told Dane to use the cash to bring back a bit of old Manor spirit. And so they had. The Griffin had a lick of paint; new window-boxes stuffed with geraniums and the old storeroom now had a little sign above the door – The Bridie Hammond Community Room. Gaynor and Dane had fitted it out and already it had groups using it. 'The Manor Credit Union' read one of the posters on the pinboard. Isaac hadn't been seen in the pub since.

Gaynor nodded her head. 'Give it a few days and I'll go and introduce myself to the new families. I'm sure they will be nice people, won't they?'

Dane raised his eyebrows as a cold breeze tickled the back of his neck. 'You never know, love, do you. Doesn't hurt to keep watch.'

ACKNOWLEDGEMENTS

To Gen and all the team at HarperNorth and Harper-Collins - thank you for all your hard work and backing. Thank you too to all my readers and followers for your continuous support and reading my books.

**Harper
North**

Book Credits

We would like to thank the following staff
and contributors for their involvement in making
this book a reality:

Fionnuala Barrett
Natasha Photiou
Peter Borcsok
Ciara Briggs
Sarah Burke
Alan Cracknell
Jonathan de Peyer
Anna Derkacz
Katie Buckley
Kate Elton
Sarah Emsley
Simon Gerratt
Monica Green
Natassa Hadjinicolaou

Megan Jones
Jean-Marie Kelly
Taslima Khatun
Nicky Lovick
Rachel McCarron
Emma Hatlen
Benjamin McConnell
Petra Moll
Alice Murphy-Pyle
Adam Murray
Genevieve Pegg
Eleanor Slater
Emma Sullivan
Katrina Troy
Daisy Watt

For more unmissable reads,
sign up to the HarperNorth newsletter at
www.harpernorth.co.uk

or find us on Twitter at
@HarperNorthUK

**Harper
North**